Last Heartbreak

A Nolan Brothers Novel ~ Book Five

AMY OLLE

Ebook ISBN: 978-1-944180-08-9
Print ISBN: 978-1-944180-09-6

DEDICATION

To the readers of romance. Your unwavering belief in love inspires me every day, in every way.

Prologue

The first time Shea Nolan broke her heart, Isobel Morales was fourteen years old.

At sixteen, he stood out among his peers at Sacred Heart High School. With black hair and smooth, taut skin, he was beautiful, almost pretty. Except for the hard scowl permanently etched into his features and the lean hunger that clung to his tall frame and burned like hellfire in his brilliant blue eyes.

While she'd known *of* him for years, ever since he and his brothers had arrived on the small island in northern Michigan to live with their uncle, she'd never actually met him or seen him up close until her first day of high school when she crashed into him in the crowded cafeteria.

The collision of their bodies jolted her, but his shocking beauty snatched all cogent thought from her brain. While she gaped stupidly at him, their classmates forged awkward paths around them.

His mean scowl evaporated when his soft lips moved. "Isobel Morales." He murmured her name with a gravity that disrupted the steady rhythm of her pulse.

Or maybe it was the lilting Irish accent that triggered the rapid fluttering beneath her breastbone, or the gravelly roughness of his voice, like crushed velvet smoothed over solid stone. More likely, it was the fact that he even knew her name at all.

He. Knew. Her. Name.

"Shea Nolan." His name tumbled from her lips as a reckless whisper.

One corner of his mouth tipped up in a lazy half smile, and a brazenly flirtatious gleam came into his bright eyes.

Furious heat rushed into her cheeks and a ridiculous noise erupted from her, like a giggle except shaky and breathless. She scurried away, already halfway in love with him.

After that, she stumbled into him as often as she could orchestrate their chance encounters. In between classes, she searched the hallways for him, hoping to catch glimpses of his dark, wavy hair, his wide shoulders, or the way his butt looked in the faded blue school-sanctioned chinos he wore.

It became an obsession, seeking him out and observing him. He made all the other girls blush and giggle, too. Most especially, she noted with a sharp pang of envy, Amber Jessop. His male classmates treated him with a measure of deference they didn't afford each other, and more often than not, she spotted Shea with his younger brother Noah, a freshman like Isobel.

One rainy fall day, as the cafeteria emptied out, she caught Shea alone. Mustering her courage, she approached him where he stood at the waste bins, his back to her as he sorted the trash from the recyclables on his lunch tray.

But when she reached his side, she pulled up abruptly. A gasp must've slipped between her lips because he froze with one hand suspended over the waste bin. In his other hand, he held half of a bagel. She blinked, hesitant to believe the information her eyes sent to her brain. He wasn't tossing refuse *into* their appropriate receptacles, he was picking them *out.*

He was picking food out of the trash?

The wrench in her stomach pulled a shocked gasp from her then. His head snapped around and his vivid blue gaze slammed into her with the force of a sea squall.

Her breath snagged in her throat. She wanted to flee or pretend she hadn't seen what he was doing, but it was too late. His fierce regard held her captive.

Her mouth went dry and she swallowed with difficulty. "You didn't get enough to eat?"

Someone else's discarded bagel disappeared into his coat pocket. "It's not for me."

"Who is it for?"

He remained silent. Defiant. The self-conscious humiliation she expected to see on his beautiful face never materialized. Rather, he stared her down, challenge stamped into every molecule and cell making up his striking features.

Reaching behind her, she retrieved a banana from her backpack and held it out to him. "I hate bananas. I don't know why my mom keeps putting them in my lunch."

He made no move to accept her offer. "If your mom wants you to eat it, you should eat it."

Then he left her standing in the lunch room holding that stupid banana as she stared after him.

That night, she lay awake in bed, her mind chewing over their exchange. If he wasn't taking the food for himself, who was he taking it for?

Before the first light of dawn tinted the night sky, she crawled from the warm cocoon of her quilts and padded barefoot downstairs. In the kitchen, she pulled a cookbook off the pantry shelf and, after a brief search, selected a recipe. When she'd laid out the ingredients and stood pondering her next steps, her mother, still dressed in her nightgown, appeared in the doorway.

Isobel gave a short, somewhat anguished explanation and then together, she and her mom set to work. By the time Isobel left for school, she carried with her a clear plastic storage bag crammed with oatmeal cookies stuffed full with nuts and raisins.

In first period homeroom, Isobel slid into her assigned seat beside Noah.

"Hi." She set the bag of cookies on the edge of her desk.

His dark eyes latched on to it. With an audible gulp, he swallowed. "Hi."

She peeled open the bag's zippered fastener. "Want one?"

Naked longing swept across his face. "You don't mind?"

She barely had time to shake her head before half of one cookie disappeared between his lips.

While he devoured the remaining half, she settled back in her seat. "With five boys in the house, I imagine it's hard for you all to get enough to eat, huh?"

He stopped chewing, and his throat worked with his heavy swallow.

Angling the bag closer to him, she kept her tone light when she said, "You're probably hungry all the time."

His mild expression suffered a small crack, which quickly filled with a defiance that reminded her of Shea. "We're all hungry. All the time."

They were all hungry. All of the time.

She had a strong heart, for it didn't break into a million pieces at that.

Her smile stiff, she scooped up the bag and plopped it onto his desk. "Why don't you share these with your brothers?"

When he opened his mouth, she knew he was going to refuse her offer.

"Please, I'm begging you," she rushed ahead of him. "Get these cookies away from me before I eat the whole bag and get fat."

With a chuckle, he slid the bag into his backpack.

The next day, she plunked a box of protein-packed chocolate bars onto his desk.

Noah lifted his head bent over his notebook, and one of his dark eyebrows inched upward.

"Do yourself a favor and do *not* read how many calories are in these things." She shuddered. "It's horrifying."

"Look, you don't have to—"

"I thought your little brothers might like them." She dropped into her seat. "How old are they now?"

That distracted him until Ms. Larkin started class a few moments later.

From then on, she brought food as often as she could manage to without being too obvious. One day she brought a loaf of fresh baked bread and a few days later, some vegetables from her mom's garden. Once, she sent him home with a Tupperware container full of tamales that her mom made from scratch before she realized the authentic Mexican dish might tip Shea off to the source of all the food Noah returned home with every other day.

She hadn't set out to deceive Shea, but neither did she wish for him to know what she was up to. Never did she dare offer him a morsel directly, and while she couldn't confirm whether any of the food she gave Noah ever made it back to him, she suspected it did, for as she got to know the brothers during that first semester, she quickly learned they shared everything with each other. They rarely fought, which seemed odd to her when she considered how often she argued with her little sister, and they never spoke badly about one another, not even behind each other's backs. They were a unit. A fortress against the world.

By Christmas, she and Shea had fallen into an easy friendship. He said hi to her in the hallways and even sat with her at lunch a couple of times. With every encounter, the butterflies in her stomach multiplied. His smiles whipped color into her cheeks and unleashed a steady stream of increasingly ardent schoolgirl fantasies.

Over winter break, Isobel longed for the day when classes would resume because it meant she'd get to see him again. The hours apart dragged on, every one more painful and tedious than the last.

On Christmas Eve, her mom appeared at Isobel's bedroom door dressed in the modest, vintage-style black dress she'd made to wear to that year's Midnight Mass.

Isobel pushed upright on her bed. "We're leaving already?"

"We're joining Mrs. Collins again this year."

Last year, when Mrs. Collins learned of a family on the island struggling to make ends meet after the dad had fallen ill and lost his job, she'd organized a small group to deliver a traditional holiday dinner and a bag full of presents to the family's doorstep on Christmas Eve.

Her mom slipped an arm into the bulky winter coat Isobel's dad held out for her. "I thought you'd like to come with us."

Uneasiness snaked up Isobel's spine. "Uh... I think I'm going to stay home this time."

Her dad misunderstood her reluctance. "Get dressed,

Isobel. It'll be good for you to do something nice for someone other than yourself."

Inside her family's car, the smell of roasted turkey hung thick in the air as her dad turned onto Bridge Street. When he pulled the car to a stop in front of a tired two-story home, Isobel's stomach twisted with knots.

Moments later, with her arms loaded down with a pile of festively wrapped gifts, she shuffled up the home's front walkway behind the others while the cold December wind nipped at the ends of her hair and coat. On the porch, Mrs. Collins pressed the doorbell, and the muffled chime set off an explosion of movement inside the home.

The door swung open and Shea loomed beneath the archway.

Isobel's heart cracked in two. Mrs. Collins launched into a wordy introduction, her shrill voice carrying on the brutal wind, but Shea ignored her. The menacing scowl tainted his handsome features as he inspected the small crowd gathered on his front stoop.

Then his gaze clamped on her, and for one fleeting moment, the hardened resentment left his expression, only to be replaced by something far worse—pure, palpable agony. A devastating mix of hurt and vulnerability, the look shattered her heart and then pulverized the tiny, irrelevant bits to dust inside her chest cavity. Her mouth opened, but no words came out, and he turned his back to her.

Numbly, she followed the others inside. The frigid outdoor air pushed in through the home's drafty walls as the loathsome stench of cooked turkey saturated the cramped room. Shea stood motionless, like a cold marble statue, while Mrs. Collins pontificated on the Lord's generosity and plucked presents from the stack in Isobel's arms to bestow upon the other boys.

In a tattered brown recliner in one corner of the room, a man wearing only a thin pair of boxers snored while he slept. Though she'd never met him, Isobel knew immediately who the man was. He was Shea's father. Like his sons, Daniel Nolan had dark, almost black hair, and if the rumors swirling around the island since his arrival the previous year were true, he had a black heart as well.

Isobel stared into the small faces of the three youngest brothers, all dark with serious, somber eyes and the same lean ranginess that Shea and Noah possessed. Their mumbled thank-yous were impossible to hear with their heads hanging so low. Only Noah lifted his gaze when he thanked Mrs. Collins, though resentment poured off him in unrelenting waves.

Instinctively, Isobel drew back and bumped into something hard.

Twisting around, she stared up into Shea's face. His eyes fixated on some point above her head when he reached for the doorknob and gave it a harsh wrench, inviting them to all leave with a bearing as pleasant as the forbidding cold that swept into the house through the open door.

As the others filed out of the house, Isobel remained rooted to the spot in his entryway. Bodies pushed past her and still, she couldn't force her feet to move. He refused to look at her, and grief compressed around her heart, choking off any words she might've uttered to make the moment end. Not that it mattered, since no words existed that could return everything to the way it was before she'd arrived at his home.

Dejected, she stepped over the threshold, but at the last second, she jerked back around. His eyes met hers when he gripped the edge of the door and, with a callous flick of his wrist, shoved it closed.

Winter break ended, and Isobel returned to school

with none of the eagerness she'd felt only days before. Her reluctance was well-founded.

The first week back, Shea avoided her so completely that she never caught sight of him. Not a peek at his retreating back or even a glimpse of his dismissive profile.

The next week, when she planted herself in front of him, he pretended not to notice her and stepped deftly by, as though she were little more than a minor nuisance set in his path.

By the end of the third week, she'd had her fill of being ignored and ambushed him as he left basketball practice. When he spotted her in front of the school, he pulled up, but then continued on his path with a determined stride.

She turned with him when he brushed by her. "Shea, wait. Please."

The soles of his gym shoes scuffed against the sidewalk when he stopped. His head jerked to one side, and he waited.

Her heart wedged in her throat. "I'm sorry."

With painful slowness, he faced her.

"I-I-I didn't know." Words poured out of her. Stupid, useless words that didn't do a single thing to erase the devastation in his eyes. "If I'd known, I wouldn't have—I didn't mean to embar—"

In an instant, his nose was inches from hers, his blue eyes burning bright as hellfire. "Damn you, Isobel Morales." His fingers bit into her arms when he grasped her and yanked her against him. "Why did you come?"

Amidst the storm of his emotion, she sought a stable point and anchored her gaze to his mouth. She touched his cheek.

His grip on her arms tightened, but she didn't flinch. She explored his face with the tips of her fingers, fascinated by the contradictions of hard and soft, power and vulnerability. When she traced the curve of his puffy bottom lip, a low growl vibrated in his throat a moment before his mouth crashed down on hers.

The kiss was bruising and demanding, and a dizzying thrill swept through her. She parted her lips, letting him inside, and he took a greedy nibble of her mouth. She tasted him, too, savoring the flavor of Shea Nolan. Of strength and light, heat and hunger. Her heart hurt but she craved more. The knot that'd twisted and coiled inside her since Christmas Eve wound ever tighter, until it finally collapsed in on itself.

He shoved her away from him, his chest heaving. "Don't you dare pity me. I'll show you, Isobel Morales. I am not just some poor, worthless kid. You'll see."

Then he left her.

The air rattled through her lungs with violent spasms, and she sagged against the school's rough brick exterior as she watched him stalk across the school grounds.

He didn't speak to her again in any meaningful way for weeks. Weeks turned into months and spring visited the island. The moment school let out for the summer break, he left her for real.

Okay, maybe not her personally, but that was what it felt like to her anguished heart. He'd kissed her, spurned her, and then deserted her, leaving her in order to work on one of the massive freighters hauling cargos full of goods to port cities around the Great Lakes.

She wouldn't see him again for three months.

When he left, he broke her heart, but even as she reeled with the terrible pain of losing him, she understood that, somehow, she'd broken his heart as well.

The next two summers, he returned to work on the freighter, and so he wasn't there when she needed him most.

Chapter One

Gray clouds loomed offshore, like angry beasts closing in on their prey. The menacing billows blotted out the late summer sun and cast the island in shadow. As they so often did, Shea's thoughts immediately veered to his wife.

Because no matter what, everything always came back to Isobel.

Droplets of rain peppered the ground, so he ducked his chin and strode across the crowded parking lot to his crew cab truck. Falling behind the steering wheel, he yanked the door closed as a streak of lightning slashed across the shadowy sky. A low growl of thunder rumbled with dark intent as he jammed the key into the ignition.

Large raindrops pelted the windshield, and the frantic sweep of the car's wiper blades whisked them away as he steered his vehicle from the lot. On Main Street, he headed inland. Toward her.

At a stoplight, he stretched forward in his seat to peer up at the inky black storm clouds smothering the island like a blanket. Though he and Isobel lived apart, a separation he'd only agreed to with the hope it might stop the fighting long enough to fix their marriage, he still knew his wife well. This storm would terrify her. So he'd left work on the busiest night of the week during peak time to go to her.

The light switched and the truck lurched forward. With agonizing effort, he eased his foot off the gas pedal and loosened his white-knuckled grip on the steering wheel. His heart thundered in his chest, revived with the anticipation of being near her again.

The loss of her gnawed at him. Every day. The ache never relented.

Much like the days when they hadn't had enough to eat. Back then he learned to live with the hunger, but he never got used to the growling pangs. The aching emptiness. Instead, he used them. If he grew tired or frustrated by the circumstances around him, the gnawing in his belly pushed him to keep going. To keep fighting, working, reaching, striving. To never give up or give in.

The trick had worked, goading him through law school to achieve a lucrative career. He'd gone years without experiencing a pang of hunger.

He turned the truck onto a secluded drive and began the long, winding journey toward the heart of the island. Near the pinnacle, he pulled into the driveway of the house he'd built. Situated among the treetops, the home had sweeping views of Lake Michigan and the island's lush, rolling hills.

It'd taken him years to build the home, the challenge made complicated and insanely expensive due to their remote location. Cut off from the mainland, building supplies and materials could be ferried across a stretch of choppy waters and out to the island in the spring and summer months, but all work ceased during the long, cold winters.

Easing his truck to a stop before one of the two garage doors, Shea killed the engine. Though far from extravagant, the four-bedroom home was infinitely more impressive than anything he'd lived in growing up. At nearly two thousand square feet, the cottage-style structure was well-built and sturdy. Of course, he wished he could've built them a bigger, more extravagant home, but it was a nice house, spacious yet charming, with all the high-end features he could afford at the time.

In the end, his lack of a fortune hadn't mattered all that much. With Isobel's talent for turning any plain, rundown, or flat-out ugly thing into something attractive and pleasing, over time, she'd transformed their respectable, sensible home into a remarkable showpiece. Charm and quaint touches abounded, from the muted beige shingle siding with extra-wide white trim, to the arched front door made of aged oak, and the overfull flower boxes and garden beds.

The two of them had made their home everything it could be and more. The same way they'd achieved so much else in their eighteen years of marriage. Together. As a team.

Or so he'd thought.

Isobel's compact sedan wasn't parked in her spot when he passed through the garage on his way to the back door. Inside the house, the familiar sounds of a baseball game streamed from the flat-screen TV hanging on the wall in the living room. Shea pushed the door shut and crossed the stylish, immaculate kitchen. Sprawled out on the overstuffed sofa in front of the TV, Shea found their teenage son, Finn.

At the sight of his dad, wariness darkened Finn's light gray eyes. He pushed himself upright on the couch and, pulling the hood of his sweatshirt over his dark hair, swiped the pad of his thumb across his cell phone's sleek screen.

The cool reception elicited a pang of regret beneath Shea's breastbone. "Where's your mother?"

Finn rolled his hunched shoulders. "She's not here."

"I can see that. Where is she? Are Connor and Maisie with her?"

"They're watching a movie down the hall. Mom's at dinner."

A ripple of alarm chased up Shea's spine. "At dinner? By herself?" In this storm? She'd be a mess by now.

"No. She went with some guy."

The words punched a hole through the center of Shea's chest. "Excuse me?"

Finn lifted his head long enough to pierce Shea with an insolent look. "She's on a date."

Beneath his feet, the ground opened up to swallow him. "Who...?" Fear and fury squeezed the question from his throat.

Finn shrugged. "I dunno."

Isobel was on a date.

With someone else.

Another man.

Another man who was not him, her fucking husband.

Reaching out blindly, Shea gripped the sofa back. "Where did they go?"

"Jesus, Dad, I don't know."

"Watch your mouth."

A sneer curled Finn's lips. "You don't get to tell me what to do anymore."

"No matter what's going on between your mom and

me, I'm still your dad."

A light flashed in Finn's heavily lashed, soft gray eyes. Isobel's eyes. "You haven't been my dad in years."

Shea shook his head to clear it and rubbed the aching wound Finn's words ripped open in the center of his chest. He couldn't banish the hurt from his voice when he asked, "What are you talking about?"

Guilt briefly softened the sharp lines of Finn's features. Shea's features. With Shea's tall, lean frame and Isobel's exotic coloring, Finn was the perfect mix of both his parents.

"Nothing," Finn muttered, returning his attention to the device cradled in his hand. "Just forget it."

"I'd like to hear what you have to say. Please."

At the "please," Finn's head came up. The expression on his youthful face wrenched the knot forming in Shea's stomach. His son looked at him now the same way Noah once had. With distrust. Derision. Accusation.

At one time or another, each of Shea's four brothers had looked at him that way. As did his wife.

Only the little ones, Maisie and Connor, didn't view him through the prism of their anger and resentment. At four and five years old, their hearts were full and bursting with love. Love without conditions. Indeed, these last tumultuous years, they'd become Shea's life raft in the raging storm of his crumbling marriage.

Finn paused a brief moment before firing his first shot. "You were never around."

"I had to work—"

He rolled his eyes. "You had to work *all* the fucking time?"

"Yes. I needed to put food on the table—"

Exasperation slashed Finn's features. "Oh, for the love of God, would you look at this place? We're not going to go hungry, Dad. Jesus Christ."

"I said watch your mouth."

Finn threw his arms wide. "Look around you. We're fucking rich, for fucking fuck's sake."

Shea balled his hands into fists so tight his nails dug into the flesh on his palms. "Because your mother and I work hard," he ground out.

He'd worked hard because he knew that one small misstep, one whiff of misfortune—a layoff, an injury or illness, a death—and everything could be lost. If he hadn't worked hard, he might've doomed them to a life of poverty and hunger, the way his dad had doomed him and his brothers.

Flinging himself back into the sofa cushions, Finn plopped his feet heavily on the coffee table. "Whatever. I don't care anymore. It's not like anything's going to change anyway."

The muscles in Shea's chest and back had bunched, instinctively readying for a fight, but Finn landed the knockout punch before Shea even set his feet.

"You want me to tell Mom you were here when she gets home? It might be late. Maybe even morning."

Dirty, disgusting images exploded in Shea's mind of his wife at dinner with another man. Tilting her face up for another man to taste her sweet mouth. Her clothes falling away from her body and another man's hands trailing over her silky skin.

Words died in his throat as Finn crammed white earbuds into his ears and dropped his head onto the couch back. He closed his eyes, oblivious to the chaos crashing through Shea.

So his wife had decided she was done with him, had she? After nearly eighteen years of marriage, three children, and a life built upon the fact of their togetherness, she figured she'd just move on without him? Discard him like the bag of trash sitting by the back door? Cut him out of her life, and while he lay bleeding out on the ground, step casually over his body and carry on her way?

Fuck that.

He wasn't about to let her walk away so easily.

ભ

Isobel's cheeks ached with the effort to keep her placid smile in place.

She kept her gaze fixated on Cooper Spence's wan face, not letting her eyes roam the interior of the island's nicest seafood restaurant or allowing her mind to recall the night Shea had brought her here on their first official date.

Six months after Finn was born.

If Shea were with her now, he'd order the whitefish.

But he wasn't with her. He hadn't been with her for a very long time.

With a pinch of sorrow, her smile faltered, so she shoveled a bite of salad into her mouth. She chewed the tasteless greenery, and when she swallowed, her stomach lurched.

Across the table, Cooper took a vicious swipe at the bead of sweat on his forehead. A loan officer at the Thief Island Credit Union, he often appeared nervous and uncomfortable. His job must be very stressful.

"Thank you for inviting me to dinner tonight." Isobel stabbed at a hunk of lettuce.

"Uh-huh." Raising a glass of ice water to his lips, Cooper drank in greedy gulps.

Isobel reaffixed her smile. "I assume you want to discuss my business plan. Did you get a chance to read it? What do you think?"

Heart in her throat, she waited while he sucked down

the rest of his water in one long, desperate swallow, trying to appear as though her entire future didn't depend on the next words he spoke.

That morning when she'd called him at the bank to schedule a meeting, she hadn't expected him to agree to see her so soon. After her initial surprise wore off, she'd opened her mouth, ready with the words to refuse his invitation to dinner, but then it hit her.

Cooper must've realized how his dinner invite might be interpreted, by her and others. The island was a small, tight-knit community, and everyone who lived there knew she and Shea were married. Everyone knew they'd been together since high school.

Everyone knew they weren't together anymore.

Though not divorced yet, in every way that mattered, Shea and Isobel were no longer married. They hadn't lived in the same house for nearly two years, and in that time they'd lived separate lives, not sharing a bank account, or a bed.

There was no reason she shouldn't go to dinner with a man who wasn't her husband.

Despair had slammed into her with the brutality of a ruthless tidal wave, and she'd sunk to the floor in the bedroom they'd once shared. She stared unseeing at the bleak future stretching out before her. Her marriage was over, whether she had accepted that fact or not.

Cooper's reedy voice poked through the curtain of anguish that threatened to suffocate her. "Isobel? Are you there?"

Blinking rapidly, she'd crashed back to reality. "I'm here," she said, though her voice was weak.

With a small shake, she threw off the shadows that hounded her and surged to her feet. No more sadness. No more waiting for Shea to change or decide whether he loved her. It was time to move on. To start over and make a new life for herself. A life without him.

It seemed impossible, and the despair had threatened to pull her under once more, but she'd steeled herself against it. She didn't need Shea, or any other man, to make her happy. She could have something better.

Or something equally satisfying anyway–a career doing something she loved. A business all her own.

But in order to do that, she needed to meet with Cooper, and the sooner the better. What did it matter if they talked at a restaurant instead of an office building?

So she'd accepted Cooper Spence's dinner invitation.

Now he set down his water glass with a table-rattling thud. "Yes. No. I mean, almost. I almost finished reading it." He tugged at the bowtie around his neck. "But that isn't why I asked you to dinner tonight."

"It isn't?" This time, Isobel took a nervous swallow of ice-cold water.

"No. You see, the thing is..."

But Isobel was no longer listening to Cooper. His words drifted past her ears without her brain absorbing them while she stared over his shoulder at the form of her tall, broad-shouldered husband bearing down on their table.

His features, usually a beautiful clash of hard angles and soft contours, twisted with his furious scowl, and his short hair, dark with moisture, stood in perfect disarray. The long-sleeved charcoal gray thermal shirt he wore was soaked through with wetness and clung to his lean, well-muscled torso.

Like an avenging angel, he stalked toward them, dragging a trail of curious glances along with him.

Isobel's heart slammed painfully in her chest. With every step he took nearer to her, the gray dullness of her world cracked and crumbled, falling away to reveal shocking Technicolor. An unsteadying rush of dizziness swept over her and she grasped the edge of the tabletop.

Shea's long shadow fell across their table. Slowly, Cooper trailed off and lifted his gaze. The color leached from his already pasty skin.

Liquid fire burned in Shea's blue eyes and Cooper shrank back in his chair. Then Shea's hot gaze swerved to her. His eyes raked over her face and lower, caressing the swell of her breasts where the neckline of her blouse dipped. Her skin prickled everywhere his probing eyes touched.

For a moment, he looked at her the way he used to, his bright eyes alight with naked emotion and hunger. Her heart tripped clumsily and she started to tremble. Once upon a time, that look, the experience of being the center of his world, had thrilled her beyond any dream she might've imagined for herself. It had calmed and comforted her.

Now it was downright violating.

Screw him.

His beautiful, lying lips curved into a vicious smile. "Hello, Coop. Mind if I borrow my *wife* for a moment?"

Chapter Two

Without waiting for Cooper's reply, Shea clamped a hand around Isobel's fine-boned wrist and tugged her to her feet with a punch of force.

"What are you doing?" Riotous color rushed into her cheeks. "I'm in the middle of–"

With a savage snarl, he pivoted and strode toward the exit.

She stumbled along behind him. "Shea, you can't barge in here–"

He whirled. She drew up abruptly but not before she crashed into his chest.

"You are my wife, Isobel." He spoke in a low, lethal voice. "Whether or not that means anything to you, it is a fact."

She lifted her chin, bringing her mouth a whisper from his. "Whether it means anything to *me*? I'm not the one who walked away."

"That isn't fair and you damn well know it."

Standing nose-to-nose with his estranged wife in the middle of the island's most popular eatery, Shea was acutely aware of the intrusive glances from their friends and neighbors. Indeed, they were all that stopped him from giving in to the primitive need to claim her mouth… and more.

A spark of fire flashed in her gray eyes. "Don't you dare talk to me about what is and isn't fair."

"Your date is over."

Her anger erupted as a shocked gasp. "How dare you."

Years of impotent rage churning in his gut, he hauled her into a darkened room off the main dining area, out of sight of the prying eyes.

"How dare *I*?" When she scurried from his reach, he pursued her until her back came up hard against the wall. "I'm not the one traipsing around town with another man."

She drove her palms into his chest, as if to hold back his fury. "I am not traipsing. I don't even know what that means."

"Are you fucking Cooper Spence?"

Emotion distorted her expression, but she ducked her chin before he could pick apart the reaction. "So what if I am?"

"I'll kill him."

She rolled her eyes, then risked a closer study of his face.

A frisson of alarm chased across her features. "Do not kill Cooper."

He promised her nothing.

She sighed, and the sound held more weariness than frustration. "Shea, what are you doing here? How did you even know where I was?"

"Finn told me."

"You talked to Finn? What did you say? If you upset him again—"

Shea cursed. "Finn's fine. I needed—" He swallowed the hard lump lodged in his throat. "I needed to know you're okay."

The spot between her perfectly arched eyebrows puckered. "Of course I'm okay. Why wouldn't I be?"

"The storm," he said. "It's a bad one."

"It's storming?" Her gaze darted to the windows on the far wall, which were covered with heavy drapery. "I didn't know..."

Instinctively, his hand sought hers. With his fingertips, he stroked the center of her palm and when her muscles relaxed, he nudged his fingers between hers, entwining them tightly together.

"It's supposed to pass quickly," he murmured while the pad of his thumb rubbed the racing pulse point on the inside of her wrist.

Her breathing hitched and her lips parted, drawing his gaze to her lush mouth. His fingers traced the curve of her cheek. Then his touch trailed lower, down the side of her neck to the elegant line of her collarbone.

"Isobel..." He pressed the length of his body against hers and dipped his head. "Let me take you home."

The column of her throat worked when she swallowed. "I have to go back."

He bristled. "I told you, your date is over."

"It's not a date." His disbelief must've shown on his face because she restated the words. "It's not. But..."

Just then, his questing fingertips stroked the crease on the inside of her ring finger. A scowl dragged at his features and a cold, revolting rage unfurled inside him.

"Where is your wedding ring?"

She blinked rapidly. "Wh-what?"

"Your. Wedding. Ring." He hated the tremor in his voice, but he couldn't suppress it any more than he could banish the anger and betrayal from his heart. "Where the fuck is it? Why aren't you wearing it?"

"Oh, uh, I..." With a frown, she disentangled their hands.

"Did you lose it? I swear to God, Isobel, if you–"

Her trembling fingers fumbled with the top button of her blouse and then yanked apart the flimsy fabric. A silver chain gleamed in the dim lighting, and there, nestled between her ample breasts, rested the small circlet of her wedding band. Over her heart.

Air leaked from him and he dropped his forehead against hers. He caressed the cold metal sphere. Beneath his touch, the smooth caramel skin of her chest rose and fell with each rapid, ragged breath she hauled into her lungs. When he skimmed the swell of one soft breast, a soft gasp escaped her.

Just like that, the flare of passion that once ruled their relationship ignited.

He swooped down to claim her mouth, devouring her with greedy nips and licks. He'd been starving so long, the hunger overcame him. It controlled him, compelling him to taste more, take more. Too ravenous and desperate to savor her flavor, he feasted on her with a wild recklessness that threatened to consume him.

"Isobel." Her name was a plea.

She made a sound like a broken sob, and he pulled back to peer down into her face.

Her eyes, the color of the summer sky before a refreshing rain, held the mystery of a thousand unspoken desires. His cock jumped, and he scraped the pad of his thumb across her bottom lip.

"Shea, what are we doing?" The quiet sadness in her voice wrenched his heart.

He knew what she was asking him, but he didn't like the answers available to him. "It's just a kiss."

Glassy moisture glistened in her eyes.

"We're... we're working on it."

"We've been working on it for two years." A despairing wail crept into her tone. "We can't even talk without fighting."

"Then let's not fight. Isobel... please..." He dipped his head and nuzzled the side of her neck.

"It's not that easy. We can't fix this, Shea. If we could, we would've done so by now."

His mouth on her throat, he tasted the bitter vileness of her words. Slowly, he lifted his head. "What are you saying?"

"I'm so tired," she whispered. "Maybe it's time we... let go."

The world tipped beneath his feet as all the agony and anger amassed in the past several years surged, slicing and slashing at him.

"No." With the denial, he gripped her arms.

"Shea—"

"We took vows, Isobel."

"Because we loved each other," she said. "But whatever we once felt, it's gone now."

"No." He squeezed his eyes shut and his mouth brushed her temple. "Never."

"Then it's too changed to be of any use to us now."

"Stop this." His hold on her tightened. "Please, just stop."

"Two years, Shea." Her voice cracked with emotion. "For two years we've been..."

Living like ghosts. Dying inside.

She didn't have to say the words. He knew. Lord, did he know.

"Maybe it's time we move on."

His world closed in on him. Hauling her tight against his chest, he buried his face in the sweet-smelling curtain of her hair. "Please, Isobel... I can't... I can't give you what you're asking."

He'd built his life around this woman. How could he go on without her? How could she ask him to? In his arms, she lifted her face up to his. A mere whisper of a breath separated their mouths.

Behind them, someone cleared their throat.

Shea turned his head to find Cooper Spence holding up a packet of trifold papers.

"I'll, uh, just leave these with you, then?"

Slowly, Shea dropped his arms and twisted toward the smaller man.

Cooper shrank back and his panicked gaze darted to Isobel. "I'll finish reviewing your application and call you when a decision has been made."

"Thank you, Cooper." She reached for the papers but Shea intercepted the packet. "Good night," she called cheerily to the loan officer's retreating back.

Then she fixed Shea with a dark scowl.

He held up the papers. "What's this?"

"Nothing." She made a grab at the documents, but he jerked his arm back and held them from her reach.

"Why don't you want to tell me?" He started to unfold the papers.

"Because it's none of your business." She slipped out from between him and the wall and snatched the documents from his hand.

"Wait, did that say business loan?"

"It doesn't concern you, Shea."

"As long as we're still married, it very much concerns me."

In her rush to get away, she slammed to a stop. A sickening sense of foreboding snaked through him as she turned by slow increments to face him squarely.

"You're right." Her expression crumpled. "I'll file for divorce this week."

He gasped with pain from the hole she punctured through his heart. Anger rushed in to fill the void.

"We're not throwing away eighteen years of marriage because you've decided you're done with me. That's not how this is going to work."

On a sob, she twisted away from him.

"Goddammit, Isobel, if you think I'm going to let you walk away from us, you're wrong. I won't allow it." Desperation tore at his insides. "You are my wife. Till death do us part. For better or worse, and believe me, things can get much, much worse before this is all over."

She sucked in a sharp breath and when she looked at him over her shoulder, a stream of silent tears stained her cheeks. "No. No more fighting, Shea. It's too late for us."

Chapter Three

Bright sunlight banished all trace of the previous night's storm, but a glum cloud hung over Isobel's head as she arrived at the Ever After Boutique.

Half bridal salon and half trendy women's clothing store, the boutique claimed two storefronts along the row of the last-century brick buildings lining Main Street. Nestled between the bookstore and the coffee shop, and across the street from Lucky's Irish Pub, Isobel had started working at the boutique eighteen years earlier when she was pregnant with Finn and awaiting her eighteenth birthday so she and Shea could marry.

Now Isobel handled most of the responsibilities managing the store, and the store's owner Celeste only bothered coming in on Saturdays, their busiest day of the week, so Isobel could focus on her chief job duty of handling the wedding and prom dress alterations.

She switched on the overhead lights and powered up the cash register at the front of the store. When she was about to unlock the doors, Celeste appeared from the back room.

"Good morning," Isobel called out to her.

"Is it?" Celeste hoisted her frail frame onto the stool behind the sales counter.

Biting back a sardonic smile at the typical sour reply from her boss, Isobel flipped the lock on the front door and turned over the sign in the window to announce that the store was officially open for business.

Never a particularly cheerful person, Celeste had grown downright cantankerous since the death of her husband some years ago. She was now in her mid-sixties, and Isobel feared her boss would retire. What would happen to the store? Would Celeste be able to find a seller who wanted to run a bridal store? Or would she, or the new owner, close it down?

Whatever she decided to do, Isobel dreaded the uncertainty and upheaval the change might bring to her own life.

Several large cardboard boxes awaited her in the stockroom, so she left Celeste with the monthly accounting ledger and headed to the back to unpack the shipment that had arrived the previous day. At one time, a batch of new dresses would have stirred a delightful hum of anticipation in her. She'd have rushed to touch the luxurious fabrics and the feminine designs would have set off a flood of creativity that might've stayed with her for days.

Now new arrivals struck a bittersweet chord, and the chore of finding the perfect bride for each gown often left her feeling shattered and hollow. It hurt, knowing what happened after the happily ever after.

She used a boxcutter to carefully slice the packing

tape, then flipped open the box top and dug out a plastic-wrapped gown. Hanging the dress on a garment rack, she unzipped the protective covering and inspected the gown, fondling the delicate fabric of the silk chiffon sheath she'd picked out of the catalogue.

The next gown managed to pull an appreciative sound from her. A heavily beaded drop-waist organza ballgown, the dress exuded fairy-tale princess more than any other gown in the store. Isobel leaned close to examine the intricate beadwork. Before long, inspiration had struck, filling her mind with a throng of ideas for a new dress. She fought the urge to reach for her sketchbook and draft a quick design.

While she'd only made a handful of dresses so far, she hoped to be able to add to her personal inventory soon. It'd started as an impossible dream, unattainable for someone like her, a high school dropout and teen mom. Then she'd watched Shea start his own business, turning Lucky's into the island's most popular destination after the public beach, and the impossible dream became merely improbable.

With her secret held tightly to her chest, she'd scraped together enough money to buy a bolt of the most incredible fabric she'd ever seen. With it, she made a dress. A vintage-style satin sheath with a sweetheart neckline and cap sleeves, the gown had a 1940s silhouette but with a sexier cut.

Isobel sold that dress to her sister-in-law, Mina. Two months later, another sister-in-law, Emily, bought the only other wedding dress Isobel had ever made, and as a guest at both of their weddings, Isobel had had a front row seat to her gowns' big days.

Of course, the brides were beautiful, but more important than that, she could see that they had *felt* beautiful. She'd overheard one guest gushing about the vintage-inspired style of Mina's gown while another guest had loved Emily's over-the-top ballgown and compared the trendy champagne-colored dress to one she'd seen at an upscale bridal salon in New York City. Even Celeste had commented on the skill of Isobel's stitching and the superb quality of the fabrics she'd chosen.

Her improbable dream sprouted wings.

With the money made from the sale of those two dresses, Isobel bought more fabric and beading. Her next gown sold in a week, and she turned the profit from that dress into two more. When the second of those two dresses sold, her dream spread roots.

That's when, recalling Shea's path to success, she worked up the courage to contact Cooper, and despite her husband's brutish interference last night, she held out hope that Cooper would approve her loan application. She wanted it with a desperation she couldn't explain, though she suspected it might have something to do with the fact that her dream was the only thing she cared about that had nothing to do with *him.*

The memory of Shea's expression when she'd told him she wanted a divorce notched a fresh gash in her chest. She'd grown accustomed to seeing anger and annoyance on his handsome features, but the wounded devastation had been unexpected.

Her vision blurred and the modified A-line gown she'd just unpacked from the box became a fuzzy ivory blob before her.

Divorce. Her heart retched at the word. It was a disgusting word, really. A series of harmless letters arranged into something so offensive. So pivotal. So final.

So painful.

That stupid arrangement of letters that didn't begin to

capture the slow torture of a crumbling marriage. Of a dying friendship, or a bankrupt love affair. Seven letters, each one containing a thousand heartaches or more.

When the faint sound of the bell over the front door chimed, Isobel let the dress fabric slip through her fingers and made two quick swipes at the tears under her eyes. Then she scurried to the salesfloor to greet the new customer.

But rather than a customer, she caught sight of Sophie Evans, her best friend since high school, handing Celeste a cardboard coffee cup from the shop next door. As Isobel approached, Sophie turned with a smile as bright as her platinum blonde hair.

"Is that the new dress?" She gestured to the gown displayed in the front window and handed Isobel one of the three remaining coffee cups from the drink carrier.

"It's too poufy, isn't it?" Isobel popped the lid of her cup and reached for a liquid creamer. "No one's going to buy it."

"Someone will buy it," Celeste said without looking up from the accounting ledger.

"And whoever she is, she'll look like a royal princess," Sophie added.

Isobel tilted her head, considering the dress with a critical eye. "I don't know about that."

"Oh, please. Everyone you dress looks gorgeous." Sophie handed Isobel a sugar packet. "Heck, you even made me look pretty when I was the size of a whale."

Isobel winced. "Don't say things like that."

"Why not? It's true."

"You're beautiful, Soph, and you always have been, no matter what size you're wearing."

"And that right there is why you're my best friend." Sophie lifted her coffee cup to her lips and took a tentative taste of the steaming brew. "I'll make you a deal.

You stop putting down your talent and I'll stop referring to myself as a ginormous mammal."

"Deal."

Isobel stirred the cream and sugar into the black liquid and watched the color lighten to a smooth brown. Carefully, she tested the temperature with her own tiny taste, all the while pretending she didn't notice Sophie's light green eyes assessing her.

"Uh-oh." Sophie set her cup on the sales counter. "What happened?"

"What do you mean?" Isobel asked innocently.

"You and Shea had a fight, didn't you?"

"How do you know that?"

"You only look this miserable after you two have a fight."

With a small shake of her head, Isobel took immense interest in the contents of her coffee cup. "I'm tired, that's all."

Sophie propped her elbows on the counter. "So it was a bad one, huh?"

Sudden emotion welled in the back of Isobel's throat. "It's not that. It's just..." She rubbed her forehead, trying to ease away the memory of Shea's ravaged expression. "We're both miserable. All the time and..."

"I'm sorry, Iz. I wish I had some advice to give you, but you know I have no experience with healthy relationships." Sophie emptied a sugar packet into her coffee. "You two have been together so long. Since high school, right?"

Isobel nodded.

Sophie placed her hand next to her mouth, as if to shield her next words from Celeste. "Have you ever been with anyone else?"

Warmth touched Isobel's cheeks and she shook her head.

"Has he?" Sophie's scandalized whisper whipped fierce heat into Isobel's cheeks.

"Don't you dare tell a soul."

"Who would believe me?" Sophie asked, her eyes wide with disbelief. "Besides, I'm not judging either one of you. I'm thirty-three years old and have been with exactly one guy, almost two decades ago, and it turns out he only fucked me because he lost a bet."

Isobel cringed at the mention of Liam Wright, remembering well the first time she'd heard that name, the same day she'd met Sophie.

Having dropped out of high school when she became pregnant with Finn, Isobel had been working at the store only a few weeks when a classmate from Sacred Heart came in looking for a dress to wear to fall homecoming. Heavily pregnant, Isobel had wanted to melt into the floorboards when Amber Jessop cornered her and demanded alterations to the slinky gold gown she'd chosen.

Isobel had cautioned against the changes, but Amber insisted, and when she returned to the store to pick up her dress a few days later, the slippery material refused to lie smoothly at the site of the alteration. She'd gone ballistic.

While Celeste dealt with Amber, Isobel had crept away to assist the only other customer in the store. A shy, sweet Sophie, who carried quite a bit of extra weight at the time.

After a brief introduction, Isobel had set to work pulling styles of dresses for Sophie to consider wearing to the dance. When she'd collected several gowns that she thought might accentuate Sophie's assets, cruel laughter pierced the air.

"Who on earth asked you to prom?" Amber had demanded.

Two bright pink spots had appeared on Sophie's chubby cheeks. "Liam Wright."

Amber's jaw had dropped and for one glorious, too-brief moment, she'd been stunned to silence. "Liam Wright asked *you* to homecoming? You're joking, right?"

"N-no."

"He can go out with any girl he wants. Why would he go out with you?"

"I d-don't know," Sophie had stammered, looking close to tears. "But he asked me, and I said yes."

Blue daggers shot from Amber's eyes as a horrid smile curled her cherry-red painted lips. "We'll see about that."

Shaking with fury, Isobel had picked a dress for Sophie and altered it in a way that flaunted her well-proportioned figure. The weight didn't disappear, but the sleek black dress was a perfect canvas for her white-blonde hair and light green eyes and looked incredible on her.

Isobel, seventeen and pregnant, the daughter of a Puerto Rican father and Mexican mother, and Sophie, an obese fifteen-year-old being raised by her grandparents, had been best friends ever since. Kindred spirits who knew how it felt to be considered different.

Unfortunately, Amber had been right, and Liam Wright asking Sophie Evans to the homecoming dance hadn't been a sincere invitation at all, but rather, was part of a cruel high school prank. Since that day, Isobel's sweet friend hadn't fallen for or even dated another guy, no matter that she'd lost a hundred pounds and more closely resembled a curvier Marilyn Monroe than that shy, overweight teenager.

Now Sophie pondered Isobel with a thoughtful frown. "You know, maybe you just need to try something different."

"What do you mean?"

"Maybe all this time you've been eating chicken when really you're a steak girl."

A snort escaped Celeste.

"You're right," Sophie said. "Shea's probably the steak. Maybe you're a vegetarian."

Isobel frowned at her friend, more than a little confused. "You think I'm a lesbian?"

"Okay, forget the metaphor." Sophie's hand sliced through the air. "What I'm trying to say is maybe you should go out with some other guys. Play the field a little bit. See what's out there and what's not. Then you'll know if it's really the end for you and Shea, or if he's truly the only man for you."

"Who would I date?"

One of Sophie's eyebrows climbed skyward. "I heard you went to dinner with Cooper Spence."

"It wasn't a date," Isobel said reflexively. "Besides, there's no chemistry there. None. Zero. Zip."

The women fell silent while they considered the handful of single men living on the small island.

Sophie brightened. "What about an online dating service?"

Isobel wrinkled her nose. "Aren't those places full of lonely, bitter divorcées?"

Sophie blinked at her, and with the slow thickness of poured molasses, Isobel realized she'd just described herself.

The bell above the door chimed and Isobel jolted when her sister, Ava, burst into the store.

"OMG. Everyone is talking about last night. You gotta tell me what happened."

"I don't know what you mean," Isobel lied. "Nothing happened."

A sly smile pulled at the corners of Ava's wide mouth. "That's not what I heard."

"What did you hear?" Sophie held out the last coffee cup to Ava.

Isobel gasped.

"What?" Sophie lifted her small shoulders. "We should know what they're saying, even if it's a complete fabrication and, more likely than not, mean-spirited in nature."

"Who cares what they're saying?" Isobel stepped over to the bridal veils and started straightening the display.

"Trust me, as someone who's been the subject of more gossip than anyone else in the history of gossip, it's better to know than to be blindsided."

Ava danced with impatience. "Come on, Iz, spill it."

"There is nothing to spill."

Sophie leaned close to Ava. "Whaddya hear?"

Ava's voice dropped into a conspiratorial tone. "Shea beat up Cooper Spence when he caught Isobel making out with him."

"That is not true!"

"No?" Ava sipped her coffee. "Then why don't you tell us what really happened?"

"Cooper and I were having a business meeting, discussing business, when we bumped into Shea. That's it."

"A business meeting, huh?" Sophie tried to hide her smirk behind her coffee cup. "I wonder what Shea thought of that."

"Nothing. He didn't think anything." Isobel fussed with a tangled mass of tulle and gossamer fabrics.

"Is that why he threw you over his shoulder and carried you out of Carter's?"

Isobel's arms dropped heavily. "Oh, for the love..."

"Tell me that's what really happened." Sophie clasped her hands in front of her. "I need this story to be true."

"It's not true," Isobel bit out.

"Which part is untrue?" Sophie asked. "Be specific."

"He did not throw me over his shoulder. I doubt he could."

"I don't," Sophie muttered. "Have you seen his butt?"

A sound like a gasp but with entirely too much laughter erupted from Ava. "You're bad."

"I can't control it. I'm sexually repressed." She turned wide green eyes on Isobel. "Then what happened?"

"Nothing. Can we please talk about something else?"

"They kissed," Ava whispered.

Sophie propped her elbow on the counter and rested her chin in her palm. "They did? Was it a nice kiss, or like an angry, possessive kind of thing?"

"I'm guessing the latter."

"Me, too." Sophie's dreamy sigh pulled a reluctant laugh from Isobel.

"Would you two please stop?"

"I bet there was tongue."

Ava nodded. "For sure."

"Fine." The word shot from Isobel and both women turned huge round eyes on her. "You win. Yes, Shea ruined my business meeting with Cooper. Yes, he was angry, and yes, he kissed me." Her skin prickled with the memory of his hot mouth on her lips, her neck, her breasts. She made a small gesture toward Sophie. "The way you described it."

Sophie smacked the counter with her palm. "I knew it."

"But we are not getting back together." The words snagged in Isobel's throat. "We're just not."

In the silence that followed her statement, a tangle of ugly, unbearable emotion swamped her. Because she didn't know how to fix what was wrong with her marriage, she'd let them all down—her friends and family, Shea's brothers and her new sisters-in-law. Most of all, her children and Shea.

"I'm sorry."

"Don't be sorry, Iz," Ava said quietly. "We know you guys have been trying. We're just rooting for you, that's all."

"Of course we are. I mean, the man's hair turned gray for you."

Isobel frowned at her friend. "What are you talking about?"

"His hair was dark until you guys split up," Sophie said. "The color changed when his heart broke."

Isobel pretended immense interest in the veils. "That'd be a romantic story if it were true."

How could she have broken his heart? She didn't leave him—he left her.

Sophie heaved a weary sigh into the air. "But if you don't love him anymore, you can't stay married to him."

"It's not that." Isobel's quick denial drew three pairs of knowing eyes to her face. "It doesn't matter what I feel. Sometimes love isn't enough."

And because she loved Shea, she couldn't let their sham of a marriage drag on another two, ten, eighteen years. Their kids deserved better. They deserved better. He would never end it—his pride wouldn't let him. Which meant she had to be the one to do it. For once, she had to be the strong one in their relationship.

"That's why I've contacted Miles Sinclair."

At mention of the island's lone divorce attorney, a sneer curled Celeste's thin lips and Sophie made a hasty sign of the cross.

Ever the peacekeeper, Ava jumped in. "Let's talk about something fun."

"Good idea," Sophie said. "Whatcha got?"

"I want to throw Finn a birthday party."

Isobel suppressed a groan. Though she was only

thirty-five years old herself, her baby was turning eighteen next month. Combine that with the end of her marriage, and a party was just about the last thing Isobel wanted.

But the absolute last thing she wanted was to disappoint either Ava or Finn. "He might like that."

"It'll be fun," Ava stated. Then she lifted her coffee to her lips and her next words were muffled behind the cardboard cup. "I'm thinking I might invite Dad."

Pain slashed at Isobel's heart, sharp and stinging.

"When's the last time you talked to him?" Ava asked gently.

"Not since he kicked me out." Isobel despised the bitterness in her voice.

"That was, what, sixteen years ago?"

"Eighteen."

"You haven't talked to him in eighteen years?" Disapproval darkened Ava's expression. "Isobel, he's our dad."

So what? Isobel wanted to shout. *I'm his daughter and he kicked me out.* The angry words built in her throat, but she swallowed them down with a ruthless gulp.

"You should call him." Ava elbowed Sophie in the ribs. "Tell her she should call him."

Sophie reared back. "Oh no, sorry. I'm not her tough-love friend. I'm the friend who enables her in everything she wants to do. Good choices, bad choices. Whatever she wants is fine by me."

Isobel offered her friend a warm smile. "That's one more reason why I love you."

"It's not about tough love," Ava argued. "He's our dad."

"And he disowned me," Isobel snapped.

Her sister was poking at an old wound, one that might have healed over with scar tissue but would forever nag and ache. Isobel tried not to take Ava's words personally.

She meant well, but she'd been only eight or nine years old when their mom died and their dad threw Isobel out of their home. She simply didn't understand all that had happened back then.

"You know how he is." Ava waved her hand with a dismissive flick of the wrist. "He was upset."

"You think I wasn't upset?" Isobel gaped at her sister. "I was seventeen and pregnant with no money and nowhere to go."

"I'm sorry." Ava's blue-gray eyes filled with misery. "I'm not trying to make you mad. I just... I just think it's sad, that's all."

Isobel's heart gave a violent lurch. "On that we can agree."

Just then, movement through the storefront window captured Isobel's attention. A man strode down the sidewalk, the morning sun picking out the golden threads in his brown hair.

Her heart spasmed in her chest to see Miles Sinclair arriving at his law office across the street, but she steeled herself against the painful wrenches.

"Celeste, I'm going to take a quick break," Isobel said as she moved toward the door.

This was it. This was the last heartbreak she must suffer before things would start to look up for her.

Wouldn't they?

She gave herself a mental shake and pushed away the doubt.

Of course they would. How could they not?

Chapter Four

Shea woke up drenched in sweat, his heart pounding and his cock throbbing. Aching for his wife.

An image of her lush breasts locked in his mind from four nights ago, when the ring he'd scraped every last penny together to be able to buy her, and the symbol of his undying love, played peek-a-boo with her tantalizing cleavage.

"It's too late for us."

With the memory of her words, a fresh agony sliced him. He was going to lose her.

Terror had him stumbling from the bed. His feet tangled in the sheets, but he kicked free of them and would've landed cleanly had the floor not dipped beneath him. On a groan, he rolled to his back, recalling too late that he'd slept on his boat, which was docked in the island's small marina.

He dropped his head on the floor with a soft thud and stared up at the cabin's low ceiling. Most days began this way, with him erupting from sleep in a panic, disoriented and disturbed to find that he wasn't at home with his family, in his own bed. With his wife.

Without her, he was lost.

Before Isobel, life had been hard. Hard and ugly. Everything about her was soft and pretty. Soft eyes, soft heart, soft breasts and hips and thighs.

Twenty some years ago, he'd crossed an ocean to come to this strange, foreign land after a hellish year filled with unbearable loss and upheaval. He'd been sleepwalking through his days, as if his soul lived outside his body, observing each new disaster that came into their lives with an anguished sort of detachment.

Then there she was. Kind and pretty, with exotic coloring and the sweetest smile he'd ever seen. The first time he saw her, she was standing at the end of the pier watching as a storm gathered and built offshore. Back then, she didn't fear the wild seas.

They were only kids then, but he knew he'd never be able to let her go. She was his, a gift from the universe that'd taken everything from him. She was his consolation. His reward for being dealt a shitty hand.

His.

He climbed to his feet and staggered to the boat's cramped bathroom. Angling his shoulders, he ducked his head and squeezed through the narrow doorway. In the shower, the weak water pressure and tepid spray pulled a string of curses from him.

When he'd moved out of the house two years ago, his dad had recently passed, and because Shea had nowhere else to go, he'd crashed at the old place on Bridge Street. It was supposed to be a temporary landing spot, but he'd stayed a year while he cleaned up the legal and physical mess his dad left behind and made repairs to the ramshackle old structure.

When the house sold last summer, he was homeless again, so he started another renovation, this time of the loft above the pub. The abandoned storage space had needed a ton of work, and Shea alternated between sleeping in his office and on his boat while he completed the overhaul. Neither place made a great home for Connor and Maisie, but to them, it was an adventure they went on every two to three days for a few nights.

Mercifully, they didn't ask why he wasn't sleeping at home, and they seemed to accept that every dad lived at Grandpa's house while he fixed it up and slept on his boat when the weather turned nice.

Last month he'd completed the loft renovation. The roomy space was cleaned out, and heat and electricity had been installed. All he had left to do was pack his truck with his belongings and haul it over there.

Yet he hadn't. Even though winter approached and his days of being able to sleep on the boat were numbered, he procrastinated. Something he'd never done before in his life. It was an odd sensation, filled with doubt and indecision. Two more things he hadn't bothered with up to that point.

Flipping open the cap on the new bottle of shampoo he'd picked up at the store, he inhaled deeply.

Damn. Still not the right one.

He wanted the shampoo that smelled like her, like them, because apparently everything in his life circled back to her. Even his fucking shampoo.

Which was the real reason he hadn't moved. The fact was he couldn't bring himself to give up his temporary sleeping quarters for something permanent. Something final. He couldn't accept living someplace without her. She was his home, and he'd not have another.

After he'd showered and shaved, he pulled on a pair of well-worn blue jeans and a black henley with the green Lucky's logo on the left breast. Then he made the ten-minute drive from the marina to the pub downtown.

The summer tourist season had begun to die down, and in the annual migration back to the mainland, Shea lost two bartenders inside a week when they returned to campus for fall semester. But despite the day on the calendar, the weather remained warm and patrons packed into the bar at lunchtime to refuel with food and drink before wandering back to the public beach or out on their boats.

When the crowd finally thinned out, Heather, his newly promoted manager, stuck her head into the kitchen where Shea had jumped in to help with the rush.

"You mind watching the bar while I do this interview?"

He wiped his hands on a towel. "For the bartender position?"

"Yep. He's out front if you want to meet him. I set his résumé down somewhere..." Her voice trailed off as she disappeared behind the door.

Shea pulled the white apron over his head and dropped it on the hook by the door as he passed.

In the dining room, Heather greeted a trio of woman that had entered the pub and seated them at a table near the front window. Then she ducked behind the bar to fill their drink orders.

"You want me to get those?" Shea asked. "Or I can do the interview."

"Will you do the interview, please?" She shot him a rueful smile. "I hate doing them."

"No problem. Where is he?"

She waved in the direction of the booths along the far wall. "I'll bring his résumé over when I find it."

"Thanks." Shea took aim at the booth. "You remember

his name?"

"Adam... something or other."

When Shea approached the booth, the dark-haired man looked up from his cell phone. Surprise crowded his expression.

"Adam? Thanks for coming in." Shea stuck out his hand.

Adam stared at it for a moment, then reached out slowly and accepted the handshake. "Uh, thanks?"

"I'm Shea. The owner here."

The color drained from Adam's face. "You're Shea? Shea Nolan?"

"That's right. And you're Adam...?"

"It's, uh, Aiden."

"Oh, sorry about that." Shea slid into the booth across from Aiden. "We've misplaced your résumé."

"My résumé?"

"You're here for the bartender position?" Straightening, Shea glanced at the nearby booths. "Or maybe I got the wrong table?"

"No." The word shot from Aiden. "I mean, yes. I'm here for the job. Of course I am. Why else would I be here?"

At the odd response, Shea's eyes narrowed.

"I'm new here. To the island. Just moved," Aiden said. "I'd heard your name mentioned around, but I pictured someone a little more..."

One of Shea's eyebrows crept skyward.

A rusty laugh knocked loose in Aiden's chest. "I don't know what I pictured. Someone different, I guess. Your accent, is it English?"

"English?" Shea's tone dripped with disgust. "Now you don't come into my bar insulting me like that. I'm Irish, and don't ye go forgettin' it."

A wide smile split Aiden's face. He had a nice face, Shea supposed. Girls probably appreciated it, anyway. If

Shea had to guess, he'd say Aiden was probably close in age to Jack and Leo.

"So, what brings ya to our little island?"

Aiden rubbed a hand across the back of his neck. "Oh, well, that's a long story."

"The long stories are the best," Shea said easily. "Why don't you catch me up on your work history? How long you been bartending?"

"All my life. I grew up in a pub."

Aiden took Shea through his work history, stopping off at bars in Montreal, Detroit, Chicago, and Vancouver. In college, he'd studied some mixology and had dabbled a little in brewing since then.

As he talked, Shea considered his unusual accent. It wasn't like any he'd ever heard before. Not quite the clipped Midwestern cadence of the locals, nor the elongated vowel patterns of a Southerner, and each word came off slightly awkwardly. Almost stilted. He must hail from some peculiar land. Minnesota, maybe?

Aiden seemed to be a perfect fit for the job. Almost too good to be true. Pushing to his feet, Shea told him as much.

"How soon can you start?"

Aiden slipped from the booth and straightened to his full height. "As soon as you need me."

"In that case, welcome aboard. C'mon over and let me introduce you to everyone."

Shea introduced Aiden to the staff and showed him the layout behind the bar. When Heather pulled Aiden aside to hammer out a work schedule for him, Shea found his attention drawn through the pub's large tinted front window and across the street to the bridal store.

He wondered what she was doing right now. Did their kiss dominate her thoughts the way it did his? Had she dropped the ridiculous opinion that they needed a divorce? If not, that kiss and her undeniable reaction to him should've dispelled the notion. Despite the anger and the arguments, she still wanted to him. He'd suspected it all along, but now he knew it to be true.

A primal, carnal satisfaction hummed in his veins.

That doesn't mean she loves you.

Whatever. He needed to touch her more. Touching her would lead to kissing. Kissing to wanting. Wanting to softening. Such a lusty concoction just might be the opportunity he'd been waiting for. The opening he needed to break through the barriers she'd erected between them.

Yes, she'd erected the walls, but his sudden optimism gave him the courage to admit she hadn't done it alone. He'd handed her the bricks.

She'd constructed her walls over years, all eighteen of them, but mostly the ones he'd spent working at the law firm. The job had been hard—and ugly. It had changed him in ways he never could've expected, and though he hadn't been able to stop the changes from taking place, he could feel them happening to him. He could feel himself withdrawing, drowning. Unable to fight his way back to the surface, he'd sunk deeper every day while his body was riddled with invisible wounds. Unseen traumas that were nonetheless life-altering, as real as a jagged scar or a chronic limp. Submersed by the pain, he'd drifted away from her. Until one day, he'd quit. He just quit, because apparently, he was too broken to care that only losers quit.

There could be no doubt that he'd had a role to play in creating the barriers between them. Which only meant he had all the tools necessary to tear them down again.

By now, Heather and Aiden were deep into a demonstration of the software system used on the cash registers. With things under control, Shea considered the store across the street. In under a minute, he could be near his wife, pulling her into his arms and reminding her how good they could be together.

He started toward the front entrance, but just then, the heavy wooden door swung open and a blinding stream of bright sunlight struck Shea. He blinked against the cruel surge of light as the shadow of a man moved toward him. When the door fell shut, the postman stood before him.

The color rode high on Postman Pete's cheeks. "Seamus Michael Nolan?"

"What are you doing, Pete? You know it's me."

Pete held out a thick envelope with a bright green certified receipt attached to the top fold. "Sign here, please."

Everything inside Shea went still.

Pete's wandering gaze didn't quite manage to meet his eyes.

With painful slowness, Shea's hand came up to accept the envelope. "What is this?"

"Certified letter."

"Yeah, I can see that." When Shea grasped the pen, he struggled to steady the trembling in his hand as he scrawled his name along the black line. Deep down, some part of him understood his life was about to be irrevocably changed.

"Have a good day." Pete spoke to the floorboards as he scurried to the exit and vanished into another blast of sunshine.

Shea turned over the envelope in his hands and read the sender's address. His stomach lurched.

Law Offices of Miles Sinclair, P.C.

Pain ripped through him and his knees buckled.

Fuck, it hurt.

She did it.

Denial screamed through him. He couldn't believe she did it. How could she?

After nearly two decades together, in which they brought three lives into the world and stood side by side as they buried two of their parents, she'd gone and done it.

She'd filed for divorce.

Chapter Five

Beneath his feet, the floor dipped and heaved. Or maybe the unsteadiness was inside him.

With a mental shrug, Shea raised the cool glass bottle to his lips. The liquor burned a trail down his throat and he prayed this would be the swallow that finally numbed the pain.

Instead, the chaos of his emotions distilled into the scalding wound of her betrayal. Her treachery wriggled under his skin and stole the bliss of oblivion from him. Unable to sleep, he'd chosen the next best thing—alcohol. Lots and lots of alcohol.

The drunker he got, the clearer things became. They were meant to be together. How could she not see that? Had she forgotten what they were to each other? How could she turn her back on them?

The boat pitched and he stumbled out onto the rear

deck. Searing sunlight blasted him. Collapsing on his back on the storage bench, he pulled the bill of his baseball cap down to shield his face from the sun's blaze.

His mind raced. He needed to reply to the summons or risk his custody status. Due to the kids, state law mandated a sixty-day waiting period before they'd grant the divorce, but that didn't mean the dissolution of his marriage wouldn't move forward. There'd be negotiations, settlements, court appearances. His lawyer mind set to work laying out his case. Stating his arguments. Building his defense. Anything that could stop the landslide her divorce filing had set off.

He squeezed his eyes shut. Shit, none of that mattered now. Whether he consented to the divorce or not, he couldn't make her stay married to him. It wasn't the 1800s.

Sometime later, when the sun had slipped halfway to the horizon, a shadow fell over him. He cracked open one eye to find two men peering down at him.

Noah nudged him with the toe of his sneaker. "We're too late."

"I get his boat." Luke settled behind the wheel.

Noah scowled down at Shea. "Are you drunk?"

Shea grunted. "Go away."

"I' hear he's been an ass ever since Isobel went on that date," Luke said, his head bent while he fiddled with something on the control panel.

"What date?" Noah's head swiveled from Luke back to Shea. "You know about this?"

A groan eased from Shea when he sat upright. Shoving unsteadily to his feet, he shuffled over to the cooler and bent to retrieve a beer from the ice.

Noah plucked the beverage from his hand. "Who's the guy?"

"You remember Cooper Spence?" Luke folded his

arms across the steering wheel.

"Not at all." With a hiss of sound, Noah twisted the cap off his beer bottle.

"He was in the class between you and Shea," Luke explained as Shea dug around in the cooler for another beer. "Brainy kid. Kind of quiet."

A frown clouded Noah's features. "The kid who wore the bow tie?"

Shea wrenched the cap off his beer and took a long glug of the draught.

"That's him," Luke said.

Noah lifted his shoulders. "He was a good guy, wasn't he?"

"And she's my fucking wife." The angry words erupted from Shea and echoed across the water.

Noah took the outburst in stride. "You don't want out then?"

"Christ," Shea muttered and sank back down onto the bench. "No." He scrubbed a hand over his face. "Jesus, no."

Noah lowered his body onto the bench across from Shea. "We heard Isobel filed." Leaning back, he propped his feet on top of the cooler. "So what happened between you two?"

Shea crammed the heel of one hand into his eye socket and rubbed. What the hell? Was he confiding in his brothers now? Good God.

But the words were pouring out of him before he could shut off the valve. "I have no fucking idea. Everything just sort of... fell apart, you know?"

"I have no idea," Noah said cheerfully. "Before Mina, I hadn't been in a relationship lasting longer than a few months. Tell me what it's like."

From beneath the brim of his ball cap, Shea glared at Noah while he searched for the words, but grief and helplessness swamped him.

Noah reached inside the cooler, snagged another beer, and tossed it to Luke.

"I thought we were fine." The air squeezed from Shea's lungs. "We were busy with work and the kids. Life was crazy, a little chaotic sometimes, but we were us. I thought we were stronger than all of that."

But it'd worn on them. Work, chores, school pickups and drop-offs, practice, dance, haircuts, doctor appointments, birthdays, holidays. The long hours he spent commuting to his soul-crushing job at the law firm, which he'd kept at for seven awful years because the money was good—excellent, actually—and because he wanted to be able to give Isobel and Finn the world.

Life had gotten in the way of living. He was too busy to talk, too tired to listen, and at the end of the day, he'd had nothing left in him to give to the ones he loved most. He was empty.

Too empty to feel.

"When we did talk, all we did was fight."

"What about?"

"Everything. Nothing. Stupid shit." Some not so stupid shit, too.

Then one day, Shea looked up from the legal brief on his computer at Finn sitting across the dinner table. A shadow of peach fuzz teased his chin and a permanent scowl hardened the increasingly masculine features on his face. When had he grown from an affable little squirt into an angry, withdrawn teen?

Stunned, he'd turned to Isobel, but rather than finding the sweet girl he once knew at his side, he discovered a woman looking more lost and alone than he could ever remember seeing her look. She should be happy, but she wasn't.

He'd never forget the wounded expression on her face

when she thought no one was watching her. He'd put that look there. No one else.

A sudden surge of bile rose in the back of his throat and he swallowed. "So I left."

Noah straightened on the bench. "Wait, *you* left *her*? Why the hell did you do that?"

The ugly memories were all jumbled in his mind and Shea shook his head. "Because she told me to."

"You've never done a damn thing I told you to do," Luke complained. "Or anyone else, for that matter."

Shea let his head fall back onto the side of the boat and stared up at the cloudless sky. "I guess I figured it couldn't get any worse if I left, and it sure as hell wasn't going to get better if I stayed."

In the silence, the cry of a seagull rang out. Shea's gaze followed the bird as it soared overhead and then dove, breaking the surface of the water with a riotous splash.

"I never thought it'd happen to us. Divorce." The beer tasted foul in Shea's mouth when he tried out the word.

"Is there any chance you can still fix it?"

"For the life of me, I don't know how." The center of his chest ached with hollowness. He hadn't felt so empty since the days following their mom's death, when they all walked around in a daze. Soulless and beyond hope. A ragged breath shuddered through him. "What the fuck am I going to do?"

"Say you're sorry and have a shit-ton of makeup sex," Luke said. "Have you tried that?"

Noah's head bobbed. "That's a solid plan."

"I've apologized for things I haven't even done yet." While Shea refused to discuss sex with his wife with his brothers, in truth, there wasn't all that much to discuss. Since he'd moved out, Isobel barely tolerated speaking to him and the chance that an intimate moment might arise between them seemed more remote than their tiny island. "I've tried everything I can think of, but nothing ever works."

"That only means you need to try something different."

Shea's gaze shifted to Noah, intrigued.

"Have you tried talking to her?" Noah asked. "Told her how you're feeling?"

Shea's lip curled. "Some."

A frown puckered Luke's brow. "Define some."

"Look, I'm not a touchy-feely kind of guy."

Two expressionless faces stared him down.

Rolling his shoulders, Shea shifted on the bench. "Sometimes I don't tell her everything."

Noah scratched his cheek. "You mean like that time you quit your job and didn't tell her?"

A vivid memory pierced the drunken haze of his mind.

Grief and fury rolled off her in pulsating waves. "Stop lying to me. For once, just tell me the truth."

The fear nearly overcame him. "I don't work at the firm anymore."

"Were you fired?"

"I quit."

The shadow of betrayal in her eyes gutted him.

"Look," he said, "we're going to be okay."

"I'm pregnant."

Fear solidified into something rigid and fierce and fiery inside him. Something that whooshed past his eardrums and thrummed in his chest.

Then, as now, Shea's heart tried to punch out of his chest. Those days after he quit his job at the law firm existed in his memory as an ugly lump of agony. A fuzzy black pit filled with anger and misery over what had happened—what he'd done—which he'd tried to drown with alcohol and self-deception. More alcohol than anything else, really.

Back then, he couldn't bring himself to tell her the truth, so he said nothing and set about formulating a new plan for their lives. He'd made a plan for them without her input.

A low whistle leaked out of Luke. "Dang, she gave me an earful about that. Like it was my fault or something. Though it wasn't as bad as the time you bought the pub without telling her."

Noah's features twisted with derision. "Seriously?"

"I was going to tell her, but she found out before I got the chance." Shea held up his hand. "It's not as bad as it sounds."

"Really? 'Cause it sounds pretty fucking bad," Luke said.

She'd been through so much and the thought of adding to her stress made Shea's stomach turn. "She worries."

"She's a big girl." Noah's voice contained no give.

"She wanted to know what was going on with you." Luke shrugged his wide shoulders. "Doesn't seem like too much to ask."

"Whose side are you on?" Shea asked.

"We're on your side," Noah said. "And if you want your wife back, you're going to have to face some hard truths."

"You should text her."

Noah dragged his gaze to Luke. "Are you serious right now? You're not helping."

"Hear me out," Luke said easily. "Emily tells me she can't get a fair fight unless we slow things down." Affection thickened his voice when he talked about his wife, Emily.

A stutterer, she sometimes struggled to get words out and Shea could only imagine how she might fare in a rapid-fire argument with his silver-tongued brother.

"At first, I flat-out refused," Luke continued. "But

now… I don't know. I kinda like it." A shadow of a smile touched his lips. "Writing it out gives me time to think about what I want to say. About what really matters. I take better care with my words."

Shea dropped his head. He stared down at the boat decking and recalled all the careless words said between him and Isobel over the years. So many stupid, thoughtless words.

When he glanced up, Noah chewed the side of his thumb while his features crowded with an intense scowl. Then he straightened and leveled Shea with a black look, like a doctor delivering a fatal diagnosis.

"The way I see it, you've got two choices." He ticked off the first option with his index finger. "One, you can let her go on that date."

"She already went on the date," Luke said helpfully. "Good ol' Coop. Cooper Eugene Spence." He overenunciated each word.

A growl built in Shea's throat.

"Then let her go out with the next guy, and the next one after that," Noah said. "Let her go on as many dates as she wants."

Shea took a long, desperate pull from his beer to hide the gnashing of his teeth.

"If Isobel's got it in her head that she wants to move on, then let her see what's out there waiting for her." A calculating gleam winked in Noah's chocolate chip-colored eyes. "Wouldn't you rather it be with a guy like Cooper Spence than, say, someone like you?"

Incredulous, Shea's gaze swung to Luke.

Luke lifted one shoulder. "He makes a fair point."

Shea's heart convulsed painfully in his chest. "I don't think I can do that."

Noah's tone turned conspiratorial. "Any chance Cooper wore the bow tie?"

That tugged a reluctant smile from Shea. "Aye, that he did."

Noah took a self-congratulatory nip from his beer bottle. "You know, you might want to educate Isobel on a few other realities as well."

"What realities?" Shea demanded.

"I overheard Amber Jessop asking you out again the other night. Maybe you should take her up on the offer." One corner of Noah's mouth lifted in a half smile. "And let Isobel see you doing it."

Pride filled Luke's expression. "Aren't you the devious bastard?"

"Amber Jessop?" Shea spat the woman's name. "Now you're just fucking with me, right?"

Noah's bark of laughter carried across the marina. "Okay, maybe not her. But how about any of the other half-dozen women on this island clamoring for your attention?"

"I'm not interested in any other women."

"I'm not suggesting you start up anything serious."

"That's good, because I'm married."

Noah dropped his chin and fixed Shea with a look. "For how much longer?"

A nasty curse erupted from Shea.

Noah pressed his advantage. "All I'm saying is would it be the worst thing in the world if Isobel thought—mistakenly, of course—that you were ready to move on, too? Maybe she'd even be a little jealous."

"There it is." Luke raised his beer. "Makeup sex."

Shea struggled to focus on just one of Noah's faces. "You're twisted."

"Thank you."

"It's not a compliment."

"Do you want your wife back or not?"

Shea drank a mouthful of bitter beer rather than

repeat himself. "You said I had two choices. What's the other option?"

With the speed of a flipped switch, Noah grew suddenly serious. "Fight for her."

An eerie quiet fell over the marina. The light in Noah's dark eyes took on a lethal glint and lifted the hairs on the back of Shea's neck.

"It's a life-or-death battle, as you well know." Emotion rode the edge of his words. "There are no rules. No gentlemen's agreement. No mercy. Fight, and don't stop fighting until the last breath has left your body."

A nauseating concoction of alcohol and fear swirled in Shea's gut. Hopelessness dragged at him. "I've been fighting all my life."

"This time is different."

"This time, you have us."

Shea had no idea what his brothers meant, but hours later, as the sweet relief of unconsciousness tried to claim him, one last cogent thought floated through his mind.

Noah was right. If he was going to get his wife back, he couldn't keep doing what he'd always done and hope for a different outcome. He had to try something else. Something he'd never done before.

No more playing by the rules. He had to do something totally unexpected. Something she would not anticipate him doing and would therefore struggle to defend against.

He had to stop fighting.

What he *wanted* to do was storm over to the house and demand to know why and when she'd stopped loving him. He wanted to make her say the words out loud and straight to his face, because maybe then his hemorrhaging heart would accept it was the end for them.

Which was the reason why he couldn't go anywhere near her. Not yet.

He'd wait until he was stronger, and sober, and if he was right, he wouldn't have to go to her at all.

She'd come to him.

Chapter Six

After three days of crushing doubt and nauseating dread, a faint thread of annoyance wound through Isobel.

Hand on her hip, she contemplated Noah standing on her front porch. "What are you doing here? Where's Shea?"

"He had something come up–"

"Unca Noah!" A thunder of footsteps erupted as Connor charged through the living room and launched himself into his uncle's arms.

Crouching, Noah scooped him up. "Hey, little man. Where's your sister?"

"Here I am!" Maisie, dressed in the pink poufy princess dress Isobel made for her, wrapped her arms around Noah's legs.

"Princess Maisie." Noah bent at the waist. "You look beautiful."

Maisie ducked her chin to hide her wide smile and twirled on the hardwood in her stockinged feet.

She studied him through narrowed eyes. Before she married Shea, Isobel and Noah had become friends, and afterward, they'd grown closer. He had even lived with them for a time, as had all of Shea's brothers. But that closeness offered her little insight into his sudden appearance now.

Connor and Maisie, competing for their uncle's attention, engulfed him in a flurry of excited chatter while he collected their bags and herded them out the door. Soon after they'd left, Finn went out with some friends and the house fell eerily quiet.

Flitting as they did from one new adventure to another, Connor and Maisie never allowed Isobel time to be sad or depressed, or really to think much at all about her crumbling marriage. Without them to keep her mind busy, her thoughts traveled a dark path.

After filing those papers, she'd expected Shea to call her, or hunt her down at the store, or charge over to the house and demand to know why she'd done it. He would confront her. Challenge her. Refuse to let her go. He would fight because that was what he did, always. He fought.

But he didn't come, and he didn't fight.

The knots in her stomach wrenched with painful twists and twinges.

She worked all day Saturday and came home to an empty house. For dinner, she made Finn's favorite pasta dish, but he failed to show and instead sent her a text to let her know he was hanging out at the beach with his friends.

Alone in the big empty house Shea had built, she put the pasta in the refrigerator and set to work scrubbing the kitchen clean, but halfway through her task, she stopped abruptly. What was the point? No one cared if the kitchen was neat or filthy. Until Shea brought the kids home on Sunday, likely no one would even notice.

Down the hall, she changed into her pajamas and crawled into bed with her cell phone. It'd been a week since she'd had dinner with Cooper, and she held out hope he might call her soon with news about her loan application.

But when she checked her messages, there were none. Doubt crept in to further deflate her mood. It was Shea's fault, she thought with a sullen scowl. Had the fiasco that was her business meeting with Cooper ruined her chances of getting the loan? That night at the restaurant, he'd put up a fight, but a week later, he couldn't be bothered?

Though she didn't understand why she'd done so at the time, she was right to hide her loan application from him. He couldn't be trusted.

Besides, his opinions about her plans were irrelevant. The fact was Shea didn't have a part to play in her plan for the future.

Purposeless and heavy-hearted, she flopped onto the bed and yanked the quilt up over her head. The bedsheets had lost Shea's smell months ago and sudden tears prickled behind her eyes.

The next morning, she didn't climb out of bed with the first light as usual. The hours slipped by while she drifted in and out of sleep, and the day passed without her ever crawling out from beneath the covers. It was something she hadn't done since those horrible months after her mom had died.

When the time approached to meet Shea at the pub to pick up Connor and Maisie, as she'd done every Sunday evening for nearly two years, she abandoned the safety of her warm cocoon and sought the refuge of a hot shower.

The water's invigorating spray restored some of her fight and after she dried off, she spent a little extra time on her hair and her makeup. Then she pulled on her blue jeans with the butt-lifting technology and the new top she'd bought at the store, which showed a little more cleavage than she normally revealed. She was about to walk out the door when a car pulled up the driveway.

Leo emerged from the dark green SUV.

Annoyance mixed with her already dark mood as she met them in the driveway.

"Where's Shea?" she demanded as Connor and Maisie scrambled out of the back seat.

"He asked me to drop the munchkins off for him."

She swallowed back a growl of frustration at the non-answer. "Why? What's he doing?"

"I assume something came up at work."

While Noah and Jack had lived with her and Shea only a few months each, Noah leaving to go overseas and Jack to pursue hockey in Detroit, both Luke and Leo had stayed in her home for longer patches time. Shortly after Luke graduated high school, he found his own place, but Leo, the youngest of the brothers, was with her on and off from the time he was twelve years old until he left for boot camp a few months before his eighteenth birthday.

After Noah, she probably knew Leo the best, which was why, despite his professional-grade poker face, she realized immediately that he was hiding something from her.

"You talked to him?" she asked. "How did he sound? Did he seem... normal?"

Leo's gaze drifted away. "How do you define normal?"

"You know, grumpy."

A thoughtful frown puckered Leo's brow. "No, he didn't. He was chill."

"Chill?" Somehow, she added an extra syllable to the

word.

"Happy."

Her heart cracked. "Happy?" she whispered.

A rare smile found its way to Leo's face. "He even made a joke. It was a crappy joke, mind you, but he tried."

Shea was happy? She hadn't seen him happy in years. Maybe not ever.

Leo's customary scowl returned. "You okay?"

Unable to speak around the lump wedged in her throat, she nodded.

As Leo drove off, she sank down on the top step of the front porch and looked on as Connor and Maisie trampled through her flowerbeds. Even when they separated several large blooms from their hearty stems, she observed the destruction with indifference.

Was that it? Had Shea signed the papers? Was their marriage over?

The thought should've brought her some relief, but the way her chest constricted and her stomach clenched didn't feel like relief. Not even a little.

Shouldn't she feel... lighter? Like a burden had been lifted? The torturous cycle of anger and self-doubt, anxiety and angst, was finally coming to an end. She could start over. Fresh. Filing for divorce was supposed to feel good. Or at least she should feel better.

Shouldn't she?

She hadn't thought it was possible to feel worse.

Three nights later, Shea sent Luke to pick up Connor and Maisie. Beneath her sorrow, a sliver of anger needled. All week she'd waited to hear from Shea, or Miles Sinclair, but her phone didn't ring. No texts. No emails. No calls. Nothing.

"Let me guess." Resentment laced her words. "Something came up?"

"He has a date," Luke said cheerfully.

With the gut punch, she sucked in a sharp hiss of air.

Alarm stole over Luke's handsome features. "I mean a meeting. It's a date, meeting. A meeting... date?"

"Who with?" She immediately regretted the question, and yet she let it ride.

Luke scratched the back of his neck. "I, uh, can't remember."

"Liar."

He dared to try his charming smile on her. "It's the baby. I haven't slept in days and I can't remember shit."

His wife, Emily, had delivered their firstborn only two months prior, and at mention of the baby, Isobel softened.

"How is the little guy?"

"Except for the not sleeping, he's great." Luke ran a hand through his hair, causing the dark strands to stand on end. "He will sleep eventually, won't he?"

The tinge of desperation in his voice coaxed a reassuring smile from Isobel. "He will. Eventually. I promise."

Luke strapped the kids into the car seats he'd borrowed from Shea's vehicle, and as they backed out of the driveway, a heavy glumness settled over her. Was Shea really on a date? He wasn't even going to talk to her? Yell at her? Say goodbye?

He must've signed those damned papers, then, eager to go out with this other woman. Isobel would put her money on the scheming Amber Jessop. The woman had been after Shea since high school. A colleague in law and now thrice divorced herself, Amber often openly flirted with him, sometimes right in front of Isobel.

She retreated inside the house and, in the kitchen, filled a coffee mug with wine. Settling on a barstool at the island counter, she gulped down the syrupy liquid and then immediately poured another. She took several greedy swallows while a tornado of angst spiraled through her, whipping up dark memories of a failed marriage.

They'd never stood a chance. She could admit that now. Married as teenagers, neither she nor Shea were prepared to handle the heap of obstacles set before them. Some hurdles were self-created, like her unexpected pregnancy, but others, such as the constant turmoil stirred up Shea's volatile father, Daniel, had been outside their control.

Their lack of money added a layer of stress on top of everything else and when Shea started work at the law firm, she'd hoped things would get easier for them. They didn't. Indeed, with the money came new pressures on their relationship. Different, and far more sinister.

Early on, Shea's new boss had invited them to dinner at his house, a lavish estate overlooking the Grand Traverse Bay. Immediately upon arriving, Isobel had felt awkward and out-of-place among Shea's coworkers and their glamourous wives. The wealthy wives of powerful men, the women chatted about things Isobel didn't understand, like frustrations with their housekeepers and their husbands' mistresses.

Stunned, Isobel had gaped at the women as they openly conversed about the fact that their husbands were sleeping with other women. There was no anger in their voices, though a touch of bitterness crept into a word or a look here and there. But mostly they spoke with a matter-of-factness that had devastated Isobel. As though they discussed the weather or traffic. Some nuisance they had no control over. Nothing of consequence which could, or should, be otherwise.

"I didn't think it'd happen so soon." Isobel detected a hint of anguish in the woman's voice who, like Isobel, was married to one of the new lawyers with the firm.

"The first affair is always the hardest," the senior partner's wife had reassured her. "It gets easier."

"It has nothing to do with you," another woman offered. "It's the stress."

"It's the men. They need it."

The experience had imbedded a kernel of doubt just below the surface, and through all the years Shea worked at the firm, it had rubbed and chafed. Isobel had tried to ignore the dark suspicions and ugly doubts, but she wasn't always able to forget what she'd heard that night, and wonder.

The years passed in a blur of anxiety and grief. She and Shea grew up and grew apart, as their lives took divergent paths, his increasingly career-focused and hers family-centered.

Until one day she felt more alone when he was there.

Slowly, she dropped her head to the countertop. The smooth granite felt cool on her forehead. She and Shea had been a couple since she was in the eleventh grade. Not a single day of her adult life had passed without him as her husband.

Until today.

And at the first opportunity, he'd stepped out with another woman. Amber Freaking Jessop, no less.

Like Shea, Amber had gone on to get her law degree and join some high-powered legal firm on the mainland where, to this day, she worked and resided but for a few months out of the year when she returned with the warm weather to her summer home on the island. In recent years, Isobel had grown to hate the tourist season.

A wave of dizziness rocked her, but not from the wine as much as from the realization that she was officially a bitter divorcée.

Saturday night, Jack dropped off Connor and Maisie, making up some excuse about spending time with his niece and nephew before he headed to training camp the following week with his hockey team, and another three days filled with wild mood swings passed while she awaited word–any word at all–from either her possibly ex-husband or her divorce attorney.

So on Tuesday morning, she greeted Mr. Sinclair at his office door, and twenty minutes later he confirmed that Shea had not returned the signed papers.

Isobel's anger turned to indignation, which quickly morphed into righteous indignation. Who did he think he was? Some carefree single dad? A bachelor? Did he think he'd just cut her loose and carry on as though their life together had never happened? Did he think that the next fourteen or so years, until Connor turned eighteen, needn't include her?

It'd been two weeks since he'd received those papers and yet he hadn't signed them. Was he going to? Or was he just going to date Amber while he stayed legally married to Isobel?

That evening, when Shea's normal pickup time rolled around, she watched from the front porch swing as Noah's black truck rolled up her driveway.

Anticipating this exact move, she waited for him.

But she bit back a curse to discover he must've anticipated her anticipation, for he brought protection.

Isobel offered Noah's wife, Mina, a genuinely warm smile.

Then her gaze sliced to Noah. "Where is he?"

"Out."

"Out where?"

"With friends."

Isobel's teeth clenched so tightly, her head started to ache. "Which friends?"

"He didn't say." Noah glanced at Mina, who looked slightly ill. "Did he say anything to you?"

Mina's mouth opened. "He–"

"Welp–" Noah clapped his hands together, "–we better get going. Mina and I are taking the kids to dinner. Then we might stop off at the beach, try to soak up some of this sunshine before the weather starts to turn on us. Then we'll be dropping off the little ones with their dad."

Isobel kissed Connor's chubby cheeks and weathered a storm of Maisie's tears, cut short by a bribe from her uncle for a post-dinner ice cream cone, before waving goodbye from the porch as they drove away.

The anger and despair that'd ruled her emotions the past two weeks suddenly seemed a distant memory. She was calm, composed, and a newfound sense of certainty overrode all else.

Certainty of one thing–that it was time she had a little talk with her husband.

Ex-husband.

Possibly soon-to-be–whatever. She needed to find his devious ass.

Now.

Chapter Seven

Ten minutes later, Isobel stifled a sneeze as she dug the formfitting red dress from the back of her closest. She brushed the dust bunnies away from the stretchy fabric and eyeballed the dress she had made for her twelfth wedding anniversary but never got the chance to wear.

Since she'd last tried on the dress, both Maisie and Connor had been born, and the reality of having two young children less than a year apart had disrupted her life in the same way a tornado might. Chaotic days followed by sleepless nights had hindered her attempts to get into a routine workout schedule or develop sensible eating habits. Then Shea left her, and the desperate wish to crawl into a hole and sleep her life away had obliterated any last traces of her willpower.

With a few unbecoming tugs and grunts, she managed to shimmy into the red dress. Then she stepped in front of the full-length mirror and inspected the image reflected back at her. The fabric had enough stretch to forgive her most severe flaws and enough structure to conceal the rest of her imperfections. After some adjustments, including the addition of a pushup bra and the removal of her panties to eliminate the lines visible through the figure-hugging material, a sly smile curved her lips.

She might not have the revenge body, but she had the next-best thing—the revenge dress.

Sophie once referred to Isobel's ability to erase flaws with well-cut, tailor-made clothing as a superpower, and in that moment, Isobel was inclined to agree with her. She added a pair of four-inch red heels and, since she'd used the flat-iron to straighten her hair that morning, as she did every morning, she applied some product to the roots of her hair to give the dark, heavy mass a sexy boost of volume.

Before the mirror, she added a touch more color to her cheeks and redrew the perfect sweep of her eyeliner before daubing cherry-red lipstick onto her mouth. Then, though her makeup wasn't quite done to the level of perfection she preferred, she turned toward the bedroom door and the task of hunting down her obstinate husband.

The setting sun cast a golden glow over the island when she steered her sedan into the marina's gravel parking lot and eased into a vacant spot. When she climbed from the car, a warm breeze kicked off the lake to rustle her hair and a flicker of apprehension disturbed her determined stride. She tripped onto the dock and inched out over the water, past the row of boats bobbing gently in the rolling waves.

A little more than midway down the dock, she picked out Shea's forty-foot sailboat at the edge of the marina,

The Fiona Mae, which he'd named after his mother.

As she drew closer, she spotted the man himself on the rear deck. Shirtless, the sun kissed his wide shoulders with a warm bronze caress. He'd pulled the baseball cap on his head low to shield his eyes from the sun's glare, and his black boardshorts hung loose on his narrow hips. Her steps slowed as her courage abandoned her.

Holding some small object in his hand, he moved to sit on one of the storage benches flanking the deck. With his movements, the muscles on his back and arms and beneath the flat plane of his stomach flexed and rippled. An appreciative sigh slipped between her lips. Unlike her, she couldn't recall him ever skipping a workout.

Once, years ago, she'd asked him where he found the discipline and willpower to remain so dedicated to his workout routine. He'd surprised her by confessing, rather matter-of-factly, that his dad, Daniel, had often hit him and his brothers, but that the first time Shea had overpowered the older man physically, when he was only sixteen years old, the beatings had stopped. In a low voice, he'd told her he had no plans to stop working out and risk a return to that place of powerlessness. Not ever.

Now, with his attention riveted by the thing in his hands, she approached undetected, until only two boats remained before she reached him.

Then his head snapped up, and his bright eyes crashed into her with enough force to knock the air from her lungs. She caught the slight slackening of his jaw before he clenched it tightly shut.

Satisfaction surged and, sucking in a sharp breath, she pressed her shoulders back and added a little extra sway to her hips.

He reclined on the bench, stretching his long legs out in front of him. Feet crossed at the ankles, he watched her with naked interest.

Heat prickled across her skin and it took all her concentration not to plunge the point of her stiletto heel into a gap between the deck boards.

At the foot of his boat, she drew to a stop. She planted a hand on her hip to create the illusion of a deeper inward curve to her waist and fixed him with what she hoped came off as a bored stare.

From beneath the brim of his ball cap, his glittering gaze raked down the length of her body. "New dress?"

She smoothed a hand down her side. "What, this old thing?"

"I've not seen you wear it before." His gravelly brogue rumbled unevenly in his chest.

"I wore it to dinner on our twelfth wedding anniversary. Oh, that's right, you weren't there. You stood me up."

The corners of his eyes crinkled, as though he experienced a twinge of pain. "I'm sorry."

Momentarily stunned by his earnest apology, her hand slipped off her hip, but she quickly re-anchored it. "I don't want your apologies."

She'd wanted her husband, the longing so fierce and full that it'd caused her heart to ache, and for every step that he took farther away from her, the pain became more agonizing and raw. Until she could no longer bear it.

"I remember that night. I stayed too late at the office and missed the last ferry out." The softness in his voice might've been nostalgia, or regret.

A clang of warning sounded in her mind. He was not himself tonight.

"You were working a Very Important Case, I'm sure." Emotion squeezed her throat. "No doubt it was more important than having dinner with me."

"No. Not more important than you." A teardrop of sorrow mingled with his words. "But important, yes. Someday I'll tell you about it, if you want me to."

"I do." The confession slipped out.

His eyes glittered in the fading sunlight. "Okay."

Flustered by the gentleness in his tone, she flipped her hair over one shoulder. "Did you receive the papers?"

After a beat, he bent his head and turned over the small piece of wood cradled in his fingers. "Yep."

"Did you sign them?"

"Not yet."

She shot an angry glower across the bow. His head down, it went unnoticed.

"Well," she bit out. "Are you going to?"

In his palm, he clutched the handle of a pocket knife, and the metal blade glinted in the sunlight as he silently inspected the miniature wedge of wood.

Why wasn't he saying anything? Or yelling at her? He was so calm. So serenely composed. The hairs lifted on her arms. When she'd filed for divorce, never in a million years would she have predicted this reaction from him.

It utterly terrified her.

She shifted her stance, only barely resisting the urge to tap her foot. "Shea?"

When he lifted his head, his eyes blazed with blue fire. "If you want me to sign those papers, you'll have to bring them to me yourself." With the knife blade, he pointed at the cabin door. "They're right there on the table."

Icy fear slid through her. It was absurd, really, that she, the daughter of a ship captain, the not-yet-ex-wife of an avid seafarer, and a lifelong resident of a remote island in one of the largest lakes in the world, was afraid of boats.

And the water.

She especially hated boats that were on the water.

Where anything might happen. Where a wind might kick up to tear up the mast or knock the vessel off course. Where heavy seas might throw the craft around as though it were an inconsequential buoy.

Where a sudden storm squall might breach the port bow, overwhelming the bilge pump and capsizing the boat, killing all onboard when it sank to the lakebed.

A complex tangle of desire and apprehension lived inside her. Though drawn to the water, experience had taught her to fear its power.

Not unlike her husband.

She looked down at the toes of her red pumps, inches from the deck flooring that bobbed gently in the rippling waves. Her mouth suddenly parched, she licked her dry lips and placed one heeled foot onto the boat.

Then the floor dipped and she promptly withdrew it.

With a huff of annoyance, she glared at Shea from the dock. "I don't have time for this. Can you just bring them to me?"

He used the knife to slice away a tiny fragment of wood. "You can't possibly believe I'd make it that easy for you, *mo chuisle.*"

My love.

His use of the endearment, spoken in the native language of his homeland, pulled a deeper frown from her. Or maybe it was the way her heart wanted to trill at its usage that darkened the scowl.

"You know what," she said. "Sign them or don't. I don't care."

More scraps of wood fell away with soft little thwacks of his knife blade.

"Since when do you whittle?"

A soft smile touched his puffy lips. "I'm trying something new."

Thwack. Thwack. Thwack.

"You can't stop this divorce."

"I can delay it."

"For how long?"

"Long enough."

"Long enough for what?" Her voice climbed with her frustration. "For one of us to kill to the other one?"

"Not that long," he said easily.

Thwack. Thwack.

Her gaze darted from him to the cabin door, to the lurching vessel floor at her feet.

Desperation goaded her into recklessness. "If you fuck Amber Jessop before we're divorced, I can claim emotional damages."

While Miles Sinclair had explained emotional damages to her when he'd asked if she wished to claim any, she was a little fuzzy on the details since none of the examples he'd listed had applied to her and Shea. Something to do with impacting division of property and custody determinations.

As a lawyer himself, she figured Shea would understand the meaning of the threat, and by the way he'd gone unnaturally still, she gathered it wasn't good.

She braced for his fury, but he only gave his head a soft shake and a smile curved his mouth, bringing to mind a fat cat, its belly full of milk. She'd given something away, though she had no idea what.

With the knife, he pared away more slivers of wood.

No matter how she might try to provoke him, it proved an impossible feat. She'd never seen him so calm. So "chill." So maddeningly, damnably restrained.

"Shea, stop this. Please."

"I've told you what you have to do, Isobel. After eighteen years of marriage, I deserve to hear you say the words to my face."

The sharp taste of fear flooded her mouth. Her gaze

darted from his insolent expression to the cabin door to the boat deck inches from her feet. She swallowed back the terror with a painful gulp.

Her heart fluttering with furious beats, she scampered across the stern and ducked inside the cabin. Twisting her body sideways, she clutched the handrail and picked her way down the steep, narrow stairs. Below deck, she rounded the kitchen counter, snatched the papers off the table, and whirled, ready to flee to safety.

But Shea's big body blocked her retreat. He skipped the stairs altogether and landed with a thud before her. The floor swayed beneath her feet.

"Here." She slapped the documents against his bare chest. "Sign them."

He took the papers and tossed them onto the counter. "Tell me why you want to end our marriage."

In the cramped space, he overwhelmed her senses. "You know why."

"I don't."

"All we do is fight." The delicious smell of his skin wrenched a pang of longing from her.

"What if I promise we'll never fight again?"

"You can't promise that."

"I can. I am." He crept closer. "I'll make you any promise, give you anything you want, just name it."

She tried to back away, but the edge of the table immediately jabbed into her bottom. "It doesn't work like that."

"You want to sell the house? Move off the island? Go to the moon?" His fingers toyed with the tendrils of hair on either side of her face. "Tell me and I'll find a way to make it happen."

"Shea–"

"Do you love me?" The hitch in his voice notched a wound on her heart.

Color rode high on his cheekbones, and in his eyes, emotion swirled like the churning waters of a stormy sea. She felt slightly seasick.

Though it'd be a lie, she wanted to deny her love for him, if only to end the pain. But the naked fear, the heartrending vulnerability visible on his face, stole her words.

The column of his throat worked when he swallowed. "If you tell me you don't love me anymore, I'll sign those damn papers. But if not…" His fingertips brushed her cheek.

At the touch, she jolted, realizing suddenly the danger she was in.

She'd never been able to resist him. Not when she gave him her virginity at sixteen. Not a year later, when he'd wanted to make love to her the night after her mom's funeral and they forgot the condom. Not when they found out she was pregnant and he asked her to marry him. She'd never been able to say no to him. Not even when she should have.

"Sign them," she said, her voice little more than a hoarse whisper.

Disappointment shadowed his features, but his expression closed, as if he guarded a sudden secret. "Fine. But before I do, I want something from you."

Wariness stole over her. "Wh-what do you want?"

"A kiss."

In an instant, her pounding pulse had nothing to do with the hazard of being trapped on a boat and everything to do with the very real danger posed by the man standing before her.

"It won't change anything."

Her gaze had riveted to his mouth, and so she watched the playful tilt form at one corner. "Then you have nothing to worry about, do you?"

A nervous laugh leapt from her throat and quickly died away.

"Just one last kiss, Isobel. It's a simple request, and you can end this right here, right now." He eased his big body close to hers. "That is what you want, isn't it?"

Chapter Eight

The small confines of the boat closed in around her and her chest rose and fell with the ragged pull of air into her lungs.

He slipped a hand beneath her hair. He kneaded the base of her neck. "You're shaking, *mo chroí.*"

My heart.

She squeezed her eyes shut with the slash of pain. "Don't call me that."

"Why not?"

Because every time she let him in, even a little, it ended badly for her.

"It hurts," she said.

"No more hurting. No more fighting." His warm mouth brushed across her forehead.

The sensation shattered her. When was the last time he'd touched her? His fingers danced across her skin.

With the pads of his thumbs, he tilted her chin up, cradling her face while he explored her mouth with tiny nips and nibbles. She couldn't keep up with her own heartbeat.

He'd never kissed her this way before. Fierce, fresh, tumbling kisses. Emotion whipped inside her, sinking and sliding darkly.

Tears prickled behind her eyes. How she'd longed for his warm, solid touch. A jagged sob snagged in her throat and her lips parted. His tongue licked swiftly inside her mouth, stealing her secrets.

Her troubled thoughts burst into flames and smoldered to ash as his hot mouth conspired with his clever fingers to seek out all the most susceptible places on her body—the center of her palm, the hollow beneath her earlobe, the notch of her clavicle.

Though she shouldn't, she reached for him. She caressed his face, his neck, his bare shoulders. Her palms smoothed over the rounded swells of his pecs and along the hard plane of his abdomen. He was familiar yet foreign to her, like coming home after a long, agonizing journey.

He cupped her through the tight dress while he tugged at the low-cut neckline. She arched her back, offering herself up to him, because even when she wanted to hate him, she wanted his touch more. She craved it. He freed her breast from the confining material and gave her nipple a firm, wet tug with his mouth.

Heat flushed her skin. Hunger coiled in her heart and belly. She whimpered like a woman willing to do anything for this man's touch because that was exactly what she was.

He tugged the dress lower and his hungry gaze clamped onto her flesh. His heavy lashes lowered until sharp shadows scored down his lean cheeks. A part of her, the part that fell instantly and completely in love with him in high school, delighted in his naked appreciation of her body.

He gripped her waist and his teeth scraped the sensitive skin where her neck and shoulder met.

"Shea." His name slipped out as a desperate plea, though, truly, there was nothing she wanted from him.

Then the long shaft of his erection brushed her stomach and the lie washed away with the flood of her desire.

Fine. She did want something from him. She wanted him to sign their divorce papers. And she wanted him to fuck her.

God, she was so messed up.

His name kept falling from her lips and he urgently rucked up the hem of her skirt, clenching the fabric in his tight fists. Cool air rushed across her hot flesh and she gasped.

Discovering her panty-less, Shea stiffened, and then a savage growl vibrated in his chest.

"Holy fuck, Isobel." Shock and arousal shook his voice.

He delved his fingers tenderly between her thighs to the patch of her curls. Questing, he found her humid flesh open to the invasion of his fingers. He nuzzled the side of her neck while he rubbed tension into her belly.

Delicious coils spiraled dizzyingly through her body. Her knees buckled, but she caught herself before she fell against him. More than anything, she wanted to lean into him, but he wasn't her safe place anymore.

Maybe he never had been.

The warm whisper of his breath teased her ear when he asked, "Do you remember the first time I touched you like this?"

The night he'd returned from that first summer spent on the freighter, he'd climbed through her bedroom window and drowned her with kisses and apologies. She'd tried to extract promises that he'd never leave her again. Rather than give them, he'd teased and fondled her flesh until, panting and sobbing, her first orgasm screamed through her. When he'd left her bed in the black of night, he still hadn't made her a single promise.

Her head moved with a jerky nod.

He skimmed over her wetness and then stroked deep, the touch so intimate, she couldn't speak for the tears clogged in her throat.

He brushed a brief, hot kiss against the side of her throat, then slipped one hand to her back as he eased her down onto the table. Shoving the hem of her dress high above her waist, one work-roughened hand rubbed slow, drugging circles over her belly while the other tenderly stroked the source of her craving.

She watched him watching her body, mesmerized by the beautiful clash of hard and soft on his face. His probing, ravenous gaze fed her arousal until the sweet torture grew impossibly high and taut. Arching her back, she swiveled her hips, unabashedly chasing the pleasure his gentle, circling strokes wrought. She neared the peak and was ready to fling herself over the precipice when his fingers suddenly left her body.

Her protests died in her throat when he frantically worked the drawstring on his loose-fitting shorts and yanked the cloth down over his hips to stand naked before her.

She swallowed with an audible gulp.

He was big. His proud erection pressed against his stomach, so long and thick that the dusky head concealed his belly button. Though she'd never been with any other man, she spent her days around women in the mood to talk. Curious about some of what she'd overheard, she once took to the internet and came away convinced Shea was large. Larger than most. By a lot.

"Open your legs." His husky voice rasped with his barely restrained control.

She never could deny him for long.

When he stepped between her thighs, his hips spread her wide. His hardness pressed against her vulnerable core and her flesh resisted him, just as her heart did. With the tip of his heavy shaft poised at her entrance, he teased her with his fingers until she'd returned to the mountaintop and hovered at the edge of the cliff.

He nudged inside.

She cried out with painful joy as her body sucked him deeper. He resisted. She shifted her hips and moaned when he slipped another fraction inside her.

Then it was a sensual altercation. With little wiggles and undulations, she tried to entice him farther inside, but he delayed, teasing and tormenting her aching flesh until she begged him in a hoarse whisper to "do it now, please." She needed him inside her.

That she begged him rankled, but her anger fractured to tiny bits of nothingness when he pushed inside the wet constriction of her body, gentle in the way only a big man could be. Her body succumbed to his power even as she squirmed at the impossible thickness of him.

"That's it, *a chuisle mo chroí.* Let me in."

Pulse of my heart.

The endearment pulled a sob from her.

His lips caught at hers while he pushed into her honeyed core, inch by glorious inch. When she'd taken him all, a shaking breath rattled through her. If he could give her more, she'd have taken that, too. There was no part of him she could refuse. Not in this moment. She wanted all of him. One last time.

He grasped her bottom, his fingers biting into the plump roundness, and set a steady, upward plunging rhythm. With every voluptuous plunge, sensation spiraled and multiplied. Each thrust drove another memory from her mind. The first time he kissed her. The first time he made love to her. The first time he took her from behind.

Moisture leaked from the corners of her eyes as all her senses burst to colorful life. Having been dulled and grayed for so long, sensation overwhelmed her. She clung to him, lifting her knees to wrap her legs around his lean waist. The position allowed him to wedge deeper and a guttural groan tore from him.

He tugged her wrists above her head and anchored them to the table. "You think another man is going to be able to give you this?"

A broken sob escaped her.

"You think you're done with me?" He thrust in a tireless rhythm, in and out, the friction slippery and sweet and carnal. "Tell me you never want me again. Tell me you can bear the thought of never being with me this way again. Say it and I'll stop right now."

No one would ever fill her the way he did. No one would ever be able to touch her so deep.

Tears streamed down her cheeks. "Never," she whispered.

His big, driving body was unrelenting, as though if he loved her fiercely enough he might be able to push out all the anger and hurt and fear.

"We are not getting a divorce, Isobel. Do you hear me?"

He couldn't stop her. They both knew it. But their bodies sang with the promise they made to each other long ago, with their words and their bodies.

"You are the only one," he rasped. "There can be no others."

His hands braced on either side of her head, she

gripped his wrists and held on while the orgasm crashed over her. Turning her head, her teeth scraped over the script tattoo on his forearm while the muscles of her pulsing core spasmed with brutal pleasure. With her throaty moans, she swallowed the Gaelic words inscribed in his flesh, translating roughly to "one heart, one way."

Inside her, Shea grew unbearably thick and hard. His long, deep plunges became short and urgent until he shuddered and his heat flooded her in violent pulsations.

In the silence afterward, their ragged breathing mingled and for one brief, painful moment, she lived in him as the beating of his heart.

With the pad of his thumb, he wiped away the tracks left by her tears. She blinked rapidly as she returned to herself. To the place where grief and doubt outlasted passion.

Unlocking her legs from around his waist, she wriggled out from under him. She tried to pull away, but he caught her easily with one hand at the small of her back. He tugged her close, drawing her against his body until her cheek rested against his collarbone.

He held her, his mouth near her temple. "I don't want to hurt you."

She swallowed convulsively. "It's all we do anymore."

"It doesn't have to be that way."

With the sharp bite of longing, her eyes filled with tears once more.

Shaking her head, she pressed her palms against his chest, but her soft shove didn't budge him. "We've tried everything. Nothing ever works for long."

Weariness filled his frustrated sigh. The sound, small and seemingly harmless, carried with it years of arguments and painful memories, and might as well have been a slap to the face.

Shame built as a sob in her throat.

Snatching the envelope off the counter, she thrust it at his chest. "Just sign the papers, Shea."

His expression hardened, and for the first time that day, she recognized him as the man she thought to divorce.

On his chest, his larger hand covered hers. Instinctively, his fingers sought the secret crevices between her knuckles.

"We had a deal," he said, his voice like velvet wrapped in steel.

Alarm bells went off inside her head. She tried to pull back her hand, but his grip tightened.

"You've had your kiss." She rattled the envelope. "Sign."

A cold sneer curled his lip. "I wasn't talking about kissing your mouth."

Chapter Nine

They belonged together, and after what had happened on his boat, she could no longer deny it.

But in case she thought to, Shea was prepared to get her naked and prove her wrong, over and over again, until he'd drilled the truth into her pretty little head.

The bell chimed above his head when he entered the store.

He knew sex wouldn't fix their marriage. Might make things worse, in fact, if he didn't handle it right. But he didn't plan to make things worse, and sex with his wife might just be the opening he needed to break through her barriers. Just a tiny crack; if he could exploit the breach, he might be able to barge the rest of the way back into her life and her heart.

There were no guarantees that he'd know what to do once inside her walls, but it was a chance. One he had to take if he was going to win his wife back.

And he had to win her back. There was no other option. Not for him.

He hadn't laid eyes on her days. Not since she'd tugged her dress down over her naked hips and scurried from his arms looking more shaken and fragile than he'd ever seen her. Though it'd gutted him to let her go, he could see she needed some space. He gave it to her, a part of him recognizing that he'd never be able to hold onto her by grasping too tightly.

But then last night, she sent Ava to pick up Connor and Maisie, and his mercy came to a swift end.

Summoned by the chime, Isobel emerged from the back room, a bulbous heap of frilly fabric in her arms. He despised the world-weary frown that pulled at her features when she spotted him.

She picked her way through the clothing racks and edged close to him. "What are you doing here?" she hissed.

She'd drawn her dark hair into a sleek ponytail, and as usual, makeup she didn't need painted her beautiful face. If he hadn't peered closely, he would've missed the puffy bags under her eyes.

A dark pleasure spread through him as he contemplated what might be keeping her awake at night. "Why haven't you returned my calls?"

She glanced in the direction of a woman rummaging through the horde of white dresses at the back of the store. "Have you signed the papers?"

"We haven't finished our negotiations."

Pink rushed into her cheeks. "That wasn't a negotiation. It was extortion."

Beneath the flowy black blouse she wore, black leggings hugged her lush bottom and shapely thighs.

"All I asked for was a kiss." He dragged his gaze back

to her face. "The rest happened because we're meant to be together."

She offered her customer a weak smile, then sliced him with a look. "Can we not do this here?"

"Where would you like to do it?"

The warm color on her cheeks spread to her neck and chest, and her lips parted with the slight hitch in her breathing. Triumph and lust tugged at his balls.

"It was just sex," she whispered, panic churning in her stormy eyes.

"It was good sex. Fucking fantastic sex." He pushed into her space. "It's a whole new ball game now, my sweet wife."

Holding the dress tightly to her chest, like a shield, she backed away. "What does that mean?"

"It means I'm not giving up on us. We're good together, Isobel. Incredible."

"Sex was never our problem." She came up hard against the counter. "Our issues are bigger than that. Sign the papers, Shea."

Slowly, he reached up and brushed a stray lock of hair that'd escaped her ponytail off her forehead. "I will never forgive myself for what's happened to us. I didn't guard our relationship with enough jealousy. But that ends now."

The pink tip of her tongue came out to lick her lips.

"I'm going to win you back, *a mhuirnín*."

Her expression softened. "Shea, I told you, it's too late."

"We'll see about that."

"You're not listening to me." She pressed her palm to his chest, as though she intended to push him away. "It's over."

"I disagree."

Her hand over his heart, her gaze locked on his

mouth. "It doesn't matter if you agree with me or not. It's wh-what I want."

His patience ran out. "Goddammit, Isobel, we are not getting a div—"

"Excuse me," a woman's voice interrupted.

Isobel's head snapped around while Shea bit down on a curse and eased away from her.

The woman with the shitty timing pointed to the dress in Isobel's hands. "Can I see that dress?"

Isobel blinked rapidly and then hoisted the crumpled gown filling her arms. "This one?"

The woman lifted the pale pink dress high, letting the fabric unfurl. "I love this color. Blush is so trendy right now." Her head bent to one side as she studied the gown. "Who's the designer?"

Words seemed to stick and slip on Isobel's tongue. "Oh, uh, she's no one you'd know."

The woman dropped her chin to glower at Isobel over the rim of her tortoiseshell eyeglasses. "What's her name?"

The pink in Isobel's cheeks heightened and spread, pulling a frown from Shea.

"Uh..." With a nervous side-eye glance at him, she offered the woman a feeble smile. "It's me. I made it."

Surprise slammed into Shea and his head whipped from the extravagant gown the woman held up to his wife. "You made this?"

"Do you have any other dresses I can see?"

After a moment of stunned paralysis, Isobel sprang forward. At a nearby rack, she rifled through garments and soon hauled a white puffy one from the throng.

"Here's a drop-waist ball gown, and I have a sheath over here somewhere..." With her free hand, Isobel shuffled through more gowns. "What style are you looking for?"

A spurt of laughter burst from the woman and she pushed a lock of her lightly graying hair behind one ear. "I'm not buying for myself. Where is the sheath?"

Isobel hauled another dress from the store rack and hooked all three gowns onto the crossbar, laying them atop the other gowns.

The woman shoved her eyeglasses on top of her head and stepped back.

Shea stared at the dresses right along with her. How had he not known Isobel made a wedding dress? Three of them. At least.

Why hadn't she told him?

"I think there's one more in the back." Isobel bit down on her bottom lip. "Do you want me to get it?"

Frowning in concentration, the woman nodded. "Yes, please."

While Isobel scurried away, Shea watched the woman inspect the gowns. She hunched close and examined the beading on one dress while on another, she lifted the hem and inspected the stitching on the gown's underside.

What in the hell was going on?

Isobel reappeared with a creamy white dress, which the woman lifted from her hands with a hum of appreciation. "Ooh, I love this fabric. Is it silk?"

Isobel nodded. "I couldn't resist making a dress with it."

Hanging the dress alongside the others, the woman plucked the eyeglasses off her head. She chewed lightly on one temple tip on the glasses.

Then she twisted to face Isobel. "Your designs are beautiful. They're trendy, but they've got a real vintage-inspired feel, don't they?"

Isobel's soft smile landed like a physical blow in the center of Shea's chest.

"My mom was a seamstress," Isobel said. "She loved vintage clothing."

"Did she teach you how to sew?" the woman asked, her no-nonsense expression softening a bit.

"She tried, but I was a brat and didn't listen to her." With a rusty laugh, Isobel gave her head a small shake. "Oh, how I have suffered for it ever since."

The woman's eyeglasses cut through the air. "No one listens to their mother. Especially teenage girls. It's the rite of passage for every woman to learn the hard way that her mother was right all along."

While the women shared a laugh, his heart battered his sternum.

"I like to look at old pictures of her." Isobel's soft voice sloped through him. "I didn't realize it when she was alive, but she was very stylish. She's inspired a few of my designs."

The woman's gaze returned to the dresses. "I love this one." She touched the delicate fabric. "The cut is amazing."

A delightful blush rushed into Isobel's soft cheeks. "Thank you."

He gaped, his mouth slightly ajar, at the sudden reappearance of the soft, tenderhearted woman he'd married. It'd been years since he'd seen her. Happy and hopeful, with no traces of worry or resentment. God, how he missed her.

"And the way you mix vintage with trendy touches is remarkable. You have a gift."

Despite her obvious pleasure, a frown puckered Isobel's brow. "You know a lot about wedding dresses. Do you work in the industry?"

The woman stuck out her hand. "I'm Vanessa Dubois. I'm the editor at *Stylish Bride* magazine."

A strangled sound erupted from Isobel. "Oh! I—I—I love

your magazine. I read it every month."

The wide smile remained on Vanessa's face as Isobel shook her hand with enough vigor to cause injury to most people. "What's your name?"

"Isobel."

"Isobel what?"

Isobel froze, then her gaze darted to his face.

She swallowed thickly. "Nolan. Isobel Nolan."

"Nolan?" Vanessa stuck her glasses on top of her head again. "Do you know Leo?"

"It depends," Shea interjected. "What's he done?"

Vanessa turned intelligent eyes on him. "He's marrying my niece."

Isobel gasped. "Prue is your niece?"

Over the odd sound of Isobel's sputtering shock, Shea said, "Well in that case, I'm Leo's eldest and most charming brother."

"The oldest brother?" Vanessa eyed him thoughtfully. "Luke?"

"Close," he lied. "I'm Shea."

"Shea and Isobel." Her gaze traveled between them. "That makes you Colin and Mary's parents?"

"You've met Connor and Maisie?" Isobel asked.

"Prue and I were at the beach scouting sites for the ceremony when we ran into... Noah? With the kids." A calculating gleam came into Vanessa's eyes. "You have a beautiful family."

Isobel suddenly appeared slightly ill.

"And we're delighted to be adding your lovely niece to the clan," Shea said easily.

Vanessa assessed him openly, and he offered her a smile, the one he knew made most women blush or giggle, sometimes both.

Vanessa didn't blush, but she did burst out with a boisterous laugh. "You're adorable."

His smile turned genuine. "I don't think anyone's ever called me adorable."

"That I can believe," she said. "I love your accent. Where are you from?"

"Ireland, originally. Our family moved to the States when Leo was a wee one, which is why he suffers the misfortune of talking like a Yank."

"But you've stayed? Did you ever think about going back to Ireland?"

"I met my wife here when I was sixteen years old." A fierce edge crept into his voice and rode just below his words. "Nothing could drag me away after that."

Feeling her gaze on him, Shea sought and found stormy gray eyes.

"How long have you two been married?"

"Eighteen years," they said together.

Vanessa missed the look that passed between them as she studied Isobel's dresses, her head tipped to one side.

"Isobel Nolan." With a shrug, she held up her hands. "I'm sorry but I've never heard of you."

Isobel's soft chuckle arrowed straight through his heart. "No one's heard of me. I'm... new."

"How new?"

"I've been sewing dresses for years, but I've only recently started to sell them here at the store."

She'd been making wedding dresses for years? He had so many questions. How many dresses had she made? How many had she sold? Why didn't he know that she liked to look at old pictures of her mom? There was so much he wanted to know. So much she'd never told him.

So damn much he'd never asked her.

Vanessa pivoted abruptly. "I have a proposition for you. What do you think about being the subject of a feature in *Stylish Bride*?"

Isobel's mouth fell slack.

"We do a monthly feature on an industry up-and-comer."

"I've read it," Isobel said dazedly.

"I want to feature you. A fresh new designer, living an idyllic life on an idyllic little island with her photogenic husband and two adorable children. Your story is exactly what our readers love."

Isobel's pretty mouth snapped shut, and Shea could practically hear the gears of her mind working. Vanessa thought they had an idyllic life. An idyllic marriage. She didn't know about the divorce summons floating in the belly of his boat or the cranky teenager at home. She didn't know that their idyllic little island would transform into a dark, frozen tundra in only a few short months.

Crushing disappointment settled heavily on her shoulders.

With a jolt, he realized that she wanted this. Badly. By her devastated expression, she needed it. Her happiness depended on it.

In the silence, Vanessa pushed to close the deal. "Look, we've had a story fall apart at the last minute, and I need to fill the spot fast. We'll do an interview, take some pictures, get you some national exposure, and then leave you to it. What do you say?"

Isobel tried to hide her sorrow behind a smile. "Unfortunately—"

"We'd love to." He slipped an arm around his wife's waist and hauled her to his side.

When she gasped, he covered her mouth with his, swallowing the sound of her tell with his kiss.

"Fantastic." Vanessa plucked a cell phone from her purse. "Whew, you scared me for a second there. I thought you were going to turn me down."

Slowly, reluctantly, he lifted his head. Isobel blinked up at him with soft eyes, glassy with shock.

"Why in the world would we do that?" Shea said. "It's the opportunity of a lifetime."

"That it is. Let me get your number." Vanessa punched the digits Shea relayed into her cell phone. "So, from your vantage point, the whole thing will only take a day or two. We'll do an interview—don't panic. We're just going to ask you some questions about yourself, your background, your creative process, etcetera, etcetera. Then our photographer will snap some pictures of you here at your store, at home, and anywhere else you'd like. Maybe grab a few shots of you two on the beach or something, I don't know. And you should select some of your more popular dresses for the photoshoot."

"My what?"

"No panicking, you promised," Vanessa said, though Isobel had done no such thing. "Maybe choose ten dresses? Enough to showcase your style but not too many."

"Ten dresses?" Isobel swallowed with an audible gulp.

"Give or take." Vanessa pressed her cell phone to her ear. "I'm sorry we don't have room to display them all, but I suspect you'll have plenty of opportunities to show off your creations after the feature runs." She stuck up her index finger. "Jen, hi, it's me. I found someone for the feature. You're going to love her. *I know.* It must be fate or something. So what's your schedule like? Okay. Okay. Call me back."

Vanessa disconnected the call and her face split with her wide grin. "Everything's falling into place. I'm so excited. Are you excited? 'Cause you look a little queasy."

"She's overwhelmed." Shea pressed a kiss to Isobel's temple. "It's a dream come true."

"It is." Vanessa winked at him and then started toward the door. "I'll be in touch with a day and time for the interview and photoshoot. I'd love to get Jen and Marcus out here tomorrow, but realistically it'll probably take a week or two to set everything up."

"Two weeks?" Isobel squeaked.

"Hopefully sooner. We need to wrap it up by the end of the month to make deadline." Her hand on the handle, she glanced back at them over her shoulder. "It was so nice meeting you both. I don't fly out until next Sunday, so hopefully we bump into each other again, but if not, I'll see you at Leo's wedding, won't I?"

Relishing the feel of his wife's body against his, Shea tightened his hold on Isobel's waist. "Definitely."

"Fantastic." Her grin wide, Vanessa shoved her eyeglasses onto her face. "Bye for now."

The bell jingled when she exited the store and they watched her pass by the front window. The moment she disappeared from sight, Isobel shot from his arms.

She whirled on him. "Why did you do that?"

He shrugged. "Because you were going to say no."

With a soft smack, she flattened her hand against her forehead. "She thinks we're married."

"We are married."

Her hand dropped heavily to her side. "She thinks we're happily married."

"You can't pretend to be *happily* married to me for a couple of weeks? Through one little interview and a couple of pictures?"

"No."

He shook his head. "I was wrong."

"Wrong about what?

"I thought you wanted this."

A dazed—no, dreamy—light flickered in her eyes, but then she fixed him with a dark look of mistrust. "So what if I do?"

Her distrust left a gash on his heart. "If you're as talented as Vanessa seems to think you are, then you have to take a shot. You deserve it."

The dreamy light flared, and for a moment he could only stare, rapt.

"But what if they find out it's all a lie?"

"Did you make these dresses?"

Color rushed into her cheeks, and she nodded.

"Then there's nothing that should stop you from seizing this opportunity."

She pulled her puffy bottom lip between her teeth and tortured it.

A punch of lust struck him in the gut. "If you want this, then I say, let's go get it for you."

Her smile tried to form before she ruthlessly bit it back. "Why do I get the feeling there's a catch?"

He clucked his tongue. "Have you always been this suspicious?"

One of her dark eyebrows inched upward in challenge. "You'd pretend to be happily married to me?"

"Of course I would." A smile curled through him. "On one condition."

"I knew it," she said, but no anger infected her tone. "What condition?"

"I'll pretend to be happily married to you, as long as I get to kiss you whenever I want."

Chapter Ten

"You cannot be serious."

Shea's puffy lips curved with his wicked smile. "Oh, but I am. Deadly."

A bark of incredulous laughter escaped her. "You're crazy."

"Nope. I'm finally seeing things clearly." His gaze held hers, startling in its intensity. "Before I sign any papers, we're going to make one last go at fixing this marriage. What better place to start than with a kiss? Or better yet, lots of kisses."

Her pulse echoed in her ears. "Kisses... on the mouth?"

"I'm not inflexible. If you want to open negotiations–"

"No, no." Heat swamped her face and chest. "The mouth is fine. I was just clarifying."

"So we have a deal?"

She shook her head to clear it. "The last time we

kissed, we got ourselves into trouble."

"Believe me, it was no trouble." His voice rumbled with a gravelly smoothness that sent the heat in her face spiraling downward.

"Kissing won't fix us."

"Worked great the other night."

Her heart gave a painful wrench. "Sex will only complicate things."

"I'm willing to risk it."

An anguishing tangle of emotions crashed through her. Wild exhilaration at connecting with him physically, the way they used to, and the thrill of feeling him inside her again after so long were crushed by the dread of certain heartbreak. How long before their first fight? How long before he shut her out again?

A low, heavy sigh tumbled from her. "Well, I'm not."

The line of his mouth thinned with his grimace. He studied her with somber eyes a moment and then turned his head in the direction of her dresses. Slowly, he reached out and touched the blush ballgown.

Her heart stuttered, tripping into a frantic rhythm as his large, masculine hand fingered the delicate fabric.

Watching him, her breath snagged in her throat. What did he see when he looked at her dresses? Did he see the creative outpouring that went into each design? Or the long hours spent drawing out the patterns, fashioning toiles, hunting for the perfect fabric, saving what little she had left over from her paychecks and scavenging for sale prices so that she could purchase the finest quality material? Did he see the fear, the work, the love that went into every stitch? Could he possibly understand the terror that, after all the parts of herself she'd poured into a dress, in the end, no one would want it?

More likely, he saw nothing but a silly exercise in losing money.

Bright blue eyes fastened on her face. "Vanessa really loved these."

A beat of pride kicked in her chest and she dropped her chin to hide her sudden smile. "She's from New York City. I'll bet she makes a big deal out of everything."

"She didn't strike me as an excitable sort, or a clueless one." His expression softened with his voice. "You have real talent, Iz."

Talent? Her? Pleasure bloomed, marching through her veins with the sweet blossom. Had she finally found something she was good at? Something she could point to and say, "Look at this amazing thing I've done. See? I am not just my dad's throwaway. I am worth something to someone."

"How long have you been making wedding dresses?"

At the vulnerable hitch in his voice, a bubble of surprise enfolded her. "I've been doing alterations for years. I made a few dresses before we separated." She tucked a loose strand of hair behind one ear and shrugged. "I think I've made eight others since then."

"Nine wedding dresses?" His features twisted. "Why didn't you tell me?"

The stab of sorrow in his tone punctured the bubble. "Probably the same reason you didn't tell me you quit your job at the firm."

He reared back. His anger flashed, swift and white-hot.

She plunged ahead before he hurled hurtful words at her. "I know. You forgot. At least I had our good friend Amber Jessop to tell me. At the summer carnival. In front of half of the island."

"Amber Jessop. Jesus–" He gulped down the rest of the curse.

She braced for his counterstrike, but it didn't come.

His anger fizzled out, to be replaced with something

soft and wounded. "Were you going to tell me?"

Uncertainty swamped her. "I don't know. Maybe. Eventually." Pain clouded his features and filled her with regret. She struggled to put words to her reasons. "I guess I thought you'd think it was silly."

"Why would I think that?" he asked softly.

Her mind chased the memories. After they married, she'd watched him breeze through college on a full-ride scholarship, tackle law school with relative ease, and then when he got bored with that, he started his own business, turning the pub into the premier establishment on the island. He'd done it all on his own, with hard work and stubborn determination, and without any help from anyone.

He was a success two or three times over and she... was a retail clerk who'd dishonored her family. Once, they'd been equals, but their paths had diverged even before that first dinner party at the senior partner's extravagant home.

She'd tried to play along. For years, she worked hard to become the woman he deserved. The perfect wife and mother with a perfect home, perfect children, perfect hair and clothing. The perfect woman. But every day she failed, and eventually she grew exhausted and defeated with the trying. Somewhere along the way, she'd taken her dreams and sheltered them away inside the secret chamber of her heart.

With a pang, she realized how unfair that had been to him.

"I don't know." His familiar face suddenly appeared strange to her. "Maybe... I was wrong."

His Adam's apple dipped when he swallowed. "I'm sorry."

The words carried the weight of a thousand sorrows and their heft slammed into her.

"I'm sorry if I made you feel like you couldn't talk to me," he said, his raspy voice rough with emotion. "That you couldn't, or shouldn't, pursue this."

A current passed between them. Not sexual, or even sensual, but intimate nonetheless. Then his gaze touched over her dresses again.

When he glanced back at her, an eager light winked in his vivid blue eyes. "Can I see the other dresses?"

She blinked away the cobwebs of confusion spun by his apology and hurtled back to reality.

"There are no other dresses." Her hand met her forehead with a soft smack. "This is it."

His brows pulled together. "What happened to the other five?"

"I sold them."

"You've sold five dresses?" A low whistle leaked out of him. "But didn't Vanessa say something about ten dresses?"

A sliver of panic shivered through her. "Give or take."

"And you only have four dresses?"

"I only have four dresses." Her voice pitched.

"How long will it take you to make the others?"

"Each dress can take weeks. Months even."

His face fell. "You don't have months."

Panic veered toward hysteria. "I have two weeks. To make six dresses."

"That's not a lot of time."

With shaking hands, she pressed her palms against her cheeks and gaped at him. "There isn't enough time. Or money."

Suddenly, his expression cleared. "You were trying to get a loan." A smug smile tipped up one side of his mouth. "That's why you went out to dinner with Cooper."

She dropped her arms. "I already told you that."

"You said it was a business meeting. You didn't tell me

the topic was *your* business."

"Cooper and I never got around to discussing business." She pinned him with a look. "Somebody ruined everything first."

The corners of his eyes creased when he winced. "You didn't get the loan?"

She shrugged to hide her disappointment. "I haven't heard from him, so I'm guessing not."

"It's only been a few weeks. It'll come through soon."

Her hand moved through the air with a dismissive wave. "I don't think it's going to happen. I mean, I'm a high school dropout who's never earned more than minimum wage. Not exactly the résumé of a successful business owner."

"Stop that," he snapped. "You're as smart as anyone I know, and a thousand times more talented. You've sold five wedding dresses totaling how much? Several thousand dollars? Don't you dare talk that down."

His words soothed the mark left by his biting tone. "Thank you. I think."

He thrust a hand through his hair. "Okay, we need a plan."

"What plan?"

"Let's start with inventory. Is there any way you can borrow back the dresses you sold?"

She wrinkled her nose. "I don't know. A wedding dress is sentimental to a woman. I don't think they'd give them back."

"We aren't going to keep them, we're only borrowing them. Every dress will be professionally cleaned before we return it. Tell them that." He dropped his chin and bright blue eyes pierced her. "And this is business now. No sentimental girly stuff. Got it?"

She touched her forehead in mock salute. "Mina and Emily each bought one of my dresses. Maybe we could ask them?"

His smile sent her pulse racing. "Can you make four dresses in two weeks?"

Pulling her bottom lip between her teeth, she gnawed on it, considering. "With my work schedule, I'll only have a couple of hours in the evening."

"Can any of your coworkers pick up some of your hours?"

"Sarah might want the extra time."

"Does she happen to sew?"

"No. But Ginny does."

"Is she good enough to help you make these dresses?"

Isobel worried her bottom lip. "She is, but I don't know... her parents are elderly and–"

He silenced her with a look. "Get her. It's only for two weeks. If she's worth it, offer to pay her double her salary."

"I definitely don't have enough money to double her salary."

A thoughtful frown tugged at his handsome features. "You're right. We need to sit down and come up with a budget." His fingertips smoothed over his puffy mouth. "How much money did you ask Cooper for?"

When she told him the amount, he surprised her with his unflinching reaction. "We might need to borrow against Maisie's and Connor's college funds to start you up."

Her jaw dropped. "You'd give me that much money?"

Confusion rippled across his face. "It's not my money. It's ours."

Except that in all their years together, she'd never pulled in even a quarter of what he had earned.

"You worked just as hard as I did," he said, as if reading her thoughts. "Maybe harder, considering you had a job, a houseful of my brothers and a colicky baby to contend with. You took care of me and everyone I care about in the world while I went to school and built my career. I can't put a price on what I owe you. What we all owe you."

The soft tenderness in his rough voice caused her skin to flush with heat.

Or maybe it was the way he looked at her, his gaze quiet and probing. "If this is what you want, then I say let's go get it for you. We've got the money. You've got the talent. And a golden opportunity has just landed in our laps." His devastating smile reached inside her. "What do you say?"

A sweet bloom of hope blossomed in her chest. He made it all seem so... possible. Probable. To make her dream reality, all she had to do was reach out and take it.

Emotion squeezed her throat and she nodded. "Okay. Let's do it."

With the quick flash of his wide smile, he brushed her cheek and pulled her close. When his lips brushed hers, sensation ricocheted through her. Thoughts of resisting him scrambled when his fingers stroked the hollow beneath her earlobe. He tasted her with possessive licks and nips that roused a gentle fire in her. The kiss was slow, drugging, and when he stopped, a whimper of regret escaped her.

"Was that so bad?" he murmured against her mouth.

"Dreadful." She extracted herself from the warm cocoon of his arms. "I guess you were serious about that kissing thing, huh?"

He studied her with the intensity he used to show his law briefs. "I was serious."

She pressed the tips of her fingers to her scalded lips. "Vanessa will probably learn the truth about us anyway from one of the island gossips."

"I doubt she'd care about a bunch of rumors, as long

as she gets her story for the feature." Storm clouds gathered at the edges of his features, contradicting his smooth tone. "But in case it does matter to her, we can be sure to give her the story she wants."

"It's a bad idea."

Dangerous and doomed to failure.

Yet she hadn't rejected the notion outright.

His broad shoulders lifted with his callous shrug. "I'm not an actor. I can't fake something I don't feel and expect people to believe me. If I have to act happy, I need to *be* happy, and kissing you makes me really fucking happy."

She bit back a smile. Would it be so bad? If she was going to make four wedding dresses in two weeks, she was going to need his help. What were a few harmless kisses if the end result was a career doing something she loved, something she was good at?

It might even be a good thing. Good for the kids if their parents stopped arguing, and maybe even got along, like they used to do. And when Shea signed those divorce papers, it'd be good for them both, for everyone, if they moved on as friends rather than enemies.

She searched the handsome face of her fierce, determined husband, who she'd never been able to resist for long.

"Those are my terms." His husky voice tickled a spot low in her belly. "Take it or leave it."

The risk of failure was great, heartbreak all but certain.

But what were a couple of days of danger for a chance at her dream? If she was going to take a shot at it, she might as well take a big, wholehearted grab. Shouldn't she?

Of course she should.

But... could she? Could she pretend to be happily

married to him? Could she let him help her? Let him kiss her whenever he wanted?

Yeah, she could.

Given the delicious tingling that remained on her lips, she might even enjoy it.

"Okay."

Blue fire flared in his eyes. Her heart fluttered wildly when he tugged her to him, and as he claimed a kiss, she experienced a flash of fear that the happiness in her heart had less to do with the realization of her dream and more to do with the delicious slide of her husband's mouth against hers.

Chapter Eleven

When Shea stepped through the back door, the familiar hollowness twisted his gut. He experienced the aching emptiness every time he entered the house that was no longer his home.

How had he and Isobel let things get so out of control that they couldn't even live in the same house? How had they gotten to this place where he made huge life decisions without her input and she hid little things about herself from him? And if she hid the little things, did that mean she was keeping bigger things from him as well?

A cartoon on the TV filled the house with noise, and he pursued it into the living room. "What's all that racket?"

Two dark little heads poked over the couch back. "Daddy!"

Connor and Maisie charged him. Bending at the knees, he scooped them up and tucked each one under an arm as if they were oversized footballs. The peal of their giggles carried to the peak of the vaulted ceiling and sang through him. This was the best part of his day every day that he got to see his kids.

Isobel appeared from the hallway, her hair piled on top of her head and a tape measure hanging around her neck.

"What are you doing here?" Her voice contained a distinct lack of annoyance.

The sound of progress.

"I thought I'd come by and see if anyone wants to go fishing." With a jiggle of his arms, he extracted more breathless giggles.

Connor gasped. "I wanna go!"

Isobel's stormy eyes widened with surprise. "Aren't you working today?"

Two weeks after hiring Aiden, Shea couldn't be happier. He showed up for his shift every night, on time, and he knew what he was doing behind the bar. By far, he was the best bartender Shea had ever had on his staff. He was fast, friendly, the staff loved him, and better yet, the customers loved him. Particularly the female customers, who'd packed into the bar every night that week for a chance to flirt and be served by the island's mysterious newcomer.

"I'm playing hooky," he said, and felt no anxiety saying it.

Disbelief parted her lips.

He resisted the urge to claim a kiss.

Though he could claim it. That was their deal.

Supreme satisfaction unfurled in his chest. She'd agreed to let him kiss her whenever he wanted.

"You two ready to go?" He set Connor and Maisie on

their feet. "Mama needs to work."

Maisie scurried to Isobel's side. "I'm helping Mama."

Isobel smoothed a hand over Maisie's small head. "Oh, not this time, sweetie."

"But I want to." Maisie slipped her hand inside Isobel's.

Shea crouched down so his face was level with Maisie's. "Do you know what Mama is doing?"

"Making a dress." She leaned against Isobel's leg. "I wanna help."

Connor bounced. "I wanna go fithing."

"Hang in there, buddy." Shea squeezed Connor's tiny rib cage and turned back to Maisie. "Did Mama tell you she's making this dress for a princess?"

Maisie's big gray eyes filled with wonder, and she bent her head back to stare up at Isobel. "A princess?"

He leaned in. "A princess who needs it right away. There's no time to waste."

Maisie's miniature mouth gaped open.

"Should we let Mama work for a little while? Then we'll hurry home to help her."

Nodding, Maisie hooked her arm around his neck. "We'll be back later, Mama."

"Thank you, *mija*."

When he stood, his gaze collided with Isobel's and the slippery softness shimmering in her gray eyes tugged at his groin.

But her small smile fell as Finn shuffled into the room, his dark hair sleep-rumpled and his eyes half open.

Connor latched on to Finn's leg, pulling a grunt from the groggy teen.

"We go fithing!"

"Cool, buddy." Finn continued into the kitchen, lugging his leg with Connor still attached along behind him.

"You want to come with us?" Hope rang in Shea's

voice.

Finn's startled gaze swung to Shea, then he ducked his chin. "Nah."

When Shea moved out, Finn had refused to take part in the shared custody arrangement his parents had agreed to. Knowing the courts wouldn't force a fifteen-year-old kid to comply, Shea had honored Finn's wishes to stay in his home with his mom, though it'd opened up a hole the size of Lake Superior inside him to see his son so seldom.

The hole splintered wide and bottomless, as it did every time Shea looked at Finn and took stock of the changes in him. The additional inch of growth, the new trendy hairstyle, the further yielding of his boyishness to the man he would become. Shea catalogued it all, though it hurt to observe how much he missed by not being a part of his son's day-to-day life.

Finn's gaze alighted on him again, but then he twisted toward the cupboard and pulled down a cereal bowl. "I've got practice later," he mumbled.

Outside, a bright summer sun bathed the island in warmth. Though the day was warm, a crispness carried on the breeze, hinting at cooler temperatures in the coming days. Guilt flooded the hole in the center of his chest. He'd meant to take Connor and Maisie fishing this summer, and it was almost over before he'd finally found the time to do it.

At the public beach, Shea grabbed the poles from the bed of his truck and set off down the pier with Connor and Maisie in tow. He knew the actual fishing part wouldn't hold their attention long, but he set them both up with a pole and a wriggling worm. As he worked, he explained what he was doing, though neither Connor nor Maisie stopped chattering long enough to absorb a single word. Gazing into their cherubic faces flushed with excitement, he decided he didn't particularly care.

They cast their lines, and less than ten seconds later, he was fielding questions such as "Now what?" and "What if I gotta go pee?"

"Impatience is your worst enemy," he said, pulling two tiny, thoughtful frowns from them.

Shea's slow smile took on a satisfied slant. In both fishing, he thought, and when trying to reel in one's wife.

They lucked out and soon Shea noticed a soft tug on Connor's line. While Connor squealed, Shea helped him haul in the lake trout. The fish thrashed and squirmed on the hook while Maisie shrieked, then started to cry.

With the wriggling fish, Shea knelt before them. Connor lunged forward for a chance to touch it, but Maisie crept close, her eyes glistening with her tears, and lightly pressed the tip of one finger to the fish's scales before snatching back her hand. Together, the three of them tossed the trout into the lake so it wouldn't die, and Maisie's tears dried.

While he packed up the gear, he couldn't recall having ever taken Finn fishing, and yet another brutal surge of regret broke over him. He'd been so focused on work, he'd sacrificed his relationship with his son. And his wife. How could he have let that happen to them?

Fear. Fear of all that could go wrong. Of what happened when the other shoe dropped. When shit hit the fan. When tragedy struck. The fear had consumed him. What others assumed was a quest to reach some imaginary mountain peak was really him running from the fear. It'd driven him. Controlled him. Filled him with the compulsion to outrun the hardships in his past. Going to bed hungry all those years had messed with his head, just as the lean desperation in his brothers' faces had warped his perception.

In the end, he viewed the world through a deceptive

lens that colored every choice he made and compelled him to work obsessively. To do more, work harder, and more than anything, never stop fighting. After all, disaster lived only a heartbeat away. Always.

Everything he'd done, he did to survive, and he became so consumed by the battle, he'd forgotten to live. What a miserable shame that was.

The next day, Shea woke early, eager to get over to the house. On his way, he stopped off at Lucky's to sign payroll and complete the liquor inventory. He let himself in the back door of the pub, which wouldn't open for several more hours, and crossed the darkened barroom to the hallway that led to his office.

He inserted his key into his office door's lock, but the heavy wood barrier gave way before he twisted the knob. Unease lifted the hairs on his neck. Had he forgotten to lock his office door?

His hand moved along the wall and when he flipped the switch, light flooded the small room.

From the corner of his eye, he saw something move, and his head snapped around as the form laid out on his couch groaned.

The lump rolled over and Aiden's eyes blinked opened. Then went wide. "Shite," he croaked and thrashed to a sitting position in the soft cushions.

"Good morning, sunshine." Shea's gaze swept the room in search of clues that might explain his bartender's presence in his office at 7:00 a.m.

"I, uh, um..." Aiden staggered clumsily to his feet. "I worked late last night and missed the ferry."

"Don't you live on this island?" Behind his desk, Shea split his focus between a flustered Aiden and the orderliness of his computer and employee files.

"I've been staying with... a friend." Aiden raked a hand through his rumpled dark hair. "But she kicked me out."

One of Shea's eyebrows inched upward. "A friend?"

"A close friend."

"What's her name?"

Wariness touched Aiden's nicely arranged features. "Her name?"

"I know just about everyone on this island." Shea moved his shoulders in a shrug. "Maybe I can offer some advice or put in a good word for you."

"Oh, uh, that's okay." Aiden turned to pluck his sweatshirt of the arm of the couch. "We're keeping things quiet for now."

Shea took his time studying the play of thoughts and emotions that chased across the kid's face. "There is no girl, is there?"

A light came into his eyes. "Not just one, no. There're several."

Shea didn't doubt that. "At your interview, you said you'd recently moved here. Why did you lie?"

Aiden yanked the sweatshirt on over his head and shoved his arms through the sleeves. Then he dragged the fabric slowly down his torso. "I didn't think you'd hire me unless you thought I lived nearby," he finally said.

"Is there anything else you're lying to me about?"

After a beat of tortured hesitation, Aiden met his gaze squarely. "Yes."

Shea stiffened with his surprise. "You want to go ahead and tell me what it is?"

"I can't. Not yet."

"But you will?"

"Yes."

"When?"

Aiden rolled his shoulders, as if an uneasy burden rested upon them. "Soon."

"Do I have anything to worry about?"

"Depends how openminded you are."

"Is it illegal?"

"No."

"Unethical?"

"No."

"Immoral?"

"No."

"Dishonest, distasteful, or dodgy?"

The shadow of a smile touched Aiden's mouth. "Yes, not exactly, and maybe. But it has more to do with righting past wrongs than creating new ones."

Shea didn't bother hiding his assessment of the new bartender, looking closely where he'd only glanced before. Beneath Aiden's pleasant features and easygoing charm, there was a leanness about him, a hunger that had nothing to do with food or sustenance. He thirsted for something all the same. Something essential and elemental.

Shea's head moved with his curt nod. "Okay. I'm going to trust you."

With his slow exhale, Aiden's shoulders slumped a notch.

Shea dropped his chin and leveled the kid with a look. "But if you prove me wrong for doing so, I won't hesitate to destroy you. We clear?"

Aiden's ease vanished. "Crystal."

Chapter Twelve

After Aiden left, Shea hurried through his tasks and over to the house. He found Isobel hunched over the dining table where she'd spread out an oversized sheet of tracing paper. At her feet, Connor and Maisie endeavored to build a fort, but by the tight set of Isobel's mouth and the severe pucker of concentration on her brow, Shea gathered the constant chatter and frequent pleas for help coming from beneath the table had thwarted her attempts to work more than a few times already that morning.

With bribes of a visit to the playground at the park and ice cream, he herded Connor and Maisie toward the door. At the last, he turned back and claimed a soft kiss from his wife.

The brush of fire whipped color into her cheeks.

Unable to resist, he toyed with the chaotic, unruly curl

at her temple. A smile curved his mouth as he pondered the last time he'd glimpsed the soft coils in her hair. Probably not since the early days of their marriage.

Ducking her chin, she tucked the curl away behind her ear. "I haven't had a chance to do my hair yet."

"Leave it," he said. "It's perfect."

Then he dropped a kiss on her scrunched-up forehead and headed outdoors to herd Connor and Maisie into his truck.

The park and ice cream were almost as satisfying as that kiss. They ate lunch downtown, then, as promised, went sailing. Blessed with calm waters and warm sunshine, all three of them sat on the boat's bow, their bare feet swinging over the edge.

He'd needed this precious time to hang out with his kids. Isobel's lucky break might just turn out to be *his* lucky break. Or would be, once he convinced Finn to join them.

The next morning, Shea returned to the house early, but when he stepped through the back door, he stumbled.

A stack of dirty dishes teetered in the kitchen sink. Clutter littered the countertops, and for a moment he thought he'd walked into the wrong house. This couldn't be Isobel's home. Her house was spotless perfection. Always. No matter what.

"Hello?" His voice held the ring of his confusion.

Pounding footsteps greeted his call and Maisie erupted into the room from the hallway. Her rounded cheeks wet with tears, she launched herself into his arms and buried her face in his neck. Words tumbled from her in a rush but, as she often did when her emotions ran high, she'd switched to Spanish and he struggled to comprehend all that she was saying.

He hugged her tight to his chest. "What's the matter, *a*

stór?"

"The toof fairy forgot." Maisie's little body shuddered with her ragged breaths.

Isobel emerged from the hall and Shea started at the sight of her. Her long dark hair a tangled mess, she wore an oversized pair of sweatpants, a T-shirt with a splotch of coffee on her left boob, and not a speck of makeup. He'd never seen her so rumpled and disheveled. Despite the look of tortured guilt on her face, she'd never appeared more adorably gorgeous.

He rubbed slow circles over Maisie's small back. "What's this now? Did you say the tooth fairy?"

Maisie pulled back and with the tip of her miniature finger, touched the hole in the row of her tiny teeth.

Shea's dramatic gasp filled the air. "You lost a tooth?"

"Uh-huh." Maisie laid her head on his shoulder. "And the toof fairy forgot about me."

A quick glance at his guilt-stricken wife told Shea the whole story.

"Well, that explains it," he said.

Maisie lifted her head. "What?"

"On my way over, just now, I saw a carrot on the dock and I thought to myself, 'What is that carrot doing here? Bunnies don't live at the beach.'" His eyes went wide. "Do you know what that means?"

Maisie shook her head. "Uh-uh."

"That means the tooth fairy came to my boat last night. She must've been confused and thought you were sleeping there. I bet if we go look under your pillow, we'll find your surprise. Should we go?"

"Right now?"

"Right now."

Maisie squirmed out of his arms and darted over to the coat rack where she sat to tug on her pink rain boots.

A smile played on his lips when he turned to Isobel.

"Omigod," she whispered, edging close. "I'm a terrible mother."

He choked down his low chuckle, but only because she appeared ready to cry. "Did you work all night?"

She nodded and shoved a hank of her hair behind one ear. "Then I fell asleep and forgot all about the tooth fairy."

A light trace of her flowery scent teased his nostrils. "How is it going? Have you gotten a lot done?"

Dark circles smudged beneath her eyes. "Everything seems to be taking longer than I expected."

"Has Vanessa called?"

"Not yet."

"No need to panic, then." The hair behind her ear came loose and he tucked it back. "I can tell you want to."

"Ready!" Maisie bounded to her feet and charged toward the back door.

"Good girl. Will you tell Connor we're leaving? I'll bet he wants to see what the tooth fairy brought you."

"Okay, Daddy." Pink boots battered the hardwood floors as she plunged down the hall, calling her brother's name as she ran.

"Jaysus, they run everywhere," he muttered, pulling his cell phone from his hip pocket.

The soft peal of Isobel's laughter startled him. Light and lyrical, the sound splashed over him as the sunshine after a storm. He laughed along with her. How long had it been since they'd shared something as simple as a laugh?

When she moved to study the paper covering the dining table, he tapped out a quick message on his cell phone, then hit Send just as the echo of frantic footsteps reverberated through the house.

Maisie burst into the room. "Can we go now?"

Shea hoisted her in his arms. "Where's your brother?"

"Here." Connor plopped his sippy cup on the dining

table.

With a smooth lunge, Isobel swiped the cup off the tabletop. "No, no, *mijo*," she murmured, then ran her palm over the markings she'd sketched onto the paper.

In his pocket, Shea's cell phone vibrated. Leo was the first to reply to the emergency text and was on his way to the marina to leave a treasure from the tooth fairy under Maisie's pillow.

Isobel helped him corral Connor and Maisie through the kitchen and toward the back door. As they passed by the kitchen sink, she pulled her bottom lip between her teeth and drifted over to the dirty heap.

"Don't you dare touch those dishes."

Her steps halted.

"Or that pile of laundry. Or the toys scattered all over this place. You can clean in two weeks."

Huge gray eyes filled with anxiety clamped onto his face.

A smile twitched at the corners of his mouth. "But if you want to take a shower, I'll allow it."

She pushed him through the back door.

Under her pillow, Maisie discovered a shiny silver dollar coin, which she immediately wanted to spend on a pair of plastic princess slippers she'd seen in the grocery store checkout lane. After they'd finished shopping, they played for a while at the beach. Then they headed back to the marina for a snack and a little rest before he took them home for dinner, bath, and bed.

As he loaded Connor and Maisie into his crew cab truck, his phone buzzed with an incoming text message from Isobel. *Totally lost track of time. Can you pick up Finn at practice?*

When Shea pulled into the school parking lot, a glower darkened Finn's features. He collapsed in the passenger's seat and yanked the door closed.

A heavy, stifling silence descended inside the truck, and yet Shea didn't want the short ride to end. While he may be struggling to connect with his son, he wasn't ready to give up even one second of their time together.

"We were about to get dinner." He snuck a glance at Finn's profile. "You mind if we stop for a bite to eat before someone has a meltdown?"

Finn flipped the hood of his sweatshirt up over his dark hair. "Whatever."

At dinner, the meltdown Shea feared became reality when Connor dissolved into a puddle of hangry tears. Before Shea could intervene, Finn slipped his phone into his pocket and within moments had turned Connor's tears into giggles with a deadly accurate imitation of Shea's gruff voice and accent.

Shea couldn't stem the kick of pride in his chest at Finn's compassion for his little brother. It had been hard on him when, at twelve years old, his mom had had a baby, and less than a year later, yet another surprise pregnancy was on the way. Two years after that, his dad moved out of the house.

In a couple of weeks, Finn would turn eighteen, and it was obvious the kid sitting across the table from Shea would be a good man. For that, he owed Isobel.

"Why are you so hard on him? He's just a little boy."

With a shudder, the memory of Isobel's heated words seared him. The truth of her words gutted him.

As a young dad, the fear had hounded Shea. Maybe it was a result of being Daniel Nolan's son. Maybe it was due to watching his four brothers weave in and out of trouble. Shea knew the lesson well. A little trouble could alter the course of one's life.

He could justify why he'd done it, but his excuses didn't make it okay. He'd tried to control everything in their lives. He'd tried to control *them.* Anything to prevent a return to those chaotic, terrifying years after their mom died.

But instead of protecting them, he'd only succeeded in pushing them away.

Well, no more. It'd taken too long, but he'd finally gotten the message. They didn't want or need him to control their lives. He had a different role to play.

But what?

In the car on the way home, uncertainty churned in him. Nearly a man, what did his son need from him? Was there anything?

His hood in place, Finn tapped away on his phone while in the back seat, Connor and Maisie dozed. As Shea steered the vehicle along the quiet roads, he catalogued all the ways he was going to do things differently with them. The list was long.

But nothing on it would help him with Finn now.

A thought clicked in his mind. If he was unsure what Finn needed from him, maybe he should just ask.

Leaning forward, Shea shifted in the seat. "So, how's football going?"

"Fine."

Tap, tap.

"You, uh, need anything? From me?"

Tap... tap, tap.

"No."

"Look, I'm sorry if I wasn't there for you."

"I'm over it."

Tap, tap, tap.

"I'd be mad, too."

"I'm not mad."

Tap, tap, tap, tap, tap.

What the hell was he doing? Dancing around the words like a nervous nelly? If nothing else, Finn deserved the truth from him.

"I'm proud of you."

The tapping noise ceased.

"And for the record, I'm glad you took your mom's side."

"I didn't take her side." Finn turned his face toward the passenger side window. "I just know how she feels."

In the fading daylight, Shea spotted a pedestrian walking along the side of the road and he eased the truck out over the center line, leaving a wide distance between the slight figure and the vehicle.

Finn straightened in his seat.

With a swipe of one hand, the hood came off and his head whipped around. "Stop the car."

"What? Why?"

"Just stop."

Alarmed by the bite in Finn's voice, Shea steered onto the shoulder of the road.

"What is it?" he asked, peering through the car's rear window.

"I think I know her."

"That girl? Who is she?"

"She goes to my school."

Unease prickled up Shea's spine. "What is she doing out here by herself?"

"I don't know."

"You want to talk to her, or you want me to?"

Without a blink of hesitation, Finn flung open his car door. "I will."

In the side mirror, Finn approached the girl with slow, cautious steps. Shea cut off the radio and eased his window down, hoping to pick up snippets of their conversation, but nothing reached him through the dusky shadows.

Just when he'd decided to get involved, they turned and walked back to the car together.

Finn's gaze briefly touched Shea's as he ducked inside the car. "Hey, Dad. This is Sidney. She needs a ride home."

The girl was all huge eyes and exposed flesh in a revealing tank top and too-short shorts. But the scanty clothing didn't bother him nearly as much as her split bottom lip. Beneath the truck's dim interior light, he caught the splotch of dried blood in the corner of her mouth.

Finn helped her into the passenger seat and then climbed into the back, wedging his body between Connor's and Maisie's car seats.

"Where's home?" Shea asked, then pulled back out onto the road, heading in the direction of Sidney's house.

While Sidney mumbled her address, Shea caught Finn's gaze in the rearview mirror.

The apprehension he felt reflected back at him.

Chapter Thirteen

In three short days, the perfection Isobel sought daily to attain had been ruined. Like red wine spilled over a pristine white wedding dress, chaos reigned. Ugly, regrettable chaos.

But since Vanessa Dubois threw her life into disarray, Isobel had selected four designs from the hundreds of sketches she'd created over the years and would attempt to make them all in the next two weeks. She'd spent hours online shopping for the perfect fabrics and had purchased several months' worth of salary for the luxurious material, paying extra to have the orders shipped as quickly as possible.

Though she hadn't skimped on her choices, she'd only spent half of the money Shea had loaned her. During their early years together, while Shea was in law school and she was teaching herself bridal design, they were so poor that she couldn't afford to make many dresses and she certainly wasn't able to splurge on things like crystal beading or lace overlays. Instead, she'd learned to use design elements to add sparkle and drama to her gowns. A dramatic neckline, a striking cut, a luxurious draping of fabric, she'd used them all to great effect and apparently still favored the style.

That morning, the first of three packages had arrived, and by the time Shea returned home with the kids that evening, she had cut out one dress, sewn the skirt, and had just started stitching together the intricate bodice when Finn steered a drowsy Maisie through the back door.

Isobel set aside her work and scooped Maisie up in her arms as Shea's large frame filled the room. Connor's slack form slung over his shoulder, he didn't speak, but his vivid gaze grabbed hers and held, eliciting a shiver of awareness from her.

Down the hall, she settled Maisie into bed and slipped quietly through her bedroom door, pulling it shut behind her with a soft click. The door to Finn's bedroom was barred, presumably with him behind it while Shea waited for her in the hallway.

For the first time in years, her foremost impulse wasn't to retreat or lash out.

She sagged against the door and offered him a small smile. "How was your day?"

"It was great." He leaned against the wall. "I think the life of leisure is for me after all."

That startled a laugh from her. Curious, she searched his face and detected the slight strain at the corners of his eyes and mouth.

Something was troubling him, and he was trying to hide it from her.

Annoyance flared. It was so typical of him not to trust

her. Did he think she was weak? Too inept or useless or stupid to be of any help? Why couldn't he–

She slammed the brake on the train of her well-worn thoughts. The ugly suspicions replayed in her mind, and dark regret seeped over her. Like that day at the store, it both stunned and hurt her to realize how quickly she'd assumed the worst about him. How quickly she assumed his low opinion of her, and just how low that opinion delved.

Why did she do that? He was a lot of things–infuriating, stubborn, controlling–but he didn't deserve her animosity. She didn't deserve it.

For so long, she'd wanted things to be different between them, but without recognizing the role she'd played in their dysfunction, her attempts to bring about a change were doomed to fail. How could she fix something when she didn't understand why it wasn't working?

Overwhelmed and baffled by her broken marriage, she'd finally given up and chucked it in the trash, accepting that she'd have to either acquire a brand new one, or forever go without.

Remorse throbbed in her chest while she stared into Shea's familiar yet foreign face. In how many and what other ways had she contributed to the breakdown of their relationship?

If she'd wanted things to be different before, now that she understood, and despite the fact she'd all but ended their marriage when she filed for divorce, shouldn't she try to make it so?

A weak smile touched her lips. "You going to tell me what's bothering you?"

His struggled played across his features. "I don't want you to worry."

"I'm too tired to worry."

He dropped his head to stare at the floor, but the spot between his brows puckered. "Do you know Sidney Shaw?"

At the mention of Finn's classmate, surprise swept over her. "I know of her. Why?"

When his head came up, his bright eyes glittered, and she was powerless to resist their magnetic pull. "We found her walking along the road out by the abandoned warehouse and gave her a ride home."

While he explained the roadside pickup and the fat lip, a frown crept across her face. "That doesn't sound good at all. I'll ask around and see what I can find out."

"Her dad comes into the pub once in a while." At his side, his hand curled into a fist and the muscles beneath his tattoo rippled. "I think I'll have a chat with him the next time."

His gaze snagged hers, and a soft, sensuous shimmer of light passed between them.

"How was your day?" he asked softly. "Did you get a lot done?"

Soft flutters stirred in her stomach. "I've pieced most of one dress together, and I'm about to start on the beadwork."

"Can I see it?"

Pleasure warmed her cheeks. "Sure."

She led him to her bedroom door—*their* bedroom door.

Her feet tripped to a stop. Through the doorway, her eyes fastened on the bed, *their* bed, and her pulse jumped with the surge of a thousand jumbled and conflicting emotions. Sorrow and regret. Guilt, resentment, rigidity. So much had gone wrong for them here. The memories assaulted her, even the ones from his boat only days ago. A whisper of arousal flickered.

Behind her, his size and heat reached out like a caress.

Though he uttered no words, she could feel his questioning thoughts. With a mental shake, she slipped inside the room.

At the end of the bed, she'd set up the dress form in the open space and the gown's lavish tulle skirt smashed against the wall. Stepping to the side, she watched his face as his eyes roamed over the ballgown.

His honeyed smile caused her heart to flip over in her chest.

"Now *that's* a princess dress," he said and then his eyes narrowed with his critical squint. "It's a little dark in here."

"I'll bring in another lamp."

He frowned at the floor, twisting at the waist to assess the entire space. "You're not going to have room for any other dresses."

"I could move to the basement, but it's a little damp down there and I'm afraid it would harm the fabric." She worried her bottom lip. "At least the other dresses aren't as poufy as this one."

His clouded expression cleared abruptly. "I know a place that might work."

"You do?" Surprise tinted her tone. "Where?"

"Get dressed. I'll show you."

When she asked him to wait while she did her hair and makeup, he flatly refused. "You don't need all that. You're gorgeous. Get in the car."

Protests fell from her lips as he crossed to the door.

"You've got two minutes." He stepped into the hall, easing the closed behind him until only a small crack remained. "And... go."

The door shut with a soft click.

She stripped out of her pajamas, tugged on a pair of blue jeans and a T-shirt, and yanked a brush through her tangled hair. Then she scampered down the hall and out the back door to his truck parked in the driveway where he sat behind the wheel with the engine idling.

She collapsed in the passenger's seat, breathless.

"Six minutes." With a quiet *tsking* sound, he engaged the clutch and the vehicle lurched backwards down the drive.

"Wait." She reached for the door latch. "I forgot to tell Finn we're leaving."

"I told him."

They descended the winding hillside road and at the bottom, turned toward downtown. Curiosity at where they were going couldn't compete with the pull of his pleasant profile and her gaze kept sliding away from the views through her window and back to him.

The deeper they journeyed into the dark, the more her awareness of him intensified. She noticed the way his broad shoulders filled the seat and his large hands cradled the steering wheel. She used to love watching him when he didn't know she looked on.

On Main Street, he parked in front of the pub. As she slipped from the cab, warmth from the sun's recently dimmed light still radiated off the pavement.

She pushed the car door shut. "What are we doing here?"

On the sidewalk, Shea pointed up, toward the top of the old brick-and-mortar building. "I want you to see the loft."

She scrunched her nose, recalling the last time she was in the space. "It's a little dirty, and I need something climate-controlled."

"I cleaned it out." He tipped his head in the direction of the building. "Come have a look. If it won't work for you, then we'll think of something else."

Between the pub entrance and the alley, a small nook led to a dark, narrow staircase. She followed him up it, and at the top, he fumbled with the door's lock before pushing open the heavy barrier. His wide shoulders blocked her view when she stepped into the room behind him.

Inky blackness engulfed her a moment before soft light flooded the sweeping loft space. She blinked as her eyes adjusted.

Shock flew through her. Rendered mute, she stared openmouthed.

"This is big enough, isn't it?"

Dazedly, she nodded. The clutter had been cleared out, the dirt and grime scrubbed from every crack and crevice. He'd refinished the wide-plank hardwood flooring and left the brick walls exposed. The wall overlooking Main Street boasted a row of oversized floor-to-ceiling windows, and in the lighting and woodwork, he'd preserved a number of details characteristic to the building's turn-of-the-century charm.

"The windows will let in a ton of daylight." He strode deeper into the space. "But we'll need to add more lighting for you to work at night. I think I have some work lights around here somewhere..." He twisted at the waist, searching the spacious loft.

"I thought this was storage." Her gaze devoured the clean, revitalized room. "When did you do all this?"

"I renovated this spring." Crouched before a box by the far window, he stole a glance at her face. "I was planning to move in before winter hit."

"You're going to live here?" A punch of distress jabbed her beneath the breastbone. "Like, permanently?"

The unspoken answer to her question glowed like embers in his vivid eyes.

He hadn't lived with her for almost two years. Why did it make her so sad to think of him in his own place?

She sucked in a shuddering breath. "I can't take your home."

He stood, dragging with him a noisy tangle of wire and work lights from the box. "Don't worry about me. I've got my sights set on another bed."

His teasing tone loosened some of the tightness in her chest. Crossing to him, she filched the other strand of lights from the box and set to work unraveling them.

"You should put your sewing machine there." He pointed to the front of the room near the windows. "We can hang the lights from the rafters."

In her mind, she arranged her cutting table and her storage caddies filled with her sewing supplies underneath the rafters. Then she positioned her dress forms where they'd catch the most daylight while she worked.

Suddenly, anything seemed possible. Buoyant optimism expanded in her chest.

"It's perfect." Emotion softened her voice. "Thank you."

His gaze wouldn't release hers. "You're welcome."

A sudden thought pulled a frown from her. "Why are you doing so much to help me?"

One corner of his sensuous mouth tilted upward. "I like kissing you."

His infectious grin coaxed a laugh from her. "You haven't kissed me today."

"You sound disappointed."

She was, a fact which sent a shiver of alarm chasing up her spine. So she enjoyed kissing him. So what? It didn't mean anything, other than she'd obviously gone too long without kisses. Or sex.

"I'm letting the anticipation build." Humor shimmered in his bright eyes. "That's sexy, right?"

The memory of him moving over her, in her, curled

through her as a warm tension.

She ignored it and shrugged one shoulder. "Meh."

His gravelly chuckle told her he wasn't buying the lie.

Ducking her chin to hide her smile, she worked a knot in the wire. Muffled sounds filtered up to them from the pub downstairs.

"You helped me," he said quietly.

Her eyes flew to his face.

"You helped me with my business, even though you were pissed at me and not exactly on board with my decisions."

"The decisions you made without me."

"That's what I meant by you being pissed off. Rightfully so." He used the full force of his intense gaze on her. "I was wrong to do that, and still, you supported me."

She shook her head. "I didn't do anything."

"That's not true." He draped his light strand over the sides of the box and moved toward the back of the room. "When I showed you the blueprints, you suggested I flip things around. I had the kitchen on the wrong side of the building, and the bar wasn't laid out right."

"I was just feeling argumentative," she admitted.

His mouth quirked when he gripped the stepladder propped against the exposed brick wall. He shot her a look as he carried it to the darkest corner of the room. "You saved us a ton of money."

"I might've been mad at you, but I had no desire to go broke."

"You fixed the interior design, too, remember?" With a scraping sound, he unfolded the stepladder and positioned it precisely beneath the rafters, then motioned for the lights in her hand. "And when you were done, it looked like an authentic Irish pub and not just a hangout for drunks. There's no way I could've done that without you."

A strange and unexpected pleasure warmed her cheeks.

"Don't forget the menu." He was in lawyer mode, building to his closing argument as he climbed to the ladder's top rung. "People actually come out to the island to eat our food and enjoy the atmosphere, all because of you. Because *you* helped *me* make the pub a success. It's only right that I help you now, in any way I can."

"Okay, first of all, you're giving me way too much credit." At his feet, she held the lights up to him. "It's not the food that draws people, it's you. It's the live music and the way you treat people. Your accent and good looks don't hurt either."

"I do know how to pick tasty beers."

Reaching up, he wound the lights through the rafters, and when he stretched to the furthermost point, the tail of his T-shirt lifted and exposed the skin of his muscled abdomen.

"That you do," she muttered distractedly.

She retrieved the second strand of work lights for him and he threaded them around the beams, then he bounded down off the ladder and returned to the storage box. Crouching, he rummaged through the contents a moment before he straightened, a bright yellow extension cord in hand.

His deft fingers worked to loosen the coiled cable. "I wish your mom were here to enjoy this with you."

Isobel stiffened. Though she thought of her mom often, she and Shea hadn't talked about her in years. Before she knew about things like divorce, her mom's death had been the most painful experience of her life and losing her as she did, with the suddenness of a storm kicking up off the lake, had only compounded her heartbreak. There'd been no illness or diagnosis to prepare her for the coming storm. No time to say her goodbyes. No chance to make her apologies. No quiet moments where she might've asked her mom all those questions she'd never thought to ask before and now wished desperately to know.

She could feel Shea's eyes on her, soft but probing. As much as it hurt to remember, she found herself eager to talk about her mom.

"Sometimes, I wonder how different my life would be if she hadn't died."

His gaze sharpened on her face. "What do you mean?"

"Would we have...?" Her throat closed around the words. "I wonder, would we have married so young?"

"I was going to marry you one way or another. Then, a year or ten later, it didn't matter. You were going to be my wife."

The edge in his voice sent a silky shiver chasing through her.

"When we moved back to the island, Celeste was the only one who would give me a job. She and my mom were friends, and I think she thought I could sew, too." A rueful smile worked its way to her lips. "Boy, was she wrong."

Some of the tension eased from his shoulders. "She must've figured it out quick."

"Lucky for me, there was another seamstress, but the poor woman suffered from arthritis. She'd stand over me and tell me exactly what to do—how to make each stitch and even how to hold the fabric. If she didn't like what I'd done, she'd make me rip it out and do it again." A light laugh bubbled up with the memory. "It was awful and intimidating, but I loved the work. It reminded me of my mom."

"That's why you wanted to work at the store."

She acknowledged the truth with a nod. "Though it's

true, Celeste really was the only one who would hire me, but even if I hadn't been a high school dropout and seven months pregnant at the time, it was the only place I wanted to work. I wanted to learn how to do alterations and make pretty dresses because, I don't know, I guess it made me feel closer to my mom somehow."

"I had no idea." He seemed to recall the extension cord in his hands then.

"Because I never told you."

Slowly, his eyes found hers once more.

Her head tipped to one side and she studied him with a frown. "I don't know why I never told you."

"I wish you had," he said, his voice taut with pain.

"I think—" Heat rushed into her face. "I was jealous."

"Of what?"

"You."

She witnessed the moment he realized she wasn't joking. A terrible torment distorted his features, and the words started to fall from her lips.

"You got a full-ride scholarship to college. You were the star quarterback. You breezed through law school and passed the bar on your first try. When you got bored with that, you bought a crappy, rundown bar and within a year it's making a profit and you're a hero to the entire island for turning the economy around. Everything you touch turns to gold."

He stared, speechless.

"You've done so much, while I"—her hand moved uselessly through the air—"haven't done much at all."

"You've done plenty."

She sliced him with a look.

"You've done so much for the kids, for me, for my brothers." He blinked at her. "For everyone... else."

A heavy silence fell between them.

"I didn't know you wanted more." Grief clung to him.

"I didn't want more. I wanted to be a wife—your wife—and I loved being a mother." Her voice and hands shook. "I just wanted different. I wanted to be creative, too."

"Did you think I would've tried to stop you?"

"I don't know." Her shoulders lifted. "Maybe?"

He dropped his head.

"I guess I should've asked you," she whispered.

When his head came up, his eyes glittered with pain even as the tension in his body melted away. "Yeah, me, too."

He stared down at the yellow wire his hands while his fingers toyed distractedly with the rubber sheathing. Then, with a nearly imperceptible shake, he cast off his melancholy.

"You accomplished something else while you were taking care of the rest of us. You honed your talent." With a hard tug, he unraveled the extension cord. "And now it's your turn."

"My turn for what?" She twisted around when he strode by her.

He scaled to the top of the stepladder and, stretching, connected the light strand with one end of the extension cord. "To find gold."

Climbing down off the ladder, he scooped up the other end of the extension cord.

"When this magazine feature is published and you become an overnight sensation, you'll have all the different you can handle." He crossed to the wall outlet and bent to insert the plug into the socket.

The lights winked on and she squinted into their soft glare. "It won't be like that."

He straightened. "Do you know that for sure?"

"Well, no."

"Then you should have plan."

"I should?"

"Picture all the success you could ever want, and then tell me, what does it look like?"

She tried to imagine it, but the critical voice inside her head distorted and dissolved the vision.

"Will you keep making dresses out of the bedroom? Will you start your own company, hire your own staff? Maybe you'll move to New York City and work for a big-time designer?" With a sheepish smile, he shoved his hands into the pockets of his blue jeans. "I have no idea how the fashion industry works, so you tell me. If you get everything you could want out of this opportunity, where will you be this time next year?"

She scrunched her nose. "Not in New York City. I want to design and make dresses... at my own store."

"If not in New York, where will this store be?"

His smile was contagious and she bit down on her bottom lip. "Here."

"You want to stay on the island?" His voice held a hint of pleasure.

"One day, when Celeste retires, I'd love to buy the store from her. Maybe. If the circumstances are right." Her smile broke loose then. "That's it. That's the dream."

"That's a great dream."

Her heart expanded with happiness, and not all of it due to talk of her dreams. Somehow, even after all the hurt and anger, his approval still mattered to her.

Their gazes collided, and a thread of awareness passed between them.

His raspy voice caused her stomach to flip over when he said, "We should probably get home."

A chorus of summer sounds greeted them when they stepped outdoors. Darkness had descended, so she didn't at first notice the man climbing into the car parked beside Shea's truck.

When she looked up, into the man's face, she recoiled.

Her heart dropped to her stomach while she stared at her dad. Lines now etched his face, and strands of gray intermingled with the light brown color of his hair.

Her dad's gaze darted away from her and over to Shea. Then his head jerked with his nod of acknowledgment.

His acknowledgment of Shea.

Shea's gruff voice reached through the dark. "Good evening, Thomas."

At the causal greeting, she sucked in a sharp hiss of air and her head snapped around. No, not casual. Shea's tone was familiar. As if he and her dad were friendly. As if they talked often.

"Good to see you." At her dad's grumbled reply, her head whipped back around.

Her dad tossed an impersonal glance her way, a glance any stranger might've imparted, before he slipped inside his vehicle and hauled the car door shut. Without speaking a word to her.

Not one word.

Her chest squeezed unbearably tight a as he backed his car out onto the quiet street and drove off into the dark night.

Her dad hadn't spoken to her in eighteen years. For eighteen years his rejection had sliced and wounded, leaving behind big blistering welts of doubt and fear, of self and love.

Not one stupid word.

The car's red taillights grew dim while a chaotic tangle of awful emotions assaulted her. Pain and panic and rage writhed and wriggled inside her until her stomach churned with nausea.

Slowly, agonizingly, she turned to her husband. "He talked to you. You talked to him."

The betrayal that slashed through her wrenched a sob from the back of her throat.

In a flash, he rounded the hood of the car and closed the distance between them. "Isobel—"

Her heart thundering in her ears, she stumbled back, holding out a hand to ward off his advance. "How could you?"

He watched her closely, his bright eyes glittering. "He came to me a couple of months ago. He asked for my help."

"Your help with what?"

"He wants to see you."

"He just saw me. He could hardly bring himself to look at me."

"I—I don't know what happened. Maybe he froze or something? Isobel, I don't know but—"

"Did you agree to help him?"

"I did not." His chest rose and fell with his rapid breathing. "I told him I was the last person who could help, and even if I could, I wasn't sure I wanted him in your life again. Not after... the way I found you."

She recoiled with his words. "You had no right to go behind my back."

"I'm sorry."

Another sob escaped her and she sucked it in, but she couldn't stem the onslaught of pain.

"Why?" Her strangled cry pierced the still night air. "Why did you do that?"

"When he came to me, I don't know, I felt sorry for him."

"You felt sorry for him? What about me? I am your wife." Her own words gashed a hole in her chest and shrank back. Shaking her head, she twisted away. "No, you know what? Forget it. It doesn't matter."

"Isobel, wait. Please. Tell me what happened between you and your dad. I want to understand. Help me understand."

"He threw me out. Like I was a dog that'd misbehaved." Her voice broke.

When she risked a glance at him over her shoulder, his eyes blazed with an intensity she couldn't bear. She turned her face away once more.

"Isobel, please, don't shut me out. Not this time."

With a gasp, she whirled. "*I* shut *you* out?"

His jaw clenched tight. "Yes."

"You were gone, Shea. I was alone and I was scared and you weren't there."

"I know. I worked too much–"

"No." Her hand shot out to silence him. "Don't say another word. Not one more word. I–I want to go home."

The trembling in her hands reached her voice, so she yanked open the door and ducked inside the car.

A tear slid down her cheek while, on the empty sidewalk, Shea stood with his head hanging down.

God, it hurt. She'd dealt with the pain of unexpectedly bumping into her dad so many times it was merely a dull ache, but to hear Shea defend her dad had cut straight through her flesh to the strike bone. And just when she'd started to soften toward her husband.

Shea rounded the hood of the car and when he climbed behind the wheel, she turned her face to the window. With the back of her hand, she swiped at the silly, ridiculous tears spilling over.

Shame on her for so quickly forgetting he was not someone she could trust. Certainly not with her heart. He never had been.

Chapter Fourteen

Fear and regret snarled and snapped at him, mauling his fragile faith in himself. In them.

On the drive home, the anger leached from her, taking with it the color from her cheeks. Silently, he followed her inside the house, but let her retreat down the hall and disappear behind the bedroom door.

He poked his head into Finn's room to let him know they were home, then peeked in on Connor and Maisie, whose heavy, rhythmic breathing told him they remained asleep.

At the doorway to their bedroom, he hesitated.

What the hell had just happened to them? One minute they were like they used to be, and the next it'd all blown up in his face. At the first inkling of trouble, all their worst instincts came rushing forth. Anger and disappointment warped reality, and the hurt made it all feel so damn real.

Their old patterns, like well-worn ruts in a muddy road, pulled them along, entrapping them and preventing them from treading a different path. Any other path.

Dammit, they could do better than this. He could do better.

He stepped quietly into the room and, with a soft click of the latch, closed the bedroom door.

She sat on the end of the bed in the dark, gazing at the wedding dress before her. Moonlight streamed in through the windows and picked out the tiny crystals scattered over the gown's full skirt like stardust.

"You okay?"

"I'm fine." Her clipped reply came too quick.

He crossed to the nightstand and switched on the table lamp. The soft light failed to banish the shadows from the room.

Moving to the end of the bed, he searched her expression. "Seeing your dad upset you."

"Hmmm? Oh." Her small hand floated through the air. "No. I'm just tired."

Her fingers touched the gown and the slight tremor in her hand gave her away. She was not detached. She was barely holding herself together.

"I have to finish this dress tonight if I'm going to stay on track," she said, rubbing the flimsy fabric between her thumb and forefinger. "I don't think that's going to happen."

A frown dragged at his features while he considered the dress. "We need to get you some help. Did you talk to Ginny?"

"She's on vacation next week."

"What about Ava? Does she sew? Or Sophie?"

She gave her head a small shake. "Anyway, they're busy right now with work and planning Finn's birthday party."

Disappointment nipped at him. "We'll think of something."

After a beat of heavy silence, she exhaled a low, leaky breath. "I'm not sure it matters."

"What do you mean?"

"If the designs aren't any good, it doesn't matter if I get them done or not."

"What do you mean, if they aren't any good? They're incredible."

She withdrew her hand and tucked it neatly in her lap.

"An editor from a national bridal magazine loves them enough to put her name behind them." He spoke to the top of her head. "Where is this coming from?"

"I'm just trying to be realistic."

He lowered his body to sit beside her on the edge of the bed.

"Doubt is natural. The ability to self-reflect, even self-criticize, can be the difference between a successful startup and a failed one." He studied her profile. "But that's not what you're doing."

She lurched to her feet. "I should get back to work."

Her back to him, she riffled through the scattered bits and pieces of her sewing supplies laid out on the dresser.

She'd retreated behind her walls. A part of him wanted to take her cue and walk away. Leave it alone. For years he'd let her build those barriers because it was easier, safer, than forcing the dark out into the light.

But not anymore. Adding more bricks to the walls would be the end for them. He knew it in his gut.

Pushing to his feet, he crossed to the dresser, turning to lean against the wall beside it.

"You never told me what happened between you and your dad."

With her index finger, she flicked frantically through her sewing stuffs. "There's nothing to tell."

"What did he say to you when he told you to get out?"

"What does it matter now?" She risked an uneasy glance at him. "It was a long time ago."

What does it matter? she'd said. Not, 'I can't remember the exact words that were said nearly twenty years ago.'

"It matters. You might not want to tell me, but it does matter," he said, his voice low and not entirely even. "A great deal, I suspect."

Her stormy eyes filled with apprehension. "I... I don't like to think about it."

"Neither do I." A cold knot twisted in his stomach and he reached for her fumbling hand. "I never once asked you to tell me what happened because I didn't want to hurt you, and because I was a coward. But we've put it off long enough, don't you think?"

At his quip, her tremulous smile broke his heart as, for just one slight moment, she appeared so like the girl he'd fallen in love with all those years ago.

She'd been seventeen at the time, Finn's age, and she'd lost her mom a few months before. He had only wanted to comfort her, to love her and take away the pain of her grief. Instead, he knocked her up.

Extracting her hand from his, she shoved her palms into the back pockets of her blue jeans and took a measured step away from the dresser. "I managed to hide my pregnancy from him until I was seven months along."

"You hid it from me, too."

"I didn't know how to tell you." Her heavy lashes swept down to hide her eyes. "And after the way my dad reacted, I was afraid to."

"I wish you'd trusted me." He swallowed thickly. "But I don't blame you for being afraid."

When she glanced up, relief swept the storm from her eyes. "Well, I do blame you for talking to him tonight."

"I never once took his side over yours." He stared into her eyes, as though he might drive the truth of his words directly into her heart. "What he did was unforgivable and he doesn't deserve to have you in his life. But I'm not gonna lie, I relished the opportunity to tell him exactly that. I'd do it again if given the chance."

A secret smile softened her lips.

"But I am sorry if I hurt you," he said. "That was never my intention."

"Thank you for saying that."

"You're welcome." He folded his arms over his chest. "You were going to tell me about your dad."

A spool of thread on the dresser snagged her attention and she plucked it up. She toyed with it a moment before she pushed a huff of air between her lips and set it back down with a clank.

But her gaze remained fixated on the spool. "It's hard to say the words."

"Luke thinks we should text."

One eyebrow lifted. "Excuse me?"

"He says it gives him and Emily time to choose their words more carefully. I imagine it'd also help if the words happened to be difficult to say."

Her brow puckered as she pondered that, then she shrugged. "I don't want to type it out either, so I guess I'll just tell you."

"I'm okay with that, too."

She studied her trinkets for a long, drawn-out moment. When she finally spoke, her voice had dropped to a quiet murmur. "He was so angry."

"Did he lay a hand you?" The burning question burst from him.

"No. He told me I'd dishonored my family. That my mom would've been ashamed of me." Her throat worked when she swallowed. "Then he told me to get out."

His dread spun into a wild fury. When he had found her, she'd been sleeping in the park for days. She was dirty, hungry, and so spooked she'd flinched when he drew near. He'd loaded her in his car to take her with him back to campus and she'd cried nearly the entire four-hour drive.

His rage must've showed on his face because a flicker of alarm chased across her features. "I can't believe he would've thrown me out unless he thought I had somewhere else to go."

"You should've come to me."

"You were four hours away, and I didn't have any money."

It took all his willpower not to argue with her. "So you slept in the park?"

A shudder passed through her. "The second night, it stormed."

He swallowed bile. "How long were you there before I found you?"

"Five nights, I think. Maybe six."

Outrage overcame him. "Jesus, Iz. Why didn't you call me?"

"You had enough pressure already."

He'd taken a short leave from work on the freighter to attend fall camp ahead of his junior year football season.

"Do you honestly think I wouldn't have left camp or made them dock that damn boat so I could get to you? You were sleeping in the park. You were pregnant and alone, and goddammit, you should've called me."

She'd clenched her fists so tightly at her sides that her knuckles had turned white. "I was afraid."

"Afraid of what?" His heart shattered. "Of me?"

"Yes. No. I—I don't know." She lifted a trembling hand to cover her face. "When my dad said those things, everything changed. I changed. All of a sudden, I doubted everything and everyone. If my dad put limits on his love like that, maybe everyone else did, too, and all it'd take was one more mistake and I'd lose everything. Even you."

He squeezed his eyes shut with the agony slashing through him.

"And then I had Finn."

His eyes flew open.

"And I realized my dad's rejection had hurt more than I'd let on. I was afraid to love him, Shea." Her voice broke with a sadness he couldn't endure. "He was just a baby, and I couldn't let myself love him." The tears were flowing as freely as her words now. "I didn't want to hold him. He'd cry and I couldn't comfort him. For days, weeks, Noah had to do everything for me."

"It's okay," he rasped.

"It's not okay. What if Noah hadn't been living with us? How could I have been afraid to love my baby?"

He tugged her to him, as much for support as to give it, and because he needed to touch her. "He's a great kid, *mo chuisle*. It's okay."

A sob slipped from her throat. Another wrenched open his heart, and another. He buried his face in her hair.

"It's okay." He repeated. "I felt it, too."

She snuffled. "You did?"

"I was terrified of him." He brushed a strand of her hair off her forehead. "My God, Izzy, we were so young. I didn't know anything about babies, about being a dad, or a husband. Between Finn and my brothers and my dad, we had the weight of the world on our shoulders, but we were kids ourselves. Of course we struggled. If we hadn't, I'd doubt we were taking things seriously enough."

With the heel of her hand, she scrubbed the tears from her cheeks. "I was so afraid to tell you that. All these years..."

"I'm glad you did. I didn't understand before, but I'm starting to now."

When she started to move away, he gripped her nape and tugged her close, pressing his forehead against hers. "I'm sorry I wasn't there for you. Believe me when I tell you, I've never forgotten that knowing me, loving me, ruined your happiness."

She pulled back so she could see his face, then her expression changed from shock to tenderness. "That's why you worked so hard all the time, isn't it? You thought you had to. To make me happy."

"I wanted to be able to give you anything you wanted. Everything, because you deserve it all." A painful lump lodged in his throat. "Instead I made you miserable."

She pushed up on her tiptoes and brushed her mouth over his. He closed his eyes and inhaled her love. Her tongue came out to take a tiny taste of him and a slow lick of arousal curled through him.

"You were always a great kisser," she murmured against his mouth. "So at least there's that."

With her smile, the anguish released him. He cupped her face and kissed both of her red, puffy eyes. A smile played on her soft lips while he dropped kisses on her nose, the curve of her cheeks, her forehead.

Her fingertips skimmed down the side of his face and danced along his jawline. "You're not awful to look at either. Especially with your shirt off."

With a flash of motion, he reached back, grabbed a fistful of his T-shirt, and yanked it over his head. Her husky laugh filled the hole in his heart when he tossed the shirt aside. Lacing his fingers with hers, he drew her toward the bed.

But her amusement died and she tugged on his hand. He turned. "What is it?"

Her troubled gaze slipped to the bed. "I don't want to

do it here. It's... where we got lost."

A small pinch tweaked him in the center of his chest. His fingers still entwined with hers, he raised her hand to his lips and pressed a kiss between her knuckles. "We're not lost, *mo chroí.* We know exactly where we are."

"We do?"

"Come." He walked backward toward the bed and sat on the edge of the mattress. Pulling her between his thighs, he lifted the hem of her shirt and kissed her stomach. Over the fabric, his eyes found hers. "Let me show you."

The proof of her consent rushed into her cheeks and showed in the way her fingers feverishly fumbled with the top button of her blouse. The fastening gave way, and so did the next, and the next, in a wanton striptease that revealed her shimmery butterscotch skin to him inch by glorious inch.

Familiar, hot longing squeezed his balls.

When her blouse parted, he reached up and slipped the material off her shoulders. As she reached for the clasp of her bra, her back arched, thrusting her full, heavy breasts before his face. A fierce flare of desire ignited in him and then her bra fell away.

The circlet of her wedding band nestled between her lush tits. He pressed the palm of his hand flat against her stomach and smoothed upward. Inserting the tip of his pinky finger inside the white gold ring, he cupped her with both hands. The necklace's chain grazed her beaded nipple and he dragged his tongue across the ripe bud, tasting warm flesh and cold metal.

Her breathing became shallow and rapid. Her breasts rose and fell with her ragged breaths.

"You're so goddamn beautiful, my wife."

At the base of her neck, her pulse throbbed as his hands roamed down her body and hooked a finger in the waistband of her blue jeans. The button popped and he dragged down the zipper. She shimmied out of the body-hugging material to stand before him in only her bright pink panties.

Hunger consumed him and he feasted on her voluptuous curves. He catalogued every dip and hollow with his fingers and tongue, lingering at a few key places—her hipbone and navel, the underside of one breast. Slowly, he stroked and tasted, licked and nibbled her skin, becoming drunk on her intoxicating softness.

His fingers skimmed the delicate skin of her inner thighs. Gripping her knee, he parted her legs and stroked her panties over the heart of her.

With her moan, her head lolled back. He toyed with her while erotic whimpers fell from her lips to stoke the fire building inside him.

When she begged him, he pulled aside the scrap of fabric and pushed a finger into her warm, wet recess. He teased her lips apart and tormented the hidden morsel. A wrinkle formed between her brows and she rolled her hips against his hand until she purred beneath his touch.

He tugged the pink panties down her thighs and then with one last, languid stroke of his fingers, he stood. Sucking his own fingers into his mouth, he tasted her. Her eyes went wide and her lips parted with her soft gasp.

He shoved his jeans and boxers down over his hips, his erection rearing hot and hard.

As he eased her onto the bed, huge guileless eyes ate him up. His cock jumped and he kneeled between her thighs on the bed. Their bed.

Emotion surged and, pressing the length of his body against hers, he touched her everywhere, her small rib cage and spine, shapely breasts and thighs, the decadent swells of her lush bottom.

Climbing over her, he pressed his body against hers, touching her everywhere—arms, torso, cheek.

The head of his cock nudged inside, stretching her softness. Pleasure lashed at him, but he didn't plunge. She gazed up at him with large, light eyes, the color of the summer sky just before a refreshing rain. Those eyes held the mystery of a thousand unspoken desires and their soft pleading almost did him in.

In one slow, excruciating slide, he pushed inside her warm heat. A moan tore from his throat as she took every inch of him into her body. Buried deep, he stilled. A shuddered racked him.

Slowly, he started to pump his hips and she squirmed beneath him. He gritted his teeth and kept his strokes even, despite the need to thrust urgently into her, to come and to claim her.

They moved awkwardly at first, as though trying to recall the steps to a dance they knew once long ago. He gripped her heart-shaped ass and probed her with slow, repetitive strokes. Then suddenly, they found their rhythm and the sky exploded.

She lifted her hips to meet his thrusts with a breathless urgency that drove his need to have her. His possession of her body was wild and fierce. When she lifted her knees to take him deeper, they cried out together.

His hand slipped between their bodies and he coaxed her to greater abandon with the light teasing of his fingers. Her plump, swollen sex wept for him. The scent of her arousal rose to torment him.

Through narrowed eyes, he watched her take her pleasure in his body. She arched her back, thrusting her breasts high while her muscles clenched and sucked his huge, hard cock. His pulsing love filled her, pushing anguished cries from someplace deep inside her. She screamed his name when she came.

Always, his name.

He was the only man to know the feel of her tight pussy and the beautiful heartbreak of her orgasm. He was the only man to know the sounds of her pleasure and the taste of her love.

Dots of light skittered across his vision. His balls tightened. The smell of Isobel and sex filled his awareness.

Sound receded. Grief and fear burned to ash in the flames of their passion.

He pressed his face into the curve of her neck, and with dirty words and hot endearments, urged her to take all she wanted from him. She dug the heels of her feet into the mattress and strained toward him with her head thrown back. His tongue lapped at the throbbing pulse point on the side of her neck.

"Shea, please." Her body and mouth pleaded.

Faster, harder, deeper.

He couldn't hold out. She was too hot, too tight, too soft and trembling.

Fiery bliss consumed him when her sex pulsed tight around him, gripping and sucking. With a roar, he plunged deep and came. It poured out of him, burning away layers of pain and sorrow. He reached the peak, but it didn't end. After the agonizing fall, the ferocious waves of his pleasure immediately rose once more. The world fractured and fragmented around him until she'd wrung the last drop of ecstasy from his aching body.

Consciousness returned to him slowly. He was still throbbing inside her when she pressed a tender kiss to his damp forehead.

Within the fire of their love, his heart beat with fierce joy.

Chapter Fifteen

Shea woke to a room painted by dawn. A miniature foot jammed under his left cheekbone and at the sound of his wife's steady, rhythmic breathing relief swamped him.

It had all been a bad dream. The angry words, the anguished glances, the tears and crushing grief were nothing but a terrible nightmare. He'd never left and had remained exactly where he was supposed to be.

With her.

He'd never wanted anything more than to be with her. Not a cheering crowd or a high-powered career. Those things were a means to an end. After growing up with a violent, volatile drunk for a dad, he wanted peace. Calm. After a lifetime of upheaval, he wanted steady.

He wanted Isobel.

Forever.

Reality crept in, wringing a pang of despair from his

chest. He hadn't yet awakened from the nightmare.

But he was rousing.

When he turned his head to look at his slumbering wife, the smile in his heart made its way to his face.

In the dusky light, her unkempt beauty stunned. He'd gazed at her face thousands of times, but she appeared different to him now. He stared at the same silky brown hair and smooth caramel skin.

Then he realized the change wasn't in her. It was in him.

It was in the way he saw her. He'd known the wound of her dad's abandonment had sliced deep, but he hadn't understood the full extent of her trauma.

Extracting Connor's tiny foot from his cheek, Shea eased from their bed and slipped quietly from the room. Since the separation, he couldn't recall the last time he'd slept through the night. Without her by his side, sleep eluded had him. Now, he felt more rested than he had in years.

He started a pot of coffee brewing and settled at the kitchen island with his cell phone. Late last night, he'd sent a flurry of text messages to his brothers and sisters-in-law and he flipped quickly through the heap of their replies.

Once done, he shuffled over to the coffeepot. As he poured his first cup, Isobel padded into the kitchen, a mildly queasy look on her face.

Dread dragged at him and he jammed the pot into the coffeemaker cradle. Was she second-guessing them already? Doubting him? What would he have to do to prove to her–

Her hand cut through the air, her cell phone clasped in her palm. "Vanessa called."

Air returned to his lungs. "What did she say?"

"There's been a slight change of plans. They want to

do the interview next Tuesday, and the photoshoot the following day." Panic darkened her light eyes. "I don't know if I can make three-and-a-half dresses in ten days."

"You don't have to do it alone." He tapped his finger on the tip of her straight nose. "I've called in reinforcements."

"What reinforcements?"

"The sisters. I sent a few texts last night asking if anyone had a hidden talent we don't know about." Steam rose from the black liquid as he filled a coffee mug. "Turns out Emily and Mina both know how to sew. That gives you three extra sets of hands."

"Three?"

"Mina, Emily, and me."

Her jaw went slack. "You sew?"

His shoulders moved with his shrug. "I grew up with four brothers. We had no mother and no money. Yeah, I sew."

Her eyes narrowed with her doubt.

"My skills are best suited for repairing holes and replacing buttons, but that has to count for something, right?"

"These are thousand-dollar dresses."

"Guess you better show me the stitch you want me to use, then." He sipped the hot brew.

She tortured her bottom lip, but the panic had left her eyes and an irresistible light peeked through the gray clouds.

Abandoning his coffee, he reached for her.

"I expect to be closely supervised." He pressed the length of his body against hers and, dipping his head, inhaled her intoxicating scent. "Very closely."

A shiver raced through her.

He couldn't stop the smile that curved his lips as she lifted her face to his.

When his mouth hovered a whisper from hers, she drew back. Pale gray eyes swirled with vulnerability. "I'm sorry about last night. I might've overreacted a little."

His heart hammered against his rib cage. "I forgive you. I don't think the kids heard your screaming orgasms."

With a startled laugh, she smacked his arm. "I'm trying to apologize." Her eyes latched on to his shirtfront. "I guess I still have some hang-ups about my dad."

He toyed with a wisp of hair at her temple. "You don't have to apologize for that."

She snuck a glance at him from beneath the sweep of her eyelashes. "When he came to the pub, what did you two talk about?"

"You." A tired habit caused him to hesitate for one heartbeat, two. "And he asked about Connor and Maisie."

"What about Finn?"

A kick of anger punched him in the chest. "Finn didn't come up."

Her lashes swept down to hide her eyes.

Was she angry? Annoyed? With him, or with her dad? Shea hoped the latter, but he didn't want to guess. For one, he sucked at it, but also, he wanted to know what was going on with her. What was really going on with her.

"That bothers you, doesn't it?"

"He's about to turn eighteen and my dad has never even met him." Her throat spasmed.

"The next time he comes into the pub, you want me to say anything to him?" Shea asked, a hopeful ring in his tone. "Deliver a message, maybe?"

The silence stretched out while a thoughtful scowl marred her features.

Then, with a hard shake of her head, the frown vanished. "No."

෬

By midmorning, Shea and Finn had hauled her sewing machine and supplies up the narrow flight of stairs and wedged an oversized work table through the loft doorway. While she set up the ballgown on a dress form in the middle of the room, they positioned the table beneath the work lights Shea had hung the previous night.

She'd borrowed three additional dress forms from the store and when Finn lugged the last two into the loft, Isobel handed him a bottle of water.

At his side, she watched Connor chase Maisie around the wide-open space until he'd taken a long, heathy swallow.

Then she pounced. "Your dad told me you gave Sidney Shaw a ride home the other night."

"Uh-huh."

"I don't know her family. Don't they live in Fishtown?" she asked, referring to the old neighborhood by the wharf.

"Yeah. So?"

Isobel noted the defensive edge in his voice. "Just curious."

Finn rolled his head in her direction and leveled her with a look. "What do you want to know?"

"Do you like her?"

The water bottle captured his attention. "She's nice."

"I mean—"

"I know what you mean, Mom." He swallowed a long swig of the clear liquid.

Isobel waited.

When he finally pulled the bottle away from his lips, he glowered. "It doesn't matter if I like her. She doesn't like me."

"That's ridiculous. I saw her talking to you a few weeks ago after your game. She seemed friendly."

His glower darkened. "She's nice to everybody. Especially the other boys. All the other boys." He tossed his bottlecap into the trash can near the door. "I'm the only one she doesn't give the time of day."

"Oh."

Light gray eyes snapped to her face. "What does that mean?"

"Nothing. You're right. If you're the *only* boy she treats differently from *all* the other boys, then she must not see anything special about you." Isobel sighed dramatically. "I guess that's that then."

She left him frowning down at his water bottle and intervened before Connor climbed onto the front windowsill. Soon Finn rounded up Connor and Maisie and headed out, leaving her and Shea alone to work.

From the heap of supplies discarded in a corner of the room, she retrieved the storage box filled with her collection of glass and crystal beads and plucked her sketch pad off the floor near her purse. Dragging the rolling cart behind her, she approached the as-yet unadorned princess ballgown.

As she flipped open her sketchbook and leafed through the pages, he came to stand beside her. She pinpointed the intricate pattern she'd designed for the bodice and as she started to explain the markings to him, he leaned close. His warm, subtle scent filled her senses.

"So we're using two different beads?" His gruff voice moved through her like a deep-bone massage.

"Yes, these two."

With large, work-roughened hands, he fingered the delicate beads.

While she threaded a needle, he studied the guide

she'd made. She picked out one sparkling crystal from the hundreds of shiny beads in her storage box and turned to the dress.

"Like this." She stabbed the fine fabric and pushed the needle through.

Then she slid the bead down the thread, and holding it gently in place, made another stab at the pristine fabric. After several more jabs, she knotted the string and then looked up into his face.

"Only one thousand more to go?" He cracked his knuckles. "Step aside and let the man work."

Over his shoulder, she observed his first few stitches. He took extreme care with the fragile fabric and, to her baffled amazement, he had a sure hand and some actual skill. She made only a few suggestions before his delicious smell and sexy needlework drove her the far side of the loft where she could finally drag a full breath into her tight lungs.

With effort, she forced her mind away from the man across the room and onto the design for the next dress. She unrolled a large swath of tracing paper and began laying out a new pattern for an elegant trumpet-style gown. A few times, she glanced up to find Shea's gaze fastened on her, and the nearly tactile touch of his watchfulness raised gooseflesh on her arms.

Sometime later, when she'd finished drawing the pattern and stood deliberating where she might find her shears, Emily and Mina arrived.

Emily took over the beading from Shea, who stood and stretched his back while Isobel hunted up the scissors and put Mina to work cutting out the pattern design. When Shea slipped out quietly, Isobel settled in a stream of sunlight pouring in through the front windows and, sketchpad in hand, contemplated how she wanted to approach the next gown's design.

After a bit, Shea returned with a card table, which he set up in the back corner, and a sound dock that he used to pump music through the loft. Another brief departure followed, and then he reappeared with a large sampling of food from the kitchen downstairs and an array of caffeinated beverages.

For the rest of the day and into the evening, they chatted and sang along to music while they worked, taking intermittent breaks to sneak bites of pub food and sips of caffeine. By the time they finally quit for the night, they'd cut out the sections for the trumpet-style gown, which Isobel had pieced together and placed on a dress form and had made progress on the ballgown's beadwork. Isobel heaped thank yous onto her sisters-in-law as they scooted out the door, then turned to the task of packing up her things to head home.

Before the ballgown, she paused. Peering closely, she examined the stitching and decided Shea's skill exceeded the others. She shook her head. How could she know someone for so long, be married to him, and not know everything there was to know about him?

"Uh-oh. Is that a look of disapproval?"

She turned as he entered the loft, after having snuck downstairs to check on things at his work.

"Not at all," she said. "You're good, actually."

A smug smile touched his puffy lips. Then he pulled a lollipop from his back pocket, peeled away the colorful wrapper and took a long lick of the bright red sucker. After a moment, he caught her staring at him, her mouth slightly ajar.

"What?"

"You're eating a sucker."

"Connor asked me how many licks it takes to eat the whole lollipop."

He rarely ate junk food, and she couldn't recall him

ever doing something so silly as counting licks of a lollipop.

"Is something wrong?" he asked.

"Who are you?" Aggrieved bewilderment strained her voice. "Every time I turn around, you're doing something... strange."

"Eating a sucker is strange?"

"For you? Yes. And sewing? Seriously?"

The sucker left a bright red kiss on his lips. "I'm a man of many talents."

"We've been married eighteen years and it's like I don't know you at all."

His arms swept wide to encompass their surroundings. "I know the feeling."

⚃

The next day, she had to work at the store. On her lunch break, she visited the loft to find Mina and Emily working together on the beaded bodice while Shea organized her thread box, which had gotten jumbled in the move.

After work, she went home to change and eat dinner with the kids and when Connor and Maisie had gone down for the night, she left Finn playing video games while the little ones slept and headed back to the loft.

Sounds from the pub downstairs carried through the floor while she sat before trumpet gown making neat stitches to connect the fitted lace bodice to the gossamer skirt. Through the row of large windows, blackness blanketed the island while inside the loft, Shea's work lights lit up the space.

When the raucous noise below had quieted, Shea appeared. Sitting back, she craned her neck to either side to stretch her aching muscles.

"It's almost two o'clock." He set a tote on the card

table and pulled out a bottle of wine. "Need a break?"

She joined him at the table as he poured wine into two Styrofoam cups. A smile curved her lips when she realized he'd chosen a wine they'd drunk once in a while in the early days of their marriage, when they were too poor to afford a decent blend.

He handed her one of the cups, then raised the other a small hitch. "To the good old days."

With a smile, she touched her cup to his.

"Did you know back then that you wanted to make wedding dresses?"

The sweet wine made her lips pucker slightly when she shook her head. "Not at all."

"What did you want to do?" The folding chair groaned when he settled into it.

"I never picked an occupation." She dropped into the chair across from him. "I don't' remember thinking I wanted to be a nurse or a teacher or anything like that." She studied the pink liquid in her cup for a moment. "There was a lot I wanted to do though."

"Such as?"

"Travel."

A flicker of surprise warmed his expression. "I didn't know that."

"When I was young, before we met, I used to dream of leaving the island."

"Where would you go?"

"Everywhere. New York, Paris, Cincinnati."

When he laughed, the years seemed to fade away.

"Then my mom drowned, and now I'm afraid to take the ferry across a mile-wide stretch of water." Shaking her head, she chuckled.

That time he didn't laugh with her.

He leaned his head back to rest against the exposed brick wall. "Lately I've been thinking about traveling more. With the kids."

Her tense muscles began to relax with the effects of the alcohol. "Where do you want to go?"

"Ireland, Mexico, Puerto Rico." His quick answer surprised her. "I want to take them to see where their grandparents come from." His voice softened when he said, "I want to visit my mom's grave."

Grief squeezed her heart. "You miss her?"

"Every day."

"Your memories of her, are they strong?"

His gaze fixed on some point on the ceiling. "Not anymore. They've faded some, but I still remember the feeling of her, you know?"

She nodded, and shifted in her chair, as if to alleviate the old pain. "What about you? Did you always know you wanted to be a lawyer?"

A thoughtful frown touched the edges of his features. "Once I realized what law could do, yes."

She propped her elbow on the table and rested her chin in the cradle of her palm. "What do you mean?"

"Growing up, I saw a lot of injustice, but I was just a kid. I wanted to fight but all I had were my fists, so I mostly just used those." His bright eyes danced with humor. "Then I discovered law, and I finally had the tools to fight with my mind. With the truth. I had a voice, and I wielded it to lay waste to bad guys. It was a heady rush."

The passion in his voice wedged a lump in her throat. "Then why did you quit?"

When he dropped his gaze, the feathery sweep of his dark eyelashes cast deep shadows over his taut cheekbones. For many long moments he didn't speak.

The silence in the room filled with tension until, abruptly, he stood. "It's getting late. We should get home."

Chapter Sixteen

Isobel returned to the loft early the next morning, but her thoughts remained at home where she'd left Shea making breakfast for Connor and Maisie.

After they'd returned home the previous night, he hadn't seemed particularly angry or upset with her, but he'd been distant. Withdrawn. The way he used to be, right before he left her.

Was it because she'd mentioned his job at the law firm? She'd always just assumed he'd quit, but given his odd reaction, she now worried something else must've happened. Had he been fired. If so, why?

Around noon, Mina and Emily arrived to take their positions in front of the beaded bodice. They chattered while they worked, but Isobel became consumed by the complicated draping of the sheath gown she stitched and lost track of their conversation until Mina's worried tone pierced her bubble of concentration.

"You look tired. Isn't he sleeping better?"

Sneaking a glance at Emily, Isobel noticed the dark circles beneath her large brown eyes.

Then those eyes clamped onto Isobel. "Shea told m-me I should talk to you."

Hunched over the work table, Isobel straightened. "He did?"

Emily's strawberry-blonde ponytail bobbed when she nodded. "He said you're the best m-mom he's ever known, and you m-might know what to do."

Surprise knocked into Isobel. "He said that?"

A fierce scowl pulled at Emily's pretty features. "The b-books all say b-babies sleep twelve to eighteen hours a day."

Isobel swallowed a laugh, only because Emily appeared so miserable. "What they don't tell you is that those twelve hours come in forty-five-minute fits and spurts."

Emily's shoulders slumped.

"He's only a few months old," Isobel said gently. "It'll take some time for him to get used to our schedules."

Soulful brown eyes glistened with tears. "Are you sure I'm n-not d-doing something w-w-wrong?"

Her helplessness was palpable and Isobel experienced a wrench of pain as the memories of her own despair came crashing back through her mind. She remembered the sound of Noah's voice reading classic novels from their English Lit class, which neither of them had completed, to Finn late into the night.

At first, she'd blamed the baby for her dad's abandonment until one day, Noah dropped Finn into her arms and disappeared somewhere out of sight. Fear had choked her. She was afraid to love him, afraid he'd be taken away from her, too, the terror eclipsed only by the horrific possibility she might not be able to love.

But holding that tiny, squirming bundle, she'd burst into tears. He was so small, so helpless, and in that moment, she was all he had in the world. She'd had no clue what to do. She was a child herself, a child who'd needed her mom, too.

The tears didn't stop for weeks. Months. When it came time for Shea to return to his work on the freighter, her fear expanded to include him out at sea and every cloud that darkened the sky, every drop of rain that plummeted to earth, had sent her into a dark cycle of panic and depression.

Isobel blinked away the memories and offered Emily a warm smile. "You're doing everything perfectly."

Emily sniffed.

"I can see how much you love him, and that's what he needs more than anything."

"I love him so m-much."

"Of course you do, Em." Mina squeezed her cousin's hand.

"I've been where you are with every one of my babies. The poor things deserved a better mom than me. At least someone who knew what she was doing." Isobel lifted and dropped her shoulders. "Instead, they got me and the only thing I had to give them was all of my heart. So I made a promise to them that no one would ever love them more than I do."

At the sound of sniffling, Isobel turned as Mina dabbed at the corner of her eyes. "Shea was right. You're a great mom."

Emily pushed out a deep, fortifying breath. "I didn't know it'd b-be so hard on us. On our r-relationship. I didn't expect that."

More painful memories lashed Isobel, of sleepless nights and short tempers. The constant, chronic inability to finish an entire conversation, or even complete a coherent thought, without interruption. The wounded pride and defensiveness, the hurt feelings, the growing apart. It was exhausting. Maddening. It could even be relationship-ending.

"That'll p-pass, too, right?" A desperate ring infected Emily's voice.

Isobel stared down at her hands for a long moment while her heart twisted itself inside out. The reassuring words wouldn't come.

"Be kind to each other, and yourselves. Be patient. You're both learning, and you're going to screw up." She recalled how much she'd concealed from Shea about her struggles, and how, at the end, she'd prayed there was a way to make him see her as the person she used to be, and not the weak, sad woman lying on the couch popping antidepressants. "Talk to him. Tell him things. Even if they seem irrelevant or ridiculous, tell him anyway. Otherwise, you'll wake up one day and you won't recognize the man you married. You might not even recognize yourself."

β

By early evening, Isobel had fitted the third mannequin with the skeleton of a gown, and when Shea appeared, Mina and Emily declared the beading project halfway complete before they knocked off for the night.

At the card table, Isobel poured a Styrofoam cup more than half full of the cheap wine and took a healthy drink, hoping the alcohol would ease the achiness in her back and hands. While she sipped her drink, Shea stood before the new dress, a soft, almost wistful expression on his face.

Her heart tripped in her chest and a flood of heat

rushed to the surface of her skin. Not unlike the way she reacted the first time she talked to him in the school cafeteria, or the way she felt every time she was naked before his probing gaze, even now, all these years later.

"Your mom would be blown away by you." His gaze swung to her and he pointed at the dress.

Maybe it was exhaustion, but the punch of emotion caused her eyes to fill with tears.

"I'm sorry," he said softly. "I didn't mean to make you sad."

"It's not that." With the tip of one finger, she wiped away a tear that threatened to fall. "I'm just so mad that I was a teenager when she died. I was mouthy, and moody, and too self-absorbed. I don't even know what her favorite song was or her favorite movie." She set her drink on the table. "The day she died... I can't remember if I told her I loved her."

"I knew you then. You weren't anything like that brat you describe. You were kind." A curious light shimmered in his eyes and she chased after it, wondering what caused it. "Did your mom help you make us all that food?"

Surprise flew through her.

His deep laugh rumbled in his chest. "Yeah, I knew."

"I never told her who it was for." A hard lump of regret formed in the pit of her stomach at the memory. "That Christmas... Shea, I—"

"It's okay." He held up his hand to cut off her stammering and as it fell away, a soft light came into his eyes. "I fell in love with you that day."

Wave upon wave of shock rolled over her.

"I don't know, maybe it was just deeper lust." His smile devastated her. "But it was a nice thing that you did. A very Isobel-like thing to do."

Her skin flushed with warmth and she searched his face, wondering if he believed his own words.

In his eyes, the inner light now burned bright enough to singe her from across the room. "You were dying to help us, I could tell, but you were so concerned about protecting my ego, you tried to hide it. Believe me, my pride took a hit that day, but not because of you. You weren't there to make yourself feel better. You were there because you cared. I saw your heart that day, and I fell in love you."

Whether from her potent husband, the wine, or the tiredness, she experienced a pleasant surge of dizziness.

"Emily told me what you said." She blurted the words.

Confusion rippled across his features. "What did I say?"

"That I'm a good mom." Her blush deepened.

"You are."

The sudden swelling of her heart pushed a smile to her face. "I thought you hated the way I parent."

The color drained from his face. "I never once thought that. Where in the hell did you come up with that idea?"

She searched her mind but could find no words or actions to point to as evidence. Was it possible she'd assigned the belief to him without proof? Had she always assumed the worst about him?

She chewed her bottom lip. "Well, I'm a lot more permissive than you."

"So? I'm too strict."

Her head tipped to one side. "Why are you so strict?"

"I was raised Catholic."

"So was I."

"Irish Catholic is different."

She gave her head a shake. "Try again."

His brows pulled together as he applied more thought to the question. "I want them to be successful."

"So do I, Shea. Truly."

He bent his head and stared down at the wood plank

flooring. "And I don't ever want them to know what it feels like to be hungry, or to be so poor they feel humiliated, or worse, trapped." When he glanced up, his expression was pained. "I guess I overdid it."

For a moment, she marveled at the man she'd married. Why hadn't she put that together about him before now? It was obvious, but she'd been so quick to assign blame she hadn't paused to consider the reasons why he might do things differently. She hadn't even considered that there might be reasons.

"Thankfully they have you to balance me out," he said.

She fiddled with the rim of her cup. "That's not why I'm lenient with them."

"Why then?" he asked, his voice gentle.

"I know how much it hurts when a parent only sees your flaws and nothing else. I don't want them to ever doubt that I love them or worry that I won't be there for them, no matter what. There's no worse feeling."

He closed the space between them and when he wrapped her in his arms, sorrow engulfed her. She couldn't escape the anguish at all they'd lost. All the years spent angry and arguing when they could've been as they were in that moment. Friends. Partners. Lovers.

That night he made love to her in their bed. When he was deliciously hard and thick inside her, a shuddering breath eased from her. As he began to move, she squeezed her eyes shut, as if she might be able to keep him from penetrating her heart.

With every touch, every kiss, every minute she spent with him, it was getting harder and harder to forget who they used to be, who she wanted them to be, and remember who they were now.

Chapter Seventeen

For what must've been the seven-billionth time that morning, the needle pierced the silk fabric and Shea pulled the thread taut. The work was beyond tedious. The pads of his fingers stung from the endless chain of tiny jabs into his flesh and his shoulders and back muscles ached from his prolonged inactivity and hunched posture.

But then, he felt the warm touch of her gaze and the pain vanished. He looked up in time to catch a glimpse of soft gray eyes before her lashes swept down to rest on her flushed cheeks.

A wide smile broke across his face. His plan was working. He'd breached her defenses, not by force or coercion, but by good old-fashioned persuasion, with a hint of flirtation thrown into the mix.

While she'd opened the gates and let him in, where

once he would've maneuvered to conquer, now he waited. He'd made his choice. Soon, she would need to make hers. Either she'd choose to come the rest of the way back to him, willingly, or she would not, but the decision belonged to her.

He was playing for keeps, not for a temporary truce or a cease-fire that lasted only until the next fight, the next separation, the next divorce filing. She must accept him, welcome him into her heart, with all his imperfections and weaknesses, or she'd never really be his.

Commitments kept Mina and Emily away the previous two days, so he and Isobel worked alone. Throughout the long hours, they kept up their dance of stolen glances and secret smiles until a delicious tension stretched between them.

Content to let the heat simmer, he remained planted on the stool before the beaded wedding dress, dutifully stitching tiny crystals into place in accordance of Isobel's pattern, until late in the day when he left to pick up Connor and Maisie from school and daycare.

At home, he made a quick dinner, suffering a moment of stunned speechlessness when Finn emerged from behind his bedroom door and joined his younger siblings at the kitchen island. He even made eye contact a couple of times while he scarfed down a healthy serving of mac and cheese and coaxed Connor into eating his broccoli with a ridiculous, seemingly well-practiced, pirate routine.

After bath and bedtime, Shea made the short drive downtown and arrived at the loft an hour or so past sunset to find Isobel on the floor before one of the dresses making small stitches along the skirt's hem.

While he'd been away, she'd set up three more dress forms, which now displayed the two gowns Mina and Emily had dropped off and the pale pink dress Vanessa had lauded that day at the store.

A little more than a week had passed since Vanessa made her incredible offer, and in that short time, he and Isobel had accomplished so much together. Right before their eyes was proof that they were good together. That they belonged together. Even she must see that now.

"What do you think?" he asked, crossing the large space. "Are we going to make it?"

"It's going to be close." Isobel climbed to her feet and stretched, giving him a tantalizing view of her uplifted breasts. "I think I'll be sewing beads on that bodice the whole time the photographer's taking pictures."

When he reached her side, he noticed lines of fatigue around her eyes. "Have you eaten?"

"I had some chips a little while ago."

"Why don't we go downstairs and get you a bite to eat before the kitchen closes?"

She groaned. "I should work."

He dropped his chin and leveled her with a stern look. "You need food—real food—or you're not going to last another hour."

She'd already let down her messy bun and was combing her fingers through the tangled tresses.

He watched her closely. "Besides, it's a special occasion."

Her hands stilled above her head.

"Or did you forget?"

Pulling the heavy mass of her dark hair over one shoulder, her fingers worked through a snarl. "How could I forget our wedding anniversary?"

A secret smile passed between them, then their gazes slid apart.

"It's getting late," she said, glancing at the wall clock. "You're going to run out of time to claim your kiss today."

His breath snagged in his throat. "The night's not over

yet."

"You've never waited this long before."

Satisfaction kicked in his veins. "Maybe I'm holding out for a reason."

"What reason?" she asked, her voice suddenly, slightly breathy.

Uncertainty gripped him and hesitated. "How about a date?"

Her lush mouth screwed into a contemplative frown. "That'd be what, our third date?"

"That's not true." Dismay crashed into him. "Is that true?"

She nodded. "It's true."

"That's fecking terrible."

Her husky laugh tugged at his groin.

Growing serious, he made a show of clearing his throat. "Isobel, would you like to have dinner with me?"

"No."

"Oh, c'mon. I thought that was pretty good."

A sound suspiciously like a giggle leaked out of her. "I will go on a date with you, but dinner tonight doesn't count." One of her small hands swept down her body. "I'm wearing yoga pants, and I haven't even combed my hair today."

With difficulty, he dragged his gaze away from her sleek black leggings and back to her face. "We'll consider tonight a practice run, then."

Pleasure pinkened her cheeks. "A practice date?"

"Might be fun."

She arched one dark eyebrow at him. "Might be as disastrous as our other dates."

"All three of them were disasters?"

"Well, no." The color on her cheeks deepened. "Our second date was quite nice, actually."

"Quite nice?" He cringed. "You gotta give me chance

to redeem myself."

Her light, lyrical laughter was contagious and his own smile lingered when they arrived downstairs.

The dinner rush had ended and a boisterous Saturday night crowd packed the bar. Then he heard it. The whispers. He glanced around the dining room at the curious gazes fastened boldly on them. They didn't even try to hide their prying.

Damn small towns.

He reached for her hand, drawing her close. "You okay?" he asked, his mouth near her temple.

Beneath her caramel complexion, she'd paled, but she nodded and clasped his hand tight.

"Because if it bothers you, we can leave."

When she glanced up at him, mischief glinted in her eyes. "Or we could give them something to talk about."

His large hand touched her face and he leaned close, but before he claimed his wife's soft mouth, movement from the corner of his eye stopped him.

Heather drew up when she spotted him.

"Hey, Boss." Her gaze bounced from him to Isobel and back again. "I was beginning to wonder if we should file a missing person's report."

Reluctantly, Shea straightened away from Isobel. "Miss me?"

"Not even a little," Heather said brightly.

He laid a hand over his still-thundering heart. "Ouch."

Her full-throated laugh rang out. "What I meant is you've trained us well and we're a finely tuned machine. I even finished payroll. You wanna sign it while you're here?"

"Not right now." He glanced at Isobel, who watched him with soft gray eyes. "I'm on a practice date with my wife."

Through her smile, Heather's brow furrowed. "What's

a practice date?"

"Never mind."

"Hi, Iz." Heather's smile warmed. "It's good to see you."

"It's good to see you, too." Isobel touched his arm. "Go sign payroll. I don't mind."

"What are the rules to this dating thing? I'm not supposed to work, am I?"

"I'll time you. You have five minutes starting–" She swiped a finger across her cell phone's screen. "–now."

In his office, Heather's payroll report lay on his desk and he glanced over the information. He made sure Heather had enough hours to support her and her young son, but not so many that she couldn't ever be home with him, and that everyone else had a good ratio of hours to days off.

When he reached the bottom of the page, he frowned. Then he started again at the top and worked his way back down the list.

His frown deepened. The entire staff was accounted for, all except Aiden.

He found Heather mixing a drink behind the bar. "Where's Aiden?"

She jerked her head over her shoulder. "Over there talking to Isobel."

He held up the payroll report. "No, I mean why isn't he on the payroll? Shouldn't he have made it into this week's check run?"

She stuck a paper umbrella into the fruity concoction. "He hasn't completed his paperwork yet. I told him he needs to bring me a copy of his social security card before I can pay him. I'll remind him again."

Shea signed the report and left it on his desk for Heather to process, then returned to the restaurant where Isobel had snagged them a booth along the far wall.

He wound his way across the room to her.

Midway to sitting, he froze. "What's wrong?"

"There you are." The recognizable female voice grated along his spine and explained the stricken look on Isobel's face. "Where have you been hiding?"

The wave of dread knocked him the rest of the way to sitting.

Amber Jessop, a black hole of toxicity and the one woman who could destroy all the progress he'd made with his wife, sidled up to their table.

He stopped her with a look. "This isn't a good time, Amber."

Placing a hand on her hip, she planted her breasts in his face. "You'll never guess who finally made partner."

"I don't care."

Shrewd dark eyes narrowed at him. "Of course you do. It's obvious you miss the mental challenge of law. Your mind needs the stimulation." She cast a side-eyed glance at Isobel. "You know what they say about the brain being the largest erogenous zone in the body."

"You haven't seen my other erogenous zone."

"Is that an invitation?"

"No," he snapped, his patience running out.

"Oh my." She leaned close to rub his shoulders. "So tense and grumpy."

Shea's voice shook with the effort not to reach out and strangle her when he warned, "Do not touch me."

With a nervous laugh that lacked humor, Amber removed her hands from his body. "Fine, you tease."

He rolled his shoulders, as if to shake off the contamination from her unwanted caress. "Now if you'll excuse us, my wife and I are trying to have dinner."

Amber's mouth turned down with an insincere pout. "I heard about the divorce. I know how much you both must be hurting."

"We're not divorced," Isobel declared with a strength in her voice that would've thrilled him, but for the unspoken "yet" she left hanging at the end of her pronouncement.

Amber ignored Isobel and focused her calculating gaze on him instead. "Let me know if you want to talk. When the divorce is final, of course. We can... talk. All night long."

Laughter burst from Isobel. "Wow. Amber, that was... incredible. You didn't sound desperate at all. A touch creepy, but overall a great performance. Honestly, well done."

A priceless scowl contorted Amber's features.

Isobel waggled her fingers. "Now shoo. My husband needs to eat so he has enough energy later tonight."

The seductive once-over she gave him then made his cock jump. But the triumph of Amber's hasty retreat was short-lived.

In the wake of her departure, a heavy, awkward silence settled over the table.

"You okay?"

Isobel's dark head bobbed.

In his chest, a hard knot squeezed. "Do you want to go?"

She shook her head.

"Look, don't let her get to you. That's what she wants. Don't give her the satisfaction."

Huge round eyes twisted his insides. "You and she haven't... been together?"

He reared back. "What? Jesus, no. Of course not."

She pretended great interest in the menu. The menu she'd created. "It's been two years. I don't expect that you've remained celibate."

Furious grief slashed through him. "Are you serious right now?"

It wasn't the first time she'd accused him of infidelity. She'd done so exactly once before.

The day he'd moved out.

"Are you having an affair?"

He stilled, frozen like a marble statue while a fire raged through him.

"How could you ask me that?" The words snapped like the crack of a whip. "How could you even think it?"

He moved deeper into their bedroom.

She stumbled back. "You lied to me about your job. What else are you lying to me about?"

A flicker of shame prickled across his face and neck, but his white-hot fury pushed out all else. "I didn't want you to worry. You needed to focus on your health. On the baby–"

"You should have told me!"

"I've given you my life," he seethed. "Every all-nighter and eighty-hour work week was for you. All the months I lived on that fucking freighter were for you. I gave up everything for you. So we could build this house. So you would be happy."

So I would be worthy of you.

"I didn't want that." Tears ran in rivulets down her pale face. "I never asked you for any of it."

"Then what do you want?" The words erupted from him as a desperate cry. "What could I have possibly given you that would have made you happy?"

"I never asked you for any of those things. Now you blame me as if I did? That isn't fair, Shea."

"You just accused me of cheating on you. Don't you dare talk to me about fair."

A sob shook her shoulders. "If you're so miserable, why don't you leave? Just go."

So he did.

He blinked until the nightmare dissolved.

With a defeated sigh, she abandoned the menu. "I don't know if I'm serious. I'm tired and—"

"What do we have here?" A female voice drew near. "Why if it isn't my two new favorite people."

Shea struggled to gain his feet on shifting ground as he looked up to find Vanessa swooping down on their table, a wineglass posed between her manicured fingers.

Isobel's spine snapped straight. "Vanessa, hi."

"Did Jen call you?" Vanessa wanted to know. "Are you all set for your interview? How about Marcus? When's he coming for the photoshoot?"

Isobel swallowed thickly. "Later this week."

"Fantastic. I'm so excited for you." While Vanessa sipped from her wineglass, her gaze shifted between them. She swallowed and struck a deceptively casual posture. "So, you two doing okay? Everything good?"

"Great. Everything's great. We're great. Aren't we, Sweetie?" Isobel's stiff smile and stilted words dragged a grunt from him.

"Great," he muttered.

At least, things were great, up until the point when all their baggage had suddenly come hurtling back at them. All it took was one random encounter and the past hurts and injustices had risen up to stab and pierce the tentative bond they'd managed to forge.

Anger gnawed at him. Never in her life had she called him Sweetie.

"We're celebrating our wedding anniversary," Isobel blurted.

Vanessa cut off the healthy swig of wine she'd just taken. "No way. How many years?"

He captured his wife's gaze and held it. "Eighteen."

Vanessa gasped and laid a hand over her heart. "Eighteen years. The porcelain year."

Porcelain. Like a toilet. Seemed fitting.

"Well, I won't keep you. Darling, it's been a treat meeting you." Vanessa tossed a couple of air kisses at Isobel and then gave Shea a wink. "You, too, handsome. You kids have fun tonight."

Vanessa drifted away and when she was out of earshot, Isobel mumbled, "Can we just go?"

Relief washed over him and he followed her to the exit. In his truck, the tension was stifling and the moment they reached safety inside the house, Isobel careened toward the hall.

"Aren't we going to talk about this?" he said to her retreating back.

She barely broke stride. "There's nothing to say."

"Who's the one walking away now?"

Predictably, she whirled on him. "Fine. What do you want to talk about, Shea?"

"You're upset. Why?"

"I'm not upset. I'm tired." To mask the lie, she gave him her back and fled.

He pursued her to their bedroom, enjoying the flash of her anger when he stepped inside the room and eased the door closed behind him. It was better than the stony-faced look of helplessness she'd worn all the way home, as if their relationship was too far gone to save and she'd given up on them.

She folded her arms over her stomach, shielding herself. "Why don't you go find Amber? It'd be so easy for you to be with her."

His jaw clenched so tightly he feared he might grind his molars to dust. "I don't want Amber," he bit out. "I want you."

"Now," she sniped. "But what about later?"

Frustrated fury lashed at him. "What do you want me to say? Whatever it is, I'll say it."

"Tell me why." Her voice shattered with her sob. "Why

did you leave me?"

"Why did you let me go?" The words erupted from his bleeding heart.

"Was it because of her? Did you leave me to be with her?"

"No." He took a step toward her.

She stumbled back. "Then why?"

"Because you told me to." The excuse was empty. Hollow. "And I was wrong."

He shoved a hand into his hair and tugged at the ends.

Just then, as he watched, her expression changed, and his hand stilled.

She blinked at him with wide, unfathomable eyes. "I was testing you."

Slowly, his hand dropped to his side. "What did you say?"

"It's true. It was a test. To see if you were like my dad." Her features twisted with agony. "You failed."

"I want a do-over."

She scoffed. "That's not how it works."

"Why not?" His jaw ticked with his building rage. "You made up the game. You can change the rules."

"Even if I hadn't told you to leave, you would've left me anyway." Bitterness infected her tone. "You were miserable."

A nasty curse escaped him and he balled his hands into tight fists. He wanted shake her to make her stop saying such awful things. Or punch a hole in the wall. Instead, he stared hard into her small pale face.

Above the defiant set of her mouth, terror swirled in her eyes.

She was testing him again now. No matter what he said, she'd throw it back at him. She'd push him until he said something he'd regret. Something that would hurt beyond the moment. She wanted him to prove himself to her, and by God, she wasn't going to make it easy on him.

He'd seen it before. She wanted a fight, and she was purposefully antagonizing him to get it. The way Leo used to do. The same way she did the day he left.

This time he wouldn't give her what she wanted. The storm wasn't inside him this time. It was inside her.

The fight left his body in a rush.

"I wasn't unhappy with you. Or the kids," he said quietly. "I wish you'd given me a chance to explain that, but honestly, I'm not sure I could have. Not then."

He rested his hand on the doorknob.

"Wait. You're leaving?" Panic shredded her voice, but she quickly recovered with a cool glare. "I knew you would."

He reached her in two strides. Slipping his hand under her chin, he gently brought her eyes to his. "I am not leaving you. I'm not even leaving the house. But it's late and we're both upset, so I'm going to sleep on the couch downstairs, and in the morning, I'll be here waiting for you."

She jerked her chin from his grasp. "Don't bother."

He gripped her nape and tugged her to him. Covering her mouth with his, he swallowed her protests. Captured by his hand, she didn't move he soothed her with his tongue and wiped the wetness from her cheeks with the pad of his thumb.

When he lifted his head, she gazed up at him, her eyes darkened with her dilated pupils.

"You haven't been able to run me off yet, *mo chroí.* What makes you think you can do so now?"

Her lips moved wordlessly as she appeared to grapple for an answer and finding none that suited her.

"The fact is, you won't win this fight." His gaze latched onto her mouth and he scraped his thumb across her succulent bottom lip.

She tilted her chin, offering herself up to him.

Because he couldn't resist her, he took one light little taste of her, then pulled back.

His mouth hovering above hers, he murmured, "Sleep tight, my sweet wife. In the morning, I'll be here, and there's nothing you can say or do to stop me."

Then he left her standing at their bedroom door, flustered and yearning for his kiss.

Chapter Eighteen

An enormous choking knot sat on Isobel's chest when she left the store. After putting in a full day of work, she wanted nothing more than to hide out at the loft and immerse herself in her own designs for a few hours before heading home to tuck Connor and Maisie into bed.

And to face her husband for the first time since their fight the previous night.

The knot in her chest tightened with a painful wrench. Their run -in with Amber shouldn't have upset her so much, except that it provided proof of the one thing Isobel had feared most when Shea had offered her his help—that she'd let him get too close. And she had. She'd let him get *way* too close.

Though her heart had ached with the loss of him, his nearness inflicted fresh wounds. Because now she knew the exact color and flavor of the anguish that awaited her if he left her a second time. She couldn't bear it, not again. Too late, she wished she'd never taken that risk.

To reclaim some of the distance between them, she'd snuck out of the house early that morning just to avoid him, leaving while he still showered, and she'd gone to bed early the night before so that she'd be sound asleep when he returned home from the pub. It was juvenile and cowardly, but she was desperate.

On the sidewalk, she careened toward the stairwell, anxious to retreat upstairs, but before she reached safety, the door to the pub opened and Sophie poked her head outside.

"C'mon," she hissed, waving Isobel inside. "Quick, quick, quick."

Isobel wavered, frowning at her friend. "What are you doing? What's going on?"

"The party, silly. *Come on.* You're late."

Isobel's stomach dropped the pavement beneath her feet. She forgotten Finn's birthday? It was the cardinal sin of parenting. Terrible guilt swamped her as she rushed inside the pub behind Sophie.

She jolted when the large cheer went up.

"Surpri–!" The burst of sound died off as a collective groan.

Ava detached from the small crowd gathered. "Relax, everyone. It's not him."

Above the bar hung a large banner with the words "Happy Birthday, Finn!"

"Wait." Isobel shook her head to clear it. "It's not Finn's birthday."

"Maisie found out and we bumped it up a few days before she tattled to Finn." Sophie smacked Ava on the arm. "I thought you were going to send her a reminder."

Ava hit Sophie back. "I did."

"Wow." Sophie rubbed the spot on her arm. "You're really strong."

Ava fixed large, light eyes on Isobel. "I sent you a text last night. Didn't you get it?"

Isobel winced to recall her fight with Shea the previous night.

"I guess I missed it." With a gasp, Isobel pinned Ava with a look. "Tell me you didn't invite Dad."

"I didn't invite Dad." Ava held up her hands in a sign of surrender. "But I wanted to."

"Yeah, well, I want a lot of things I can't have either," Isobel muttered.

Sophie looped her arm under Isobel's elbow. "C'mon. Let's get you a drink."

At the bar, a handsome bartender took their drink orders.

"Sorry I haven't been able to help you out more." A sardonic smile tugged at Sophie's mouth. "Though given my sewing ability, maybe that's a good thing."

Isobel leaned in, as if imparting a secret. "Ava's worse."

Sophie's green eyes danced with humor. "Is she?"

Isobel nodded. "And it's okay. I know how busy you are with the business. How's it going?"

Sophie rolled her eyes. "It was great, up until this week."

"What happened this week?"

The bartender set two glasses half filled with pink wine on the bar and Sophie scooped one up. "I don't want to talk about it right now." She took a long, hearty swallow, then returned the wineglass to the bar top. "Let's talk about your week instead. I noticed you and Shea having been spending a lot of time together."

The bite of uncertainty pinched Isobel in the center of her chest.

Sophie winced. "Uh-oh. That's the sigh."

Despite herself, Isobel laughed.

"Is it true you two were on a date?" Sophie prodded gently.

"It was a practice date."

Sophie scrunched up her nose. "What the heck is a practice date?"

With a flick of her wrist, Isobel waved off her question. "I don't recommend it."

"But that means you guys are trying?" Sophie nudged. "So there's hope, right?"

Isobel's throat squeezed, and she stared down into her wineglass. "I don't know. Every time I think we've turned a corner, that we might be past the worst of it, something always pulls us back down again. Like gravity." Tears prickled behind her eyes when she risked a glance at her friend. "Really sucky gravity."

"I'm sorry, hon. I wish I knew how to help." Sophie raised her wineglass to her lips, but before she could drink, a choked sound erupted from her. "What the—?"

Isobel twisted around. "What? What happened?"

"Who put the balloons there?" Sophie bounded off her barstool. "They can't go by the cake table. Seriously, people."

Sophie's aggrieved protests died off as she scurried away to rectify the situation. Isobel turned back to her wine and lifted the glass to her lips.

"Can I say something?" asked a voice at her side.

At the sound of his thick Irish accent, Isobel groaned. Apart from her husband, she only knew one other man with that accent.

Her head swiveled in Noah's direction. "Depends what it is."

Noah propped his elbow on the bar and leaned his long frame against the wood. "Of all the people in the world, I think you and I probably know Shea the best.

Wouldn't you say?"

"Yeah, probably." She searched his dark eyes and found herself pulled in by their gooey warm centers.

"The two of us, we know more than anyone what he did for the rest of us."

Her heart lurched. "You mean what he did for you and your brothers?"

"He carried the weight of the world—of all our worlds—on his shoulders." A wistful smile curved one side of his mouth. "For a long time, I resented him for that. But I was only looking at things from my point of view. I didn't see what it cost him."

"I know it was hard on him, but he wouldn't have wanted it any other way."

"Maybe not, but he gave up an awful lot us. He gave up everything to try and save us. All of us." He tipped his pint of Guinness at her. "Except you. He wouldn't give you up. Even when you tried to make him."

"I didn't make him give me up." Heat flushed her cheeks. "He did that all on his own."

"Did he?"

Her blush deepened, not with outrage but with shame. Because she knew he was right.

Emotion clogged in her throat. "I'm still annoyed with him."

"No doubt." Noah's white teeth flashed with his wide grin. "I intend to hold it against him for the rest of our lives. It's great fun, that."

If she'd been able to laugh, his probing gaze would've smothered her mirth.

"I don't know what's happened between you two, and honestly, I don't care." Dark brown eyes gripped her. "I knew you both before you were together, and I knew you as a couple. You're good together."

Unable to bear the intensity of his gaze any longer,

she ducked her chin.

"Izzy, don't end your marriage because you think it will end the pain. It won't. And don't end it because you're mad or hurt or because you think it's too hard." A gentle anguish touched his voice. "Isn't that what your dad did to you?"

The words impaled her heart. A direct hit.

On that traitorous note, he slipped away into the crowd.

Twisting on the barstool, she called after him, "I never did like you."

His easy laughter carried back to her.

When she turned back for her glass of wine, she caught the bartender watching them, an intense scowl on his pleasant features. Hastily, he dropped his gaze and made vigorous swipes at the bar top with a wet towel.

"You must be the new bartender." She offered him a stiff smile. "How do you like the job so far?"

He tossed the towel across one of his broad shoulders. "I like it."

"I'm Isobel. Shea's... wife."

Golden brown eyes regarded her outstretched hand warily. "I know who you are." He jerked his chin at something behind her. "That was his brother?"

She curled her untouched hand into a fist and let it fall to the lap. "One of them, yes."

"Which one?" he asked tightly.

"Noah."

Confusion puckered his brow. "So Shea, Noah, Leo, and Luke?"

"And Jack."

He straightened. "Jack?"

"He doesn't live on the island year-round." Proud of all Jack had accomplished, details about his life and career gathered in her throat, but at the bartender's troubled expression, she swallowed them. "He travels a lot."

His scowl turned severe when he ducked his head and resumed his assault on the bar. Collecting her drink, she slipped off her barstool and moved away.

"What happened to their parents?"

His question stopped her midstride and she glanced back at him over her shoulder. In the dim lighting, his deep-set eyes were hooded by shadow, and the straight line of his nose over his full, plump mouth plucked a familiar chord that reverberated through her.

The hairs lifted on her arms and the back of her neck. "They died," she said softly.

A muscle ticked along his jawline while he appeared to wrestle with another question, but when another guest leaned across the bar, he flashed the woman a dazzling smile and fetched her drink.

Isobel's heart thrummed while the jovial sounds of her family and friends swirled around her. With a mental shake, she tried to throw off her discomfort with the odd exchange. She took a swig of wine, chasing its calming effect, and turned her back to the barkeep.

Through the crowd, she spotted Sophie wrestling with a tangle of balloons while Ava offered input that made Sophie's mouth pinch at the corners.

Then, she saw *him*.

Dread sat on her chest. His back to her, he wore a black sweater that stretched tight across his wide shoulders and hung loose around his lean waist. When he bent to scoop up Connor, his dark blue jeans hugged his tight butt.

As though sensing her regard, he turned, and his vivid blue eyes captured hers.

An army of butterfly wings beat furiously in her stomach as the pull of his gaze started her feet moving under her.

In his arms, Connor squirmed and as she drew near, Shea set Connor loose to launch his little body at Isobel. Dropping down, she pressed a kiss on his chubby cheek before he wriggled free of her arms to chase after his sister.

She stood, and a startled laugh burst from her.

"Why are you laughing?" Shea smoothed his large hand the length of his torso.

"Nice sweater," she said, chewing at her irrepressible grin.

"Don't you like it?"

"It's... uh... Is that a Unicorn?"

He looked down at the white and pink and yellow mess knitted onto his shirtfront.

"I think so?" His playful smile grabbed at her insides. "I have no idea."

She stared, dumbfounded as, for one brief moment, the Shea she thought she'd lost forever stood laughing before her. "I'm sorry, but it's hideous."

He feigned offense. "I'll have you know my baby girl picked this sweater out for me. I think it might be the most beautiful sweater in the history of all the sweaters."

Isobel's heart swelled. "You may be right about that."

Just then, a boisterous cheer erupted and she caught a glimpse of Finn, a wide smile lighting up his handsome face, before the crowed closed in around him. The ruckus captured Shea's attention, but he didn't leave her side. Standing together, they watched their oldest son work his way through the gathering of his family and friends.

Ava engulfed him in a hug and Sophie fussed with his rumpled hair. A sheepish smile whipped color into his cheeks, and when he reached his uncles, he muttered something through one side of his mouth that set off a round of deep male laughter.

"I can't believe we made that." The warmth in Shea's

voice spread through her like a soothing balm.

She swallowed thickly. "I can't believe it's been eighteen years."

Then, with a hitch of surprise, Isobel noticed the pretty girl at Finn's side. She had straight, light brown hair and tilted, sea-green eyes, and she hung back awkwardly while the mob bathed Finn with their adoration.

Isobel glance at Shea. "Is that Sidney Shaw?"

A grim set to his mouth, he nodded.

"You like her?" Isobel asked in a low voice.

"I don't know her well enough to have an opinion one way or the other." Lines of worry bracketed his eyes and mouth. "Her dad was here last night."

Finn leaned close to whisper something in Sidney's ear. A shy smile curved her mouth, which heightened the color on Finn's cheeks.

"What happened?" Isobel whispered.

"He got drunk, started a fight. I had to call the cops." Shea's voice sounded tight, strained. "I guess he lost his job last week and was taking it out on anyone within reach."

Isobel's stomach gave a wrench and her gaze clamped on Shea's face. "Should we tell Finn?"

"I think we better. Soon."

Chapter Nineteen

Agitation churned inside Shea when he arrived at the pub Tuesday afternoon. First thing, he sent Finn a text and asked him to stop by after school, then he sought refuge in his work. Old habits and all that.

While he filled drinks behind the bar, his mind kept coming back to the problem of his wife, much the way his tongue might worry a spot on the roof of his mouth. In a few hours, they'd sit down for an interview with the bridal magazine and pretend to be a happily married couple, and it suddenly bothered the piss out him that they'd have to fake it.

Or at least, she would. What he felt was real.

Aiden clocked in for his shift and Shea reminded him to turn in his paperwork so they could get him paid.

Aiden gave Shea his back and went to work wiping down the counter. "Will do, Boss."

Shea left his bartender to tend bar and turned to his other tasks. In his office, he attacked the stack of paperwork waiting for his attention. Shortly after the time when Finn's school day ended, he returned to the pub room and, clipboard in hand, went behind the bar to finish the liquor inventory.

But more than an hour after school had let out, there was still no sign of Finn. Shea waited as long as he dared, and just when he'd made the decision to leave to meet Isobel at the house, the door opened and a beam of late-afternoon sunlight spilled across the pub room.

At the sight of Finn strolling toward him, a grimace pulled at Shea's mouth.

Catching the look, and misreading it, Finn slowed. "Look, whatever you have to say, just save it. You've made your point loud and clear."

Behind the bar, Shea folded his arms over his chest. "What are you talking about?"

"I know you don't like me." Finn's eyes brimmed with vulnerability. "Just know I'm trying, all right?"

The sting of shock was drowned out by the flood of agony that crashed into him. with an agonizing shock. He peered into his son's face, searching for signs of spite or misguided humor. Anything that might explain such a wildly inaccurate statement.

He found none.

Finn meant every word. He truly believed his own father didn't like him.

Pain ripped through Shea with the chaotic destruction of a tornado, tearing him apart.

At one time, he'd considered himself an honorable person, but the facts were stacking up against him. He could no longer deny the truth.

He was a failure. As a brother, a father, a husband. In one way or another, he'd failed every person he'd ever sought to protect.

When his mom died and his dad spiraled out of control, he'd had no skills to hold his family together. Not one. With only ignorance and desperation, he'd tried to do it in a lot of boneheaded ways. He'd been cold, controlling, and too hard on his brothers. He was older, bigger, stronger, and he'd used every advantage he had to keep things under control. Grudgingly, they'd respected him, maybe not for his tactics but because he was a better alternative than their dad. Until eventually they came to resent him.

But rather than learn from his failures, he turned around and repeated the same mistakes with his son.

Shame and regret tunneled through him, grotesque and sickening.

All he'd ever wanted to do was take away their pain—which was also his pain. Instead, he'd driven them away. Worse, he'd made them doubt his love, and themselves.

"I like you." His voice shaking, Shea held his son's gaze with his own. "A lot."

Finn appeared unconvinced.

With a steadying breath, Shea plucked a pint glass from the dry rack and filled it with Coke. "Have a seat."

Finn jerked his head over one shoulder. "I've got a thing I gotta get to..."

"Please." Shea gestured to a barstool. "There's a reason I asked you to come by today."

"What reason?"

"Sidney Shaw."

Unease visibly settled on Finn's shoulders. "What about her?"

Shea opened his mouth, but the words to explain suddenly wouldn't come and he snapped it shut. He scrubbed a hand over his face.

"Don't," Finn snapped. "I know what people say about

her."

He peered at Finn through the cracks of his fingers. "Huh?"

The color heightened on Finn's cheeks. "They think she's... too friendly or whatever."

The nasty curse shot from Shea before he could stop it. "People talk too much," he growled.

One corner of Finn's mouth twitched. "Yes, they do."

"But that's not what I wanted to talk to you about." Shea slanted forward, leaning with his elbows on the bar. "It's about Sidney's dad and that fat lip she had the other night."

A storm cloud rolled across Finn's features. He dropped his backpack to the ground with a thud and slid onto the barstool. "You think her dad did it to her?"

"I don't have proof he hurt her or anything like that," Shea was quick to say. "But he's been causing some trouble around here lately. He's a hothead with a mean streak, and I believe he's capable of something so disgusting. I wanted you to know I think so, in case."

"In case what?"

He lifted his shoulders. "That's the thing with a man like Ray Shaw. You never know what they're going to do or when, only that they will lash out again. Guaranteed. Just be careful around him."

"Okay." Gray eyes, Isobel's eyes, latched onto Shea's face. "Thanks."

An awkward silence fell between them while behind Shea, Aiden worked at restocking the pint glasses.

Words knocked around inside Shea's head a moment before he arranged them into a sensible order. "I can't believe I never told you this, but I grew up in a home a lot like the one Sidney's living in now."

Finn drew a low, nearly imperceptible hiss of air between his teeth. "That's why you never wanted me around him, isn't it?"

"He drank a lot, all the time, and it changed him. He was short-tempered. Violent. I didn't want you anywhere near that." A weary breath escaped him. "I know I haven't been a great dad to you, and I won't insult you with some bullshit excuses, but growing up like that, it has a way of messing with you, you know?"

Finn sat still as a statue on the barstool. "Actually, I have no idea what it's like."

That pulled a reluctant smile from Shea, which quickly dropped away. "One minute everything is calm, sane. The next, the whole world is turned upside down and you have no idea how it happened. You start to feel like you're losing your mind." With the tip of one finger, he traced the line of a scar that nicked the bar's hard wood surface. "If you live with it long enough, you forget which way is up and which is down, and once you've lost your bearings, it's hard to know what to believe or who to trust."

A wrinkle disturbed Finn's smooth brow as he slurped a swig of Coke through his straw.

"I should've trusted you," Shea said. "But I was so afraid of letting you down the way my dad let me down that I couldn't see what was right in front of me. You're a good kid, Finn, and a great person. I'm proud of you."

Twin spots of pink touched Finn's cheeks and a faint smile teased his lips before he ducked his chin. He appeared young and self-conscious, and Shea's heart pinched.

"I'm sorry I mucked this fatherhood thing up so badly. In my defense, my example sucked."

Finn rolled his eyes. "Geez, Dad, you weren't *that* bad."

"Well that's a relief." Shea straightened away from the bar. "If it's not too late, maybe I can still figure it out. Though I might need your help."

The thoughtful frown played across Finn's features while he sucked on his soda. Then his expression cleared. "Okay."

"Okay?"

"Yeah." Finn slipped easily off the barstool. "I'll help you, and in return, you can help me."

"Oh? How so?"

A mischievous light winked in Finn's eyes when he slung the strap of his backpack over his shoulder and backed toward the exit. "Tell me everything you know about women."

The bark of laughter erupted from deep inside Shea's chest.

"I mean, they're kind of confusing."

"Tell me about it," Shea muttered.

The humor on Finn's face faded and his steps slowed. "I didn't think I wanted to hear your excuses either, but I'm glad I did. Thanks."

Finn ducked through the pub door and a wide smile split Shea's face. Feeling lighter than he had in years, he turned and nearly collided with Aiden.

"Sorry, man," Shea said. Then, he drew up. "Everything all right?"

His feet planted shoulder-width apart, Aiden stood blocking Shea's path, his golden-brown eyes blazed in his stony expression. "You got a minute?"

"Not really." Shea glanced at the wall clock. "I have to—"

"It'll only take a minute."

At the cold edge in Aiden's tone, alarm stole over Shea. "My office?"

With a curt nod, Aiden allowed Shea to pass by him. The two men moved silently down the short hallway to the office door. Shea twisted the knob and motioned for Aiden to enter ahead of him. Then he closed the door quietly behind them.

"What's going on?" he asked the moment the latch clicked into place.

Aiden's calm veneer crumbled and he paced the small room like a caged animal. "Your father was Daniel Michael Nolan?"

A breath wheezed from Shea. "You heard all that, did you?"

"Aye, I did." His odd accent slipped, and for a moment, the inflection of his tone lilted. "He was a drunk, was he?"

Through narrowed eyes, Shea watched Aiden march back and forth. "That he was."

"He did a number on you and yer brothers." Aiden drove a hand through his dark hair. "That's what you said?"

"How do you know my dad's name?" The words were thick on Shea's tongue. "And why in the hell are you suddenly speaking with an Irish accent?"

Abruptly, Aiden stumbled to a stop. He faced Shea fully.

A thousand lifetimes might've passed in the seconds Shea waited for Aiden's reply.

The bartender's throat convulsed with his heavy swallow. "Because Daniel Nolan was my dad, too."

Chapter Twenty

Ominous gray clouds gathered beyond the glass door.

"You have a beautiful home."

Isobel wrestled a smile into place for Jen, the writer from *Stylish Bride* magazine. "Thank you."

Jen turned away from the French doors and the sweeping view of Lake Michigan beyond Shea and Isobel's large deck.

Isobel placed a steaming cup of coffee on the dining table. "I apologize for the delay. My husband is running a little late."

Jen slid into a dining chair and reached for the coffee mug. "It's fine. This isn't anything too formal. It's supposed be fun and relaxed."

"Maybe I'll send him another text..."

With a flick of the wrist, Jen halted Isobel's quest for her cell phone. "Sit. We'll chat until he gets here."

Isobel managed a tremulous smile as she sank slowly into a chair at the table.

"So, how long have you been designing wedding dresses?"

"Not long, actually." Isobel's fingers found the hem of her blouse under the table. "I've been sketching designs for years, but only recently started to create the gowns."

Jen retrieved a notepad from her oversized leather bag and flipped to a stark-white page. "Where did you study?"

"Study?"

Jen propped an elbow on the table and cradled her chin in the palm of her hand. "Did you go to one of the New York schools, or did you stay closer to home?"

"Oh. Uh, I don't have a formal education." Isobel folded and refolded the gauzy fabric of her blouse. "Since high school, I've worked in a bridal store doing alterations. I guess I picked up the elements of design and dress construction that way."

"How clever of you." Jen's warm smile was filled with sincerity. "I can't wait to see your gowns. Vanessa was so pumped, and trust me, it takes a lot to impress her."

With a soft buzzing noise, Isobel's cell phone vibrated on the kitchen island and she lurched to her feet. "Do you mind if I grab that? It's probably Shea."

But when she scooped up the device, she didn't recognize the number on the phone's display. Worry bit at her as she silenced the call, letting it go to her voicemail. Where was he? Was he held up at work, or had something happened to delay him?

She returned to the table, but before she lowered herself into the chair, a noise sounded at the back door. Soft hope to bloomed in her chest and she rushed forward.

Then Shea stepped inside the house. He filled her

world and the tension in her shoulders instantly began to melt. The blue sweater he wore caused his eyes to sparkle like precious jewels in his handsome face, but at his expression, the words on the tip of her tongue dissolved like sugar in the rain.

"Is everything okay?" she whispered, keeping her voice low so Jen wouldn't overhear them.

White teeth flashed quick and bright. "Of course."

The bite of her disappointment stung. He was late and there was a reason, a reason he was now hiding from her.

He'd pushed the sleeves of his sweater past his elbows, and the script tattoo on his forearm briefly passed by her vision when he slipped his hand to the back of her head.

He drew her to him and dropped a soft kiss on her forehead. "We'll talk later," he murmured.

She pulled back enough to see his face. "Is it Finn? Did you talk to him?"

"It's not Finn."

Her concern deepened.

"Finn's okay." He tapped his finger lightly on the tip of her nose. "Everything's okay."

"No one ever says everything is okay unless everything is *not* okay."

A smile quirked on his soft mouth, but the shallow lines of his worry remained. "Trust me. Just this once."

Too preoccupied to argue with him anyway, Isobel reached for his hand, prepared to pretend great happiness that he'd finally arrived.

A seismic tremor jolted her when she realized she wouldn't be faking it. Not completely.

He squeezed her hand. "You're shaking."

Unable to explain the source of the nervous tension coiling through her, Isobel shook her head.

A part of her had feared this moment since she'd

agreed to Vanessa's offer. What if their lies were found out? What if Jen discovered there was no happy marriage, no booming wedding dress design business, no story they wanted to print in their magazine? Who wanted to read about a no-name wannabe designer going through a divorce?

But another part of her, the rational part, understood the magazine feature was an incredible opportunity and the anxiety rattling her the past several days derived from something else. Something entirely unrelated to any future business ventures.

"I just want to get this over with," she muttered.

They returned to the dining room, and after quick introductions, Shea settled into the chair beside Isobel.

"This island is so charming." Jen reached for her coffee. "Have you lived here all your lives?"

"I have, but Shea emigrated from Ireland with his family when he was young."

"Ireland?" Jen sipped her coffee and returned the cup to the table. "You don't happen to know anything about that delightful Irish pub downtown, do you?"

"As a matter of fact, I do," Shea said. "I own it."

Jen's face lit up. "You're kidding. We ate there last night and had a blast."

From there, their conversation meandered, and Isobel relaxed. Jen had a way of talking as though she were an old friend that'd stopped by for a visit, and it wasn't until she picked up her pen to scrawl something in her notebook that Isobel remembered they weren't old friends catching up.

Jen was a pro. A truth seeker at work, collecting information and hanging substance on her shadowy sketch of their perfect lives. Idyllic small town. Good-looking Irish husband. Adorable children. Beautiful home. Talented, happily married couple owning not one but two successful businesses.

"When did you two meet?"

Isobel glanced uneasily at Shea. "In high school."

"You were high school sweethearts?" Jen scribbled something in her notebook. "How romantic."

Isobel's throat tightened with the surge of her emotions. She didn't find teen pregnancy or extreme poverty and hunger all that romantic.

Jen shot Isobel a conspiratorial smile. "Is he the first boy you kissed?"

Working at a bridal store for so many years had its perks and Isobel mimicked the brides that paraded through her life, their sweet faces lit up from inside with love and hope for the future.

"He's the only boy I've ever kissed," Isobel admitted, her words true, but her smile fake.

Jen's clear blue eyes slid to Shea. "When did you know she was the one?"

"The first moment I saw her."

He said the words so convincingly, even Isobel wanted to believe him.

"Did you meet in class?"

A shudder passed through Isobel and she shivered. She didn't want to talk about high school, or that blasted cafeteria, or any of the things that happened back then.

"At the beach," she blurted. "We met at the beach."

They were faking a happy marriage, she might as well add some fake happy memories to go along with it.

"That's not true," Shea said quietly.

Her fake smile faltered.

"It was the pier." His warm gaze landed on her face and the icy fear wrapping around her heart began to melt. "I'd been on the island, I don't know, a month maybe, before I discovered the public beach. I remember it so clearly. The wind was biting, but the sun was out, and all of a sudden, there she was, standing at the end of the pier. I don't think she even saw me, but I knew right then that I would marry her one day."

Isobel's heart beat wildly against her breastbone.

"*Aww.*" Jen flipped the page in her notebook. "Tell me about your wedding. Was it a big family affair or a small gathering? Or maybe a destination wedding?"

The question landed like a gut punch knocking Isobel's memories loose.

After Shea had found her in the park, he took her with him back to campus, where he was about to begin fall semester. But once there, Isobel didn't fit in to Shea's new life. He had a large group of friends that she didn't know, and when he introduced her to them, found she had nothing in common with. She was fat, and she missed her mom with a grief so sharp and strong she frequently, often unexpectedly, dissolved into tears.

On top of that, the devastation of her dad's rejection still tormented her, and with every day that her due date drew nearer, fear of her impending labor intensified. Fears that turned out to be well-founded.

Shea's large, warm hand closed around hers, pulling her back to the present.

He intertwined their fingers. "We were young and broke." The shadow of a rueful smile darkened his handsome face. "I couldn't give her any of what she deserved. We had a small ceremony, just the two us and the justice of the peace." His lips brushed her palm. "It was perfect."

Perfect.

She flinched.

In the old courthouse, they sat hand in hand in the clerk's office, waiting for the justice of the peace. A deep furrow puckered the spot between his dark brows.

"Why do you want to marry me?" she whispered. "Is it

because of the baby?"

"Absolutely not." The column of his throat worked when he swallowed. "You're everything. Smart and kind. Beautiful. You're everything that's good and true in this world. You're perfect."

His words had lived like a threat inside her heart ever since. At first, she'd thought he teased. That his words were nothing more than a cruel joke, because of course she was anything but perfect. Her own father was ashamed of her.

But almost immediately, she realized he wasn't joking. He believed what he said, and for the next eighteen years, she lived in fear of the day he discovered the truth. That she was hopelessly, irrevocably imperfect.

"You two are too stinking cute." Jen's conspiratorial smile widened. "Let's talk about the important stuff—your dress. Did you make it yourself?"

Fake smile affixed, Isobel recounted the details she could recall through the haze of her depression. "Well, it's true we didn't have much money, so I found a dress at a secondhand store." It was at least four sizes too big, but it was the only one they could afford that also fit around her eight-month pregnant belly. "It had huge puffy sleeves and a lace overlay that looked like a doily, so I removed them both. I tried to convince myself it was vintage, but really it was just an old, ugly dress."

"Do you have pictures?"

"Thankfully no, no pictures."

"Wait." One of Shea's long legs stretched out under the table and he pulled his wallet from his hip pocket.

He flipped open the leather billfold and pulled a small, cracked picture from one of the protective sleeves. Isobel caught a glimpse of a dark-haired girl on the beach, possibly in a wedding dress, before he passed it off to Jen.

"What is that?" Her head snapped to Shea. "Is that

me?"

"It is."

"Where did you get that?"

He hitched one shoulder. "I took it."

A faint smile on her face, Jen studied the aged photograph. "The dress isn't nearly as awful as you describe."

She held out the photo, and Isobel reached for it with a trembling hand.

The picture had been taken the day she and Shea married, and the girl in the photo didn't appear nearly as fat as Isobel remembered feeling. Nor was the dress she wore quite so horrid as her mind recollected. Her face was turned away from the camera, but even in profile, she could make out the youthful roundness of her features and the soft expression that played on her face.

Despite all the grief and fear and doubt she'd experience during that period of her life, that day, the day she married Shea, Isobel was at peace.

"So, what's next for you?" Jen asked.

Isobel peered at the young girl in the old photograph. What would she have answered in response to Jen's question? What had she wanted for her life?

"I have no idea," Isobel murmured.

Jen's infectious laugh pulled a reluctant smile from Isobel.

"It's true. I have no idea what's going to happen next." Her gaze touched the dog-eared photograph again. "I hope more of the same. I'm enjoying my happily ever after. What more could I want?"

Jen closed her notebook. "It has been so much fun talking with you both and I can't wait to write your story."

Sliding the notepad into her bad, she climbed to her feet. The three of them walked to the front door together, then Shea and Isobel watched Jen slip behind the wheel of her sleek black car and back out of the driveway.

"That was nice." Shea spoke in a smooth, even tone. "What you said about happily ever after."

Jen's car had rolled down the street, growing smaller and smaller until the tiny black dot eventually disappeared, before Isobel found the courage to face her husband.

A soft sadness clung to the corners of his eyes. "Did you mean a word of it?"

Chapter Twenty-One

Her guarded gaze darted over his face. "Jen didn't come here looking for the truth about our marriage. She sells dreams."

"So that's what you gave her?" His chest tight, he winced. "Your dream?"

"I don't know. I never had any dreams." She brushed by him and went to the table where she scooped up Jen's coffee mug, but she didn't carry it to the kitchen sink and instead, stared down into the cup while the moment stretched taut with tension.

Slowly, he crossed the room to stand at the opposite end of the dining table.

"Everything happened so fast for us and I... I was too afraid to have dreams." When she lifted her head, her gray eyes churned with emotion, like a roiling sea. "You don't know what it's like to be that scared."

A sharp punch of anger struck him in the ribs. Would

she only ever look at him and see his flaws? His failures? Would he never figure out a way to change her mind about him? To change her heart?

"How can you say that?" His voice shook with the flash of his fury. "You think I wasn't afraid every time the food ran out again?"

Her expression suffered a crack. "Of course you were. I'm sorry—"

"You think I wasn't afraid when Finn was born? When the doctors told me they couldn't stop the bleeding and I should prepare for the worst?" The memories of those awful, frantic moments at the hospital while her life was slipping away threatened to overwhelm him.

"I'm sorry," she whispered. "I didn't mean it."

"My God, Isobel, it's like you don't know anything about me."

She didn't deny it and the truth pressed down on him.

She didn't know him. Because he hadn't allowed her to.

All his life, he'd tried to control things. People. His brothers, his kids, and most especially his wife. He'd wanted to protect her, and he thought that to do so meant he needed to keep her at a distance. He'd only let her get so close, giving her as much as he wanted and holding back everything else.

It was past time he stopped trying to control her thoughts and feelings.

An old anguish filled his heart when he said, "Do you know why I left you?"

With a quick intake of breath, she froze to the spot.

"Don't take this the wrong way, but it didn't have all that much to do with you." His gaze dropped to the floorboards. "I needed some time."

"Time away from me?"

At the hitch of vulnerability in her voice, he squeezed

his eyes shut with the slash of pain. "That's what I thought. At the time." He forced his gaze back to her face. "But I was wrong."

She lowered the coffee cup back down on the table.

"In reality, I needed you. I needed to be with you, and the kids. If I'd been stronger, I would've realized it then." Sand filled his mouth and he swallowed with difficulty. "I thought you deserved better than me, and that if I went away, I might be able to make myself into the man you deserved. Stronger. Saner. Sober."

"Sober?" She came around the table. "What are you talking about? I don't understand."

He drove a hand through his hair while he wrestled with the words that could explain. "When I picked law, I was being naïve."

"Idealistic."

"Same thing."

"It's absolutely not the same thing," she snapped. "You wanted to help kids like you and your brothers. Kids who had no one else. That's not naïve, Shea. It's incredible, actually."

His heart wanted to smile, but the painful memories darkened the lightness. "I thought I'd be a hero. That's why I picked that law firm over all the others, because they had a reputation for taking on the kinds of cases I wanted to argue."

She crept closer.

"But the reality of it was... different. Difficult." A shallow breath shuddered through him. "The work ate at me. For years, it took everything, and by the time I'd get home at night, I had nothing left in me to give you or Finn."

When she touched his face, he didn't flinch, but only because his body was coiled so tightly.

"The last case I worked was the hardest. The abuse

done to those kids..." Images flooded his mind and his stomach roiled. "It was the worst I'd ever seen. I started drinking too much. I couldn't concentrate."

He took a step back, and another, as though he might be able to outpace the truth. Instead, he came up hard against the wall. "I made a mistake. A procedural error." His voice barely reached a whisper. "The sick bastard got off on a technicality."

A wave of nausea crashed into him with the shame and his knees buckled. "I couldn't bring myself to tell you what I'd done."

She rushed to his side. "You didn't do anything wrong."

"It feels like I did."

"It won't always." Her fingers closed over his and he turned his palm over to grasp her hand. "I'll help you."

The seconds melted away while he stared down at their clasped hands. His large and work-roughened. Hers small and elegant.

"You were so distant," she said quietly. "I thought maybe... you'd found someone else."

Without lifting his head, his eyes captured hers. "Since I found you in the park, all I wanted to do was protect you. I knew you were struggling. I could see it, but I had no idea what to do. So I stopped telling you things that I thought would upset you. I hid a lot from you, but not that. Never that."

"I should've asked you." A deep frown puckered her brow. "Instead, I let Amber Jessop get to me."

"I should've talked to you before I quit, but I couldn't bring myself to do it."

She conducted an intense study of their clasped hands. "Maybe I had something to do with that."

"What do you mean?"

"When I realized I was pregnant again, I..." Her throat

worked with her heavy swallow. "I don't know. Maybe I closed myself off, not just from you, but from everyone. If you had tried to talk to me, I doubt I would've made it easy for you."

"When you told me about the baby..." He squeezed her hand tight. "I don't think I've ever been so scared in my life. It's not that I didn't want another baby, because I did. But not if it meant I had to watch you suffer. I couldn't lose you."

Her eyes glittered. "I cried when I found out. Then I cried some more because I knew I was the worst person in the world."

Lifting her fingers to his lips, he pressed a soft kiss to her warm skin.

She shifted to stand beside him, her back against the wall, and laid her head on his shoulder.

He rested his cheek on the top of her head. "I'm sorry I didn't dance with you at our wedding. Or smash cake in your face."

Her throaty laugh floated up to him. "I'm not sorry about that. No, really, I'm not. I wouldn't have wanted a big wedding, not right then, when I'd just lost my mom. It was more special with only the two of us."

"Technically the three of us."

"The three of us." The soft wonder in her voice eased the gnawing ache that'd been tormenting him for years.

Just as an easy silence descended, her head popped up off his shoulder and she looked up at him with huge round eyes. "You haven't told me why you were late today."

A curse slipped from him with the renewed shock. "I don't even know where to start."

"At the beginning."

He dragged a hand over his face. "Okay, let's see. Well, it's about Aiden."

"Your bartender?"

He nodded, then forced out the words. "He says he's Daniel Nolan's son."

"*What?*" Eyes huge in her small face, she gaped at him. "But... when? How?"

"Uh..."

"I mean, who is his mother?"

"I don't know. He's five months younger than Leo."

A small gasp slipped through her lips. "That means..."

"My dad was cheating on my mom." Bitter resentment twisted Shea's gut. "I always thought losing her was what changed him, but I guess he was an asshole all along."

"Is there a chance he's wrong. Maybe he's lying."

"Why would he lie?" Then, because his mind had already traveled that road, added, "There's no inheritance to speak of. No money, no land. Not even a family legacy or reputation to try to stake a claim to."

She tortured her bottom lip. "Maybe his mom is wrong about his paternity?"

"Maybe." He studied her face closely. "But you believe him, don't you?"

She winced. "Honestly, he looks a little like your dad. Like all of you. Around the eyes and here." With the tip of one finger, she brushed the length of his straight nose.

He let his head fall back to rest against the wall. "I see it, too." Now that it was right there in front of him.

"What do we do?" she asked softly.

"I want to make sure he is who he says he is, but beyond that, there's not much else we can do."

"That's driving you crazy, isn't it?" A hint of humor infected her tone.

"You have no idea." His deep chuckle vibrated in his chest.

She returned her head on his shoulder, and the tender touch sent warmth spreading outward from his center to the farthest reaches of his limbs.

"You have another brother," she said, her quiet words filled with wonder.

He rested his cheek against the crown of her head. "It would seem so."

"Are you going to tell your brothers?"

"Of course."

"When?"

"First thing in the morning, before we meet with the photographer."

"Do you want me there with you?"

"I'd like that." Emotion roughened his voice.

Whatever was happening between them didn't feel like a game anymore and hadn't for some time.

Nonetheless, in the space between their heartbeats, the faint drum of victory echoed.

⁍

Isobel flopped into bed. Exhaustion dragged at her, but not the empty, overwhelmed tiredness she'd grown accustomed to.

After making dinner, all five of them ate together for approximately ten whole minutes before Connor had a potty emergency and Finn dashed out the door to meet up with some friends. The chaos of bath and bedtime followed, but rather than depleting her, she came away from Maisie's bedroom feeling revitalized.

The house fell quiet, and she and Shea retreated to their bedroom together. For the first time since he'd returned home, none of the doubt hassled her. Instead, she lay on her back on the bed and stared up at the vaulted ceiling while her eyelids grew heavy.

In the adjoining bathroom, the sound of running water from Shea's shower lulled her and sleep beckoned.

An arrow of surprise poked through the drowsiness at how easily she'd accepted his presence in the house. How familiar it felt for him to be home. Ordinary, but also completely different.

Normal, but odd. Exhausted, but energized.

In the bathroom the water stopped, and a few minutes later, Shea emerged, nude and wet from his shower. Somehow, in his nakedness, he seemed even more powerful than he did with his clothes on. Large and muscular, his taut strength and brutal gracefulness seized her gaze.

His body responded to her notice.

Rolling to her side, she openly watched him. "It's still weird, having you here."

He moved to the edge of the bed and slowly lowered his body to the mattress. A dark look shadowed his features as he gazed down at her.

"I wish I'd been strong enough to stay." He bowed his head, as if in supplication. "Of all the regrets I have, that's one of the hardest to live with every day."

Her heart kicked in her chest. She never thought he'd let her go. Tears tightened the back of her throat.

A hank of his hair fell across his forehead, and she curled her fingers through the silky soft strands.

His shoulders shook when a shudder passed through him.

"The color is beautiful." She twirled the lock around her fingers. "Sophie thinks our separation grayed it."

Without lifting his head, his eyes found hers. "The day you asked me to leave, it was dark. By the end of that week, it'd turned. The color left my hair the same way it'd left my life."

Her fingers detangled from the short locks when he shifted to stretch out on the bed beside her.

Damp heat from the shower clung to his large, naked

body. "But I don't mind it. It's a scar I wear with pride. A reminder of the mistakes I've made. The battles I've lost. The war I've so far survived."

Despite herself, she smiled. "You think of our marriage as a battle?"

"Not the marriage, the break up, and not a battle—a war."

Her battered heart wailed with its agreement. By the bone-deep weariness and constant aching in her body, she felt like she'd been through a war. Neither one of them had set out to hurt the other. It'd just happened. She could see the innocence in what they'd done to each other. All of it. And though they both wished to stop the hurting, they were powerless to do so.

Why, when they loved each other, was it so hard to keep from wounding one another?

"I wish we could rewind." Needing to touch his warmth, her hand moved to his chest. "Go back to the early days and start over."

The ghosts of impossibility haunted the dark corners of their bedroom.

"Shea, can we fix this? Can we fix us?"

His soft smile surprised her. "We can. We aren't broken."

"Sometimes, it feels like we are."

"We're injured, but we can heal."

"How?" she whispered.

"With time, and with love. The answer is always love." He tapped a finger on the tip of her nose. "You're the wedding dress designer. You know this."

But the humor in his tone didn't reach his eyes.

His hand closed around hers. Gently, he turned her palm face up and pressed his warm mouth to the sensitive skin on the inside of her wrist. His fingertips lightly traced the underside of her arm. and there she saw reflected all the aches in her own heart.

When he nudged the hem of her sleepshirt, she arched her back to allow him to tug the garment up. When she was naked before him, his gaze swept over her body. The color rose high on his cheekbones and amidst the dusty glow, his eyes burned like blue fire, leaving a trail of sensation heat everywhere his gaze touched.

He traced the line between her breasts, and his fingers toyed with the silver chain and the band of her wedding ring before circling each of her budded nipples with whisper soft swirls. His hand roamed lower, leisurely dropping to her navel. He lingered a moment, then slipped through the curls between her thighs.

His sweetly provoking fingertips pulled a soft gasp from her throat. Oblivion beckoned when he kneeled before her and grasped her knees. Easing her legs apart, his wide shoulders pressed into her thighs when he brought his mouth to her body.

With the silky glide of his tongue, pleasure surged and she clutched his head hard, holding him close while she rocked against him. Reaching up, he clasped her wrists, pulling them down to her sides.

Manacled in his grip and spread open, her passion ignited. Incoherent sounds vibrated in her throat as he licked and ate into her softness. His mouth savored her with a tenderness that brought tears to her eyes. Searing need flooded her honeyed core. Every sweep of his tongue unleashed more delicious sensations and she rode the undulating tide of desire.

Her moans grew in volume and frequency. Commanded by his hot mouth, her hips swirled, chasing the promise of shameless bliss. Gentle gave way to wild and reckless, and soon he rose up between her thighs.

She drank in the sight of him. The well-defined muscles of his chest and the flat plane of his stomach.

Heavily aroused, the prominent length of his thick shaft captured her attention. Taut and dusky, his erection gave an eager jerk. She let her knees fall open.

Barely restrained emotion poured off him as he lowered his body over hers. When his pulsing heft nudged at her opening, she gasped and gripped his shoulders. He entered her slowly and pushed deep.

On a cry of pleasure-pain, she arched her back and he suckled a beaded nipple into the wet heat of his mouth. His rough hands rushed over her sensitive skin. Passion lashed at her and she grasped his butt with both of her hands, feeling his muscles clench as he pumped into her.

He impaled her with relentless strokes, and she struggled beneath him, wanting it faster, harder, deeper. She told him so, and he cursed, uttering the naughty words against her flesh in his gravelly voice.

Sensation swelled. Emotion expanded in her chest as she couldn't contain the sweet, horrible love his body delivered to hers. The ache became unbearable and tears leaked out the corners of her eyes. Shattered, but unable to stop, she raced toward her own destruction, lifting her knees to take him deeper. To take him all.

Gripping her hips, his eyes clamped on her breasts as they bounced with the force of his penetration. With his wicked words, he described all the ways he loved her body.

Too soon, she succumbed to the power of his raspy voice and probing eyes, crying out as lush spasms rippled outward from the center of her body. The climax rolled through her in delicious waves, rising and falling again and again, before giving one last, voluptuous lurch.

He collapsed on top of her and his mouth latched on to the throbbing pulse point on her throat. His thickness grew impossibly large inside her and he made a series of plunging thrusts before his roar of pleasure vibrated against her skin.

He remained wedged inside her while their breathing returned to normal. When he finally withdrew, her body made a soft sound of regret. Rolling off the bed, he crossed to the dresser and pulled out a clean pair of shorts. Then continued rummaging through the drawer. Languidly, she watched his bare backside and the way the muscles of his back rippled with his movements.

Then he glanced at her over his shoulder, his disheveled hair in perfect disarray, and held up his faded green T-shirt.

She cringed inwardly.

"Is this my T-shirt?" He rumpled the cotton in his grip. "I've been looking everywhere for this."

"Hmm? Oh, you must've left it here by mistake. I sleep in it sometimes."

A smug smile curved his impossibly pouty mouth.

"And I also wear it when I clean the toilets."

The shirt muffled the sound of his laughter when he yanked it on and his head poked through the collar. His gaze touched her face, then lazily, seductively, swept over her nakedness.

Though her body was sated, she experienced a sharp longing.

A painful, dangerous longing.

He returned to the bed, and as he coaxed another orgasm from her satiated body, the longing only intensified. Exquisite and awful, it devastated her.

Chapter Twenty-Two

He jolted awake.

A loud noise reverberated through the house. Slowly, Shea's sleep-addled mind soon identified the impatient punch of the doorbell and he staggered from the bed.

Isobel gained her feet as he stuck his head through the collar of his T-shirt.

"It's almost three o'clock." Fear infected her tone.

In the hallway, Finn hovered outside his bedroom door, shirtless and barefoot. Together, they moved toward the sound of furious fists pounding on the front door while Isobel hurried after them.

At the door, Shea peered through the transom window and flicked on the porch light. "What the...?"

When he opened the door, Sidney Shaw and her father, Ray, confronted them. Fury contorted Ray's blunt features, and his fingers bit into his daughter's upper arm. He glared at Shea with blurry, bloodshot eyes.

But Shea's focus had riveted on Sidney's ravaged face. Tears had ruined her heavy makeup, which streaked down her cheeks in thick rivers of black, and her left eye had nearly swollen shut.

"You bastard." Finn lunged.

Shea jumped between the two men and shoved two hands into Finn's torso to hold him back.

"Easy," he said, leaning hard against his son's coiled body. "Easy now."

"Finn, I'm so sorry," Sidney whispered.

"You son of a bitch," Ray slurred.

"Do not talk to my son that way," Shea warned the intoxicated man.

Ray's face reddened with rage. "Do you know what he did?"

Sidney struggled against Ray's brutal grasp. "No, Dad—"

Ray's hand came up, his intent clear, and Sidney covered her head with both of her arms.

But Ray's strike was thwarted when Finn burst through the barricade of Shea's bigger body and clamped a hand around the man's wrist. "Don't you dare touch her."

Shea gaped at Finn, marveling at the change in him from gangly teen to menacing man.

Jaw clenched tight, Finn stared daggers through Ray Shaw. "Sidney, come inside."

Huge tears clung to Sidney's eyelashes. "Finn, I..."

Finn's gaze shifted to her then. "It's okay. Just come inside and we'll talk."

Sidney scurried across the threshold and Shea pulled the front door closed. With a disgusted shove, Finn released Ray.

Shea moved to stand beside his son.

"This is your fault, you little shit." Spittle propelled from Ray's mouth as he backpedaled.

Then, the heel of his foot the caught empty space of the top porch step and he tumbled backwards down the short flight of stairs to land on his ass in the lawn. He staggered to his feet and his hands balled into fists at his sides.

"If you think I'm going to take care of your mistake, you're wrong." Ray weaved as though a breeze disturbed his balance. "You knocked her up, you deal with it."

Shock and alarm whipped through Shea and his head snapped around, but Finn appeared unaffected by Ray's accusation.

Coolly, Finn jerked his chin. "Go home, old man. And stay the hell away from Sidney."

"You little—" Ray charged.

White teeth flashed in Finn's dark face and he braced for battle, but Ray drew back his arm with an overexaggerated windup that Shea caught easily in midair. With a vicious wrench, he twisted Ray's arm behind his back and slammed him face first into a porch beam.

"What the hell is wrong with you? You come to my house and threaten my son?" Shea slammed him again. "And if you put that bruise on your daughter's face, so help me God, I'm going to tear you apart."

Ray squirmed and kicked out with his leg, so Shea wedged his arm against the man's throat until his eyes widened with panic and his face mottled with red. In an instant, the past came rushing at him. The terror and chaos of life with a violent drunk reawakened his rage, and with it came the knowledge of the most efficient and ruthless means to take the asshole down.

He increased the pressure on Ray's throat by slow, steady increments, until finally his smaller body sagged.

In the next moment, Shea experienced a flood of relief that Sidney had gone inside so she didn't hear her father's next words.

"She's a whore," Ray wheezed. "Just like her mother."

Hatred surged. Shea clamped a hand around Ray's throat and squeezed. Then he flung the weaker man into the darkened void of the yard. "Get the hell off my property."

Together, Shea and Finn advanced toward Ray as he climbed clumsily to his feet.

Eyeing them with his unfocused gaze, Ray dragged a hand across his mouth. "Fine. She's your problem now. You tell her not to come running back home this time."

"To you?" Finn sneered. "Never."

His chest expanding with his deep breaths, Ray glowered at them. He was outmanned and slowly, his alcohol-soaked mind realized it. He gave his head a shake, which disrupted his balance as he lurched toward his battered truck. The headlights came on and he whipped out of the driveway, spewing a spray of gravel with his tires.

The uncomfortable silence that followed had Finn driving a hand through his dark hair.

Shea looked into his son's face, a face both similar and unlike his own. Chaos churned across Finn's sharp features and brought to Shea's mind the terrifying moment nineteen years ago when he had just learned that he was about to be a dad.

Reaching out, he slipped a hand to the back of Finn's neck and squeezed. The breeze rustled the leaves on the trees.

"What do you want to do first?" Shea asked quietly. "Talk to me, or talk to Sidney?"

The color left Finn's face, but he set his chin with a resolute nod. "Sidney."

When they stepped through the front door, Sidney sprang to her feet. On the couch beside her, Isobel rose slowly.

Sidney rushed forward, clutching a blanket tightly around her shoulders. "Finn..." Her mouth opened and closed several times, but no words came out.

"What's going on, Sid?"

"I'm so sorry." Her gaze bounced around room, landing briefly on each of them. "I didn't mean for any of this to happen."

"Is it true?" Finn asked softly.

Tears welled in Sidney's large eyes while shame and humiliation burned on her pale cheeks.

Finn approached her with caution, as though she were a frightened animal he expected to bolt at any moment.

"It's okay, Sid. I just need you to tell me the truth. Nothing bad is going to happen, I promise." Finn tucked a strand of her hair behind one ear. "We're going to help you. How far along are you?"

A gasp escaped Isobel and her gaze collided with Shea's. A violent sea of panic and pain tossed him around like a ragdoll.

"There's nothing for you to do," Sidney said.

Quiet, Finn considered her. The moment drew out, long and terrible, until he detonated a dirty bomb in their midst.

"Then I'm going to marry you."

"*What?*" Isobel's shrill cry pierced the air. "No, absolutely not, no way. You cannot get married. Finn, you're in high school."

"So?" Finn lifted his shoulders and perched his hands on his hips. "I'll work on the weekends until we graduate. If it's too hard, I'll quit school. It's no big deal."

The past was playing out before him. It was there in the cornered look in Isobel's soft eyes and the pale, stricken expression on Sidney's youthful face. Even in Finn's reckless attempt to put an end to the terrifying uncertainty. Like a recurring dream with no escape, or a slow-motion nightmare, Shea relived every detail in vivid horror.

"You are not quitting school," he said over the steady stream of his wife's flabbergasted sputtering. "But we aren't going to figure it all out tonight. Let's get some sleep and in the morning, we'll talk. Finn, why don't you make Sidney a bed in the family room?"

Shea and Finn exchanged a look, one man to another, and the trust brimming in Finn's light eyes did much to lessen the tension bunching Shea's muscles.

"She can sleep in my room," Finn said, then over his parents' vehement protests, quickly added, "I'll take the couch."

After Finn took Sidney down the hall, Shea made a quick call to the police station while Isobel paced in front of him. A sad fact of his job as pub owner was that he had the number to the dispatch desk memorized. Bonnie took his call, and he told her about their visit from Ray.

"He's been drinking."

"Got someone on it, doll. Hey, tell that cute brother of yours we miss him around here."

"Will do. Thanks, Bonnie."

The second he disconnected the call, Isobel whirled on him. "What are we going to do?"

He shrugged. "There's not much we can do."

"We can forbid him. You're his dad. Tell him no, he's not getting married."

"He'll be eighteen in a few days. He's his own man."

"Oh. My. God." She pressed the flat of her hand against her forehead. "I'm going to be a grandmother."

Shea chewed the smile from his lips.

Her hand dropped heavily to her side. "Why aren't you

freaking out about this?"

"We don't even have all the facts. Let's wait—"

"He just asked her to marry him." Isobel's voice climbed with her mounting hysteria. "What other facts do we need?"

"Do I want him to get married? No. I want him to go to college, date some girls, study hard and find the thing that's going to give him the best shot at being truly happy in life. But what if she's that thing?"

"They're children!"

"We did it."

"And look what's happened to us." She was shaking her head. "No. We can't let him make the same mistake we made."

Pain sliced him. "Is that what you think? That our life together is a mistake?"

"Shea, I..."

Her silence slashed at his bleeding heart. It was true. Had she felt that way all along? Since the day they married, and even until the day she filed for divorce?

"That's not what I meant." Frustration glistened in her eyes. "This isn't about us. It's about Finn, and we can't let him throw his life away for this girl."

"If it's what he wants, how will we stop him?"

"We'll—we'll forbid him."

"And if he doesn't listen?" He let the question hang in the space between them. "Will we disown him, Isobel? Throw him out of the house and out of our lives?"

Tears brimmed in her eyes, then spilled over to stream silently down her cheeks.

"I won't tell Finn how to feel about her—it'd be the height of hypocrisy—and I won't abandon him." For every tear she shed, another notch gashed his heart. "No matter what he's done. Even if you can't forgive me for it."

Her chin trembled and her hand flitted uselessly

through the air. "I've been that girl. Lost and lonely. He'll marry her because he has a good heart, but he won't be happy and..." She shook her head. "You know the rest."

"I do." He swallowed thickly. "I was in love with that girl. And you're right, I wasn't happy. Happy doesn't begin to describe my life with you."

Such a silly word to describe the sweet, maddening joy. The essentialness.

"Please don't."

"Don't tell you the truth?" The hole in his chest ripped wide open. "I've never lied to you, Isobel, but I haven't been completely honest with you either."

Apprehension filled her eyes.

"I'm glad you wound up pregnant."

Her lips parted with her shocked gasp.

"I didn't set out to make it happen, but when you told me, I was happy, because it meant I could make you mine. And I've never regretted marrying you. Not once. Not even a little."

Her tears had stopped and she wiped a trail of moisture from her cheeks.

"If given the chance to do it all over again, I'd make the same choice." Emotion roughened his gruff voice. "A thousand times, a thousand different scenarios, I'd pick you. I loved you and I wanted to be with you. I loved our baby, though I had no idea who they might turn out to be. My life was you. Period. Everything else was just white noise.

A sickening wrench twisted his gut. "But I'm just now realizing I was the only one who felt that way."

Suddenly, her gaze snapped to something behind him.

He turned to find Finn hovering at the edge of the kitchen. A terrible torment clung to him when shuffled over to the refrigerator and tugged open the freezer door. After a brief search, he retrieved an ice pack and eased the door shut.

"How is she?" Shea asked.

Finn raised the ice pack. "For her eye. She wanted a minute alone."

"You okay?"

His dark head bobbed.

Shea experienced a pang of sympathy. "You didn't know she was pregnant, did you?"

"No." Finn scratched a spot on his shoulder. "She keeps apologizing. Says she doesn't want to stay here."

"She doesn't have to stay," Isobel began.

"I don't want her to leave," Finn blurted, raw emotion shredding his voice.

At the possessive outburst, Shea captured his son's panicked gaze. "She can't keep you from your child. There are laws. I'll help you."

Surprise siphoned the blood from Finn's face. "Oh, uh, that's not... The baby isn't mine."

In the heavy silence, Shea and Isobel exchanged a look.

"Are you certain?" Isobel prodded gently. "Condoms can break."

"We didn't use a condom."

A deluge of castigations erupted from Shea and Isobel until Finn held up his hands.

"We didn't use a condom because we didn't... do it." He flushed miserably.

"But...?" Isobel frowned with her confusion. "You knew you weren't the father when you offered to marry her?"

Finn hitched his shoulder. "I thought it would help."

Isobel stared after him as he shuffled down the hall.

Then she turned to Shea with a feeble smile. "He reminds me of you. Always trying to be the hero."

The words were innocent enough, but they chafed his wounded pride. "Maybe he wasn't trying to be a hero.

Maybe he just sees something he wants, something he needs, and he isn't willing to let it go. Did that possibility even occur to you?"

She stared, stunned and mute.

"I'll take that as a no."

"Why are you so angry with me?"

"I'm not angry, I'm tired. I'm tired of being the bad guy. I'm tired of explaining myself to you. You want to assume the worst about me? Go right ahead. I won't stop you. Hell, I won't even get offended. Not anymore. You wanna know why?"

He didn't wait for her to answer.

"Because it has nothing to do with me. This is about you, and why you can't believe anyone would love you."

She stumbled back a step and her face crumpled with hurt. Hurt he'd caused. She appeared fragile, as though she might crumble into a pile of broken pieces on the floor. In the past, he would've held her together. But not this time. This time, she had to do it for herself. She had to collect all her shattered parts and fit them back together again. That, he couldn't do for her.

Without speaking the words screaming inside his heart, he left her alone to figure it out. Without him.

Chapter Twenty-Three

Doubt squirmed inside Isobel, nasty and gnarled. Unable to settle down to sleep, she padded barefoot into the kitchen before the first slivers of sunlight peeked over the horizon.

She left the overhead light switched off and used the nightlight on the microwave to navigate her way around as she started a pot of coffee brewing. In pantry, she rummaged about for the bottle of Irish Cream to add to her coffee. Liquor in hand, she turned back just as the dark silhouette of a figure moved across the living room.

"Sidney?"

The girl started and spun.

Isobel flipped off the closet light and crossed the kitchen. "Are you okay?"

Sidney's gaze slid longingly to the front door and she gripped the backpack strap slung around her shoulder. "I was, um, leaving."

"Where are you going?" Isobel lowered the glass bottle onto the island countertop.

Sidney stared down at her sneakers. "The first ferry starts boarding in a couple of hours."

Isobel folded her arms over her stomach. "You're leaving the island?"

"I'm, um, going to my aunt's house. In Texas."

"Does she know you're coming?"

Sidney's light brown hair shimmered when she nodded. "She bought my plane ticket."

In a gentle voice, Isobel asked, "Does the baby's father know you're leaving?"

Sidney's face flushed with her mortification. "It isn't Finn's."

"I know. He told me." Isobel worried her bottom lip. "But if Finn's not the dad, who is?"

"Nobody."

Isobel's eyebrows shot up.

"I'm not pregnant." The words erupted from Sidney. "I just told my dad that so he'd... do what he did."

She dropped her arms heavily to her sides. "You wanted your dad to throw you out to get of the house?"

"Yes."

"But... why?"

Huge eyes clamped onto Isobel's face, pain-filled and darkened with more misery than Isobel had ever witnessed up close. Her stomach lurched.

With a curt nod, she gave Sidney's thin arm a soft squeeze. "Okay. It's okay. You're not going back there. Your safe now."

The coffeemaker beeped and both women jumped.

Isobel returned her gaze to Sidney. "Can I talk to your aunt before you go?"

"It's, like, four in the morning where she is."

Slipping past Sidney, Isobel snagged her purse off the hook by the door. "You can leave me her number."

With one hand, she rummaged through the bag for her cell phone, then made Sidney recite the digits to her. "Do you have any money?"

"Some."

"How much?"

"Three hundred and forty dollars."

"Not bad," Isobel muttered, pulling her checkbook from an interior pocket. "More than I had."

"Um... what?"

"Nothing." Isobel flipped to a blank check and started writing.

When she'd finished, the amount matched the funds remaining from Shea's loan, which meant she would have to put her business plans temporarily on hold. She wasn't even a little sad about that fact when she ripped the slip of paper from checkbook and held it out to Sidney.

"When you get to Texas, I want you to open a bank account and put this in it."

Sidney recoiled, as though Isobel held out an invitation to drink poison. "I don't want your money."

"I insist."

"Th-that's not why I came here."

Isobel tilted her head to one side. "Why did you come here?"

"I didn't know where else to go. I've been planning to leave for a while, but then I-I had to get out a little sooner than I expected and I-I knew Finn would help me." Sidney's voice and eyes softened when she said Finn's name. "He's always been so nice to me."

Isobel's heart swelled pride, constricting her chest. She jiggled the check. "Just take it."

"I don't want it."

Dropping her chin, Isobel leveled Sidney with the look

all three of her kids immediately responded to. "It's my fee for coming here tonight."

Sidney twisted around and careened toward the door. "I'll go."

Isobel slid into her path. "You don't even have to spend it. Think of it as insurance. It's there if you need it. If you don't spend it, you can send it back to me. Maybe include a note to let me know you're okay." A sudden surge of emotion piled in her throat. "Take it, please. For my sake, if not yours."

"Why are you being so nice to me?" Sidney's voice cracked with a hitch of desperation.

Isobel peered into the girl's youthful face and a pang struck her beneath the breastbone to realize how young she was. "I've been where you are. I know how scared you must be."

Sidney ducked her chin. "I'm not scared."

"Then you're a lot braver than me. I didn't have the courage to leave. I waited until my dad tossed me out like garbage.

Sidney swallowed, the sound an audible gulp. Then a silent sob shook her shoulders, and Isobel wrapped her arms around Sidney's small body. More sobs escaped, and Isobel wanted to weep right along with her. She was only a child. The same age as Isobel when her own father had kicked her out of the house.

All these years, she'd carried the shame of what had happened. But the shame wasn't hers. It belonged to her dad. If he could be so cruel to his own daughter, a frightened child, then he was the one lacking. Not her. She hadn't done anything wrong, except love too hard, too soon.

"It will get better," Isobel promised. "Soon it won't hurt so much."

When that storm kicked up off the lake and blew

across the island, the fear and the shame broke her. Exhausted, hungry, the terror had overcome her and she'd laid her head down on the ground. She didn't care if the storm killed her or if she got sick. At least death would take her away from the nightmare.

"Eventually the storm passes," she murmured into the smooth mass of Sidney's long hair.

In her case, the storm had ceased the moment his sneakers appeared in her line of sight. After that, she knew only warmth and love and the soothing comfort of his raspy voice as he talked to her, jabbering away for hours while she slept and cried in the passenger's seat of his car.

Sidney lifted her head and wiped her eyes with a shaking hand. "Please tell Finn how sorry I am, and how much I appreciate what he's done for me."

"You don't want to tell him yourself?"

Sidney shook her head.

"Give me a minute to grab my shoes and keys?" Isobel moved toward the hallway. "I'll drop you off at the ferry."

Protests fell from Sidney's lips. "You don't have to do that."

"It's another one of my fees," Isobel called over her shoulder as she darted for the hallway.

She slipped into the bathroom and shut the door, then quickly pulled up the number for Sidney's aunt. The woman's groggy voice grew instantly alert when Isobel explained who she was and why she was calling. Though they talked briefly, Isobel learned Sidney's aunt, Becca, was eager for her niece's arrival and had indeed booked her airfare. By the time Isobel disconnected the call, she felt a little better about letting Sidney go.

Thirty minutes later, Isobel waited while Sidney boarded the ferry and soon after, the boat cast off. A bright orange sun peeped over the horizon when she returned home.

She let herself in through the back and slammed into a thick wall of tension that halted her steps. At the kitchen island, Shea perched on a barstool, a cup of coffee in one hand.

Slowly, he set down his cup. "Where've you been?"

She opened her mouth to tell him all that had transpired while he slept, but the thundering of footsteps cut off her reply.

Finn burst into the kitchen, his chest heaving from his dash to reach them. "Sidney's gone."

Isobel laid a hand on his arm. "She left, *mijo.*"

Finn jerked away from her touch. "What?"

"I just dropped her off at the ferry," she said, setting her purse and car keys on the island counter.

"You let her go?" Fiery anger contorted Finn's attractive features. "Why didn't you stop her?"

Isobel gaped stupidly at him. Not only had she never witnessed so much animation in her son, but in that moment he so strongly resembled Shea that a thunderbolt of shock jolted her.

"She didn't want to stay." Isobel licked her parched lips. "Finn, she lied about the baby. She's not pregnant."

With a confused shake of his head, he snarled a hand through his hair. "Where did she go?"

"To her aunt's in Texas." Isobel tugged open her purse and tunneled through the oversized handbag. "I have the phone number."

Hands on his hips, Finn stared at the floorboards while she fumbled for her phone. Pulling up the call log, she scribbled the number on a piece of scrap paper and thrust it at him.

His gaze flickered to the note, but he didn't reach for it. He stared so long and so hard at that tiny slip of paper in her hand, she felt it warm from the heat of his gaze.

"Keep it," he said finally. "She obviously didn't want me to find her."

Then he crossed to the refrigerator and disappeared behind the open door.

Isobel glanced at Shea, who studied the refrigerator door with a concentrated scowl.

Finn banged around inside the fridge. He cursed.

She tucked Sidney's number inside her purse. "You okay?"

More noises tumbled across the kitchen, but there was no reply.

"Finn?"

At Shea's stern tone, the door slammed shut. "No, I'm not okay. I'm pissed off. She should've talked to me before she left."

"So call her," Shea said.

A snarl curled Finn's upper lip, but a wounded light glittered in his eyes.

Her heart squeezed. "I know it hurts right now, but you're a little relieved, too, right?"

"Relieved?"

It could've been Shea, the man she married eighteen years ago, ensnaring her in his defiant glare.

"Sidney is s-safe." Her nerves stretched taut, she stammered. "She isn't pregnant, and you aren't marrying a girl you hardly know. You couldn't have wanted that for yourself."

Finn's expression turned scornful. "Mom, you know me. Do you honestly believe I'd ask a woman to marry me if I didn't want to marry her?"

Shock stole her voice.

"The answer is no, Mom." Then, his shoulders slumped, he retreated down the hall.

Her gaze swung to her husband. Belatedly, words dropped from her lips. "I—I—what was that?"

Shea sipped his coffee. "I tried to tell you."

"You tried to tell me what?"

Brilliant blue eyes pierced her. "Not every man who asks a woman to marry him is doing so because he thinks he has no other choice."

"That's what you still think, isn't it? That I married you out of some outdated sense of duty or obligation?"

His words plucked a chord of truth in her heart and she ducked her chin to hide the fact that's exactly what she believed. Though it was perfectly understandable, given the circumstances of their marriage, that she might've wondered, but icy fear tightened her throat, strangling the admission.

If she confessed the truth, he'd be mad, and they'd fight. Again. She was so tired of fighting, but more terrifying than that, what if this fight was the last fight? What if, like all the other fights, it fixed nothing, and they had to face the fact that their marriage couldn't be saved? What if the last fight, the last heartbreak, was the last light to be turned out on them?

Slowly, he pushed to his feet and at the sink, set his coffee mug in the basin.

When he turned back around, his expression had changed. "I've got to go talk to my brothers."

Her hand flitted over her hair, touching the sagging ponytail and uncombed tendrils. "Let me go change—"

"No."

She froze, and her hand fell uselessly to her side.

His gaze touched hers briefly, then dropped away. "You look exhausted. You should get some sleep before we meet with the photographer later."

Inwardly, she groaned. In the chaos of the night, the photoshoot had fled her mind. She hadn't finished the last dress, but truthfully it didn't seem all that important to her now. Certainly not as important as being with Shea when he told his brothers about Aiden.

She opened her mouth to tell him exactly that, but he moved close and dropped a quick kiss on her forehead. "Get some sleep. I'll meet you later at the loft."

Then he slipped quietly through the back door without her.

She wanted to scream at him to stop. To wait for her. She wanted to demand he tell her why he no longer wanted her to go with him.

But that question had been answered by the devastation in his eyes. Devastation that she had somehow triggered.

Chapter Twenty-Four

Still hours before opening, the empty pub echoed the hollowness inside Shea as he worked his way around the room overturning chairs which had been stacked on top of the tables to allow the crew to sweep the floors.

When he'd passed the halfway mark in his task, the back door groaned open, letting in a stream of morning sun, and the silhouette of a man and moved inside. As the door fell shut, the man's shadowy form took the shape of his youngest brother, Leo.

"Wait, I'm the first one here?" Leo held his arms out at his sides. "Has that ever happened before?"

"Never." With a smile, Shea set down the chair in his hands.

Though it'd been only a few weeks since Shea had last seen his reclusive little brother, the change in Leo sent a ripple of surprise chasing through him. His deep-set hazel-green eyes glimmered in his sun-warmed face and he'd added some much-needed weight to his rail-thin frame.

"How you doing?" Shea palmed Leo's hand and gave him a one-armed man-hug. "You good? You look good."

"Yeah?" An unmistakable hint of humor glinted in Leo's eyes when he threaded a hand through his short dark hair. "I got a haircut."

"That must be it." Shea's gaze lingered while the knot that'd formed in his chest years ago and twisted itself around all things Leo eased somewhat. "It suits you."

"How about you?" Leo lowered his body into a chair. "Got any hair appointments coming up?"

Slipping into a chair, Shea stated simply, "Nope."

Leo's deceptively casual gaze grabbed him, but Shea ignored it.

He didn't want to discuss the problem of his marriage. The aching was constant and if he gave in to it, it could easily overwhelm him. Down that road loomed a dark bleakness he'd never thought he'd feel when it came to his wife.

If she considered the life they'd built together a mistake, what did that mean for their future? If all that existed between them was their haunted memories, what could he possibly hope for? An end of the fighting? Good sex? Dare he hope for companionable friendship?

Or, as the years piled up, did a sadder fate await them? More growing apart, more fighting, more assuming the worst about each other, until the torment wore them down and they retreated into themselves? Good sex could only take them so far. Soon, it'd become awkward, impersonal, draining. Unsatisfying.

Their relationship cold. Loveless.

Could he do it? Could he accept such a marriage?

"Don't worry," Leo said. "I'm not going to pretend I

have some sage wisdom to offer or some such crap."

A reluctant smile tugged at Shea's mouth. "I appreciate that."

"I mean, what the hell do I know about sustaining a relationship for twenty years."

"Not much, I gather," Shea said dryly.

Leo slanted forward in his chair and propped his elbows on his knees. "But let me just say this."

"Here we go," Shea muttered.

"Whether you and Isobel stay married or go your separate ways, don't sell yourself short." Green eyes locked with blue. "You deserve to be happy."

Shea's heart slammed against his chest cavity with the tempest of emotion Leo unleashed inside him. A bead of moisture broke out on his forehead and he swiped at it.

"Ah." Leo reclined in the chair. "I see how it is."

His chest tight, Shea dragged a painful hiss of air into his lungs. "What the hell are you talking about?"

"You're out of time," Leo said softly. "The excuses aren't working anymore. There are no more lies you can tell yourself, or her. That means there's only one thing left to do."

Exasperated, Shea snapped. "Give up?"

"Give in."

Bitterness colored Shea's harsh, humorless laugh.

"If there's enough there pulling you together, then you have to let go of whatever it is that's keeping you apart," Leo said. "Pride, anger, fear, whatever it is."

"Just let it go, huh?" Shea's lip curled with his sneer.

Annoyingly, Leo chuckled. "I didn't say it was easy, but it is simple. You have a choice—hold on to your anger or your wounded pride or whatever it is that's keeping you apart and end the relationship. Put yourselves out of this misery."

Shea glared at his little brother. "Or?"

"Surrender. Forgive her, and yourself. Be happy."

"You're right," Shea said. "You don't know shit."

Leo's rare smile flirted with forming. "That may be true, but I know the stink of desperation when I smell it. You're out of other options. It's time to choose. You can go left, or you can go right, but you can't have it both ways. Pick one. Yes or no. Go or stop. What's it gonna be, brother?"

Shea sat back in his chair and, stretching his legs out in front of him, contemplated Leo. "You've changed," he said, his tone accusatory.

Leo shrugged. "I stopped drinking."

Understanding stole over Shea. "That's why you don't come into the pub anymore."

"I've got other things occupying my nights now." The light in his hazel-green eyes glinted. "Better things."

"How is the wedding planning going?"

"Don't know. Don't care. I went left. Now I'm just enjoying the ride."

Shea couldn't recall ever seeing Leo so open and relaxed. "Looks like you made the right choice for yourself."

Leo's features pulled into a thoughtful frown. "You know, now that I hear you say it, it really wasn't a choice at all. At least, it didn't feel like a choice."

"What did it feel like?"

"Death."

A rusty laugh rumbled through Shea.

"And not the good kind of death either," Leo said.

"Is there a good kind of death?"

"Sure. There's the kind that brings relief. This wasn't that kind of death. It was the awful, painful kind," he said happily. "You know, where you're kicking and screaming and praying to a God you don't even believe in, but you're just that desperate to avoid your fate."

Weariness pulled at him. Damn, but he was tired. Tired of living half-alive but half-dead.

"You've thought a lot about this," he said.

White teeth flashed in Leo's tanned face, then a beam of sunlight fell across the floor when the back door opened, and Noah filed into the bar with Jack close behind him.

Shea and Leo pushed to their feet.

"Surrender," Leo said. "You can thank me later."

Dark desolation churned in Shea's gut. He tried to listen as his brothers discussed Jack's week at training camp and the upcoming hockey season, but the misery swamped him, darkening the world around him.

Through the gloom closing in around him, Shea recognized the light of truth in Leo's words. The time had come for he and Isobel to decide their fate. Would they stay married or go their separate ways?

For Shea, the choice was easy. He wanted Isobel. He wanted her heart. All of her heart. But how was that possible when, for her, their marriage had been one long drawn out trauma? Why would she choose him?

Despite the fallout with her dad, and after the initial shock, a steady thrum of excitement had hummed inside Shea to be marrying Isobel. For years up until that point, his life had been entirely focused on shielding his brothers from Daniel and scrounging up enough food for them to eat. He hadn't been living, he'd been surviving. Until her.

Then, she was everything. His life, his love, his adventure. Everything inside him was wrapped up in her and their baby. But he didn't mean to make marriage and kids her only adventure, and he certainly hadn't meant to make her do it alone. Could he blame her if she couldn't forgive him for that?

His gaze touched over his brothers' faces, and the

shadows lifted just a little. "Where's Luke?"

Noah frowned down at his cell phone screen, his thumb moving across the display screen. "He overslept. He's on his way now."

"What's going on?" Jack kicked the leg of a chair out and straddled the seatback.

"I have some news."

Wary alarm rippled around the trio.

"Good news or bad news?" Noah asked.

"Good, I think." Shea didn't bother to hide his concern. "Though honestly, I don't know for sure."

Alarm turned to alertness.

"Hit us."

"We'll wait for Luke," Shea said. "This is something we have to do together."

℣

Clouds gathered overhead, darkening the sky darkened with impending doom. Fear gripped her. But beneath the terror twisting her insides into knots, an edge of annoyance prickled.

She was tired of being afraid all the time. Fear of storms. Fear of boats. Fear of heartbreak. Fear of love. It'd grown tiresome, and she, exhausted.

She turned away from the window overlooking Main Street. The photographer from *Stylish Bride*, Marcus, roamed the loft, snapping pictures of her gowns displayed on the dress forms she'd arranged throughout the large space.

With each soft click of Marcus's camera, her stomach coiled tighter, every shutter closure a new opportunity for her work to be judged.

Judged and found lacking.

She resisted the urge to snatch the camera from him,

chuck it out the window, and watch it shatter on the concrete sidewalk below. Instead, she fisted her hands into tight balls until her fingernails bit into the flesh of her palm.

At her side, Shea appeared amiable and relaxed while he chatted with Marcus about the building's history, but tension gathered in the pinched corners of his mouth. His gaze refused to connect fully with hers and she experienced a painful relief that she didn't have to witness the disappointment in his eyes.

Marcus turned his camera on the two of them, firing off a round of soft clicks. She fought to hold her stiff smile in place, but the persistent rapid-fire was too much.

Her smile faltered.

The camera lens glared, like a spotlight bringing her flaws into sharp focus and amplifying them.

Shea's hand slipped to the small of her back waist. Her tripping heart steadied, until his assessing gaze landed on her. it reminded her of the days shortly after he quit working at the law firm. Thought it'd hurt, she'd grown accustomed to his absence from their lives, and when suddenly, he was there, his singular attention focused on her, she couldn't bear it.

That's when their real troubles began. She grew to fear the times when he noticed her. She'd never survive the brutal devastation of his rejection.

Click, click, click.

Just when she'd become convinced that Marcus's irritating camera clicks would never cease, he pulled the heavy piece of equipment away from his grizzled face and smiled. "I think that'll do it."

Air leaked out between her teeth.

Marcus packed up and Shea helped him lug his gear downstairs. After they'd loaded the trunk of Marcus' rental car, Shea returned to the loft alone.

Tension crept into the room as he hovered near the doorway, his expression inscrutable. "Congratulations," he said. "You did it."

She anticipated a ripple of joy, or at the very least, relief, but neither emotion affected her. There was a touch of pride at what she'd accomplished, a sort of impartial self-respect that was new to her, but beyond that, no emotion landed with a noticeable impact.

Rather, she experienced an odd absence of feeling. A numbness she didn't understand.

"So, that's it, huh?"

"That's it." At the unusual hitch in his voice, she risked a glance at him. "I guess there's no need for us to pretend any longer."

A bite of alarm broke through her numbness. "Pretend?"

"If we want, we can go back to the way things were." His Adam's apple bobbed when he swallowed. "Before Vanessa stopped by the store."

The words struck her like a blow. Panic whooshed through her. The echo of her heartbeat ricocheted around the inside of her skull.

"Is that what you want, Isobel? To go back to the way things were?"

Denials screamed inside her head, but icy fear crept up her spine.

"I don't want that." Her throat constricted. "But I... I'm afraid."

"Me, too, *mo chroí*. But it's time to decide."

At the sound of raindrops tapping against the windowpane, she turned. Drawing close to the windows, she pressed her hand against the glass. With the tip of one finger, she traced a droplet as it snaked downward.

The steady patter of raindrops pierced her defenses,

releasing the memories of those nights she'd slept in the park. The rain had soaked through her clothing and left her shivering even before the heart of the storm struck the island. The wind howled and the terror flowed through her like a toxic sludge to mix with the poison of her dad's abandonment.

She loved Shea. She loved him for finding her in the park that day, for rescuing her from the paralyzing fear and that dark place inside her that doubted everything and everyone. She loved him, and yet she hesitated. How could she want something so badly that her body became physically ill at the prospect of losing it, yet be too afraid to reach for it?

Shame washed over her at her cowardice, but so too did pity for that young, scared girl who believed so strongly that her marriage had to be perfect, that she had to be perfect, or else she'd suffer—even deserve—her husband's rejection.

With a jolt, she twisted around, only to realize she was alone in the empty loft.

Chapter Twenty-Five

The bell above the door chimed, and Isobel poked her head around the clothing rack as Sophie plopped a drink carrier filled with cardboard coffee cups on the front counter.

"Good morning." Sophie began removing cups from the carrier. "How'd the photoshoot go yesterday?"

With a shrug, Isobel abandoned her work. "Okay, I guess."

Sophie set a creamer and two packets of sugar on one of the coffee lids. "How long until the issue is out?"

"Not for a few months." Isobel reached for the cup with the creamer and sugar packs.

"Izzy, I'm so proud of you." Sophie pried the lid of her coffee. "I hope you get everything you could ever want from this."

The words knocked into Isobel and sudden emotion

piled in her throat. "I don't know what I want."

Sophie pursed her lips to blow on her steaming coffee. "We're not talking about wedding dresses anymore, are we?"

Isobel shook her head. She swallowed convulsively. "He thinks I'm perfect."

Laughter erupted from Sophie and rolled across the store in gusty waves. "I hate to burst your bubble, but he knows you're not perfect."

"Forget I said anything," Isobel muttered.

Sophie wiped a tear of mirth from the corner of one eye. "No, I get it, Iz. I really do. You and I are a lot alike. It's why we're such good friends."

"Well then, do you mind telling me? Because I'm freaking out a little bit."

"You're afraid of going through what you went through with your dad." Sophie's voice softened. "No one can blame you for that, but Shea isn't your dad. Not only are they, literally, different people, but they are completely different kinds of men."

"He left me," Isobel said, but her statement lacked the heat of betrayal.

Shea hadn't cruelly abandoned her. He lost his way, and for a time, he didn't know how to return to her.

"Look, I'm an expert on overly critical people." A teardrop of sadness hung in Sophie's green eyes. "And while your dad may be one of them, your husband is not. He just isn't."

"But what if my dad was right?"

Confusion clouded Sophie's features. "Right about what?"

"About me." A pang of anguish struck Isobel in the center of her chest. "What if my dad was right and Shea is wrong?"

Sophie waved off Isobel's words with a flick of the

wrist. "Shea isn't wrong. I'm not wrong. Your kids and Ava aren't wrong. Half this damn island isn't wrong. It's not like there's some list of traits and once you tick enough boxes you get to be loved. Love is an all-or-nothing thing and Shea loves you. The end."

"My dad loved me. Until he didn't," Isobel couldn't help but point out. "What if Shea changes his mind, too?"

"Have you talked to him about any this?"

A snort of disgust slipped from her. "God, no."

"Why not?"

Isobel fiddled with a sugar packet, crinkling the paper between her fingers. "I was afraid to bring it up."

A smile twitched at the corner of Sophie's mouth. "Afraid it would ruin your marriage?"

Isobel's watery laugh dissolved with her groan. "Something like that." Leaning over the counter, she dropped her head into the cradle of her arms.

"So you're not perfect. So what? Unless..." Sophie let the word hang like a threat. "It's not Shea's judgment you're worried about."

Isobel pressed her cheek against her forearm and glared up at her friend. "What does that mean?"

"There is one person I know who hates disorder and messiness and general imperfection more than anyone else I've ever met."

Isobel's spine snapped straight. "Don't you dare."

Sophie's hands shot up, palms facing out. "I'm just saying."

"You're just saying what? That I let my marriage fall apart because I'm... I'm–I don't even know what, intolerant?"

"No, that's not what I'm saying at all. I'm saying you let your marriage fall apart because you thought it'd save you from having to face the fact that you're not perfect. You're the one who can't stand it. Not Shea."

Isobel sucked in a sharp hiss of air. Was it true?

The answer came in the form of a vise clamping around her heart. She clasped her fist against her chest.

When her dad tossed her out, shame took root inside her. A dark, ugly shame that had twisted and warped, and started her on the impossible quest for perfection. If she were calm and confident, competent and serene, flawless, outwardly at least, then maybe no one would notice all the yucky stuff underneath. They'd believe she was more than a piece of trash her own father didn't want. Shea would believe it. If she played at the game long and hard enough, maybe she'd even believe it, too.

So she'd turned herself inside out trying to become someone Shea had never asked her to be. Then she blamed him for letting her do it.

Sophie's blonde curls bounced when she shook her head. "Seriously, I thought I was messed up." She shot Isobel a pointed look. "You need help."

Heat seared Isobel's cheeks and a curse slipped from her.

"You know what's crazy?" Sophie nudged Isobel with a soft elbow. "Your only real flaw is your perfectionism."

Isobel narrowed her eyes. "I don't want to be friends with you anymore."

"Tough," Sophie said, taking the threat as seriously as Isobel intended it. "You're stuck with me."

With the jingle of the door chime, Celeste breezed through the front door.

Her cell phone pressed to one ear, the sound of her tinkling laughter shattered the quiet inside the store. "Yes, yes, I accept their offer. I can't believe this is happening. Okay. Uh-huh. Call me when they're ready and I'll stop by to sign them."

Celeste disconnected the call and blasted Isobel and Sophie with a full-wattage smile. "Good morning, ladies."

As one, Isobel and Sophie turned as Celeste floated by them and rounded the store counter.

"Celeste? Are you okay?" Sophie asked. "You look a little flushed."

Celeste's small shoulders lifted when she pulled in a deep breath and held it, as if to contain her excitement. "I have news."

Sophie gasped. "Are we the first to hear it? Oh, please say we are. I'm never the first to hear any gossip on this damn island."

Celeste drew in a deep breath, which then burst from her. "I sold the store."

The announcement dropped like a sledgehammer on Isobel. "You did what? To who?"

A severe crease added wrinkles to Celeste's brow. "Oh. I don't know." Her expression cleared. "Anyway, I had lunch with my realtor yesterday, just to talk about the idea and see what I needed to do to get the ball rolling. Just now, she called me with an offer. A great offer. Now, I can retire and not have to worry about my money running out before I die."

"There's our Celeste," Sophie said.

"But... is the store going to stay the store?" Isobel's heart pounded with wild, frantic beats.

Celeste's beady eyes fluttered rapidly, as though Isobel had asked her for the answer to a complex math problem. "Oh. Um, I'm going to meet with my realtor later today. I'll know more after that."

Isobel gripped the edge of the counter to keep from being dumped off the side of her tilting world. With the store under new ownership, would she still have a job? Would the store remain a bridal store, or did the new owner have a new endeavor planned? A bitter slash of disappointment sliced through her to realize any chance she may have had of ever owning the store had likely vanished.

The line of Celeste's thin mouth twisted with a regretful frown. "I wish I could go another twenty years, but it's time for me to enjoy what's left of my life."

Isobel's vision blurred. "I'm happy for you, Celeste. I am. It's just that, you're the only boss I've ever had." She sniffled. "I'm going to miss you."

"You're not getting rid of me that easily." Celeste plucked a coffee cup from the drink carrier. "I'm not leaving the island. We'll still see each other plenty."

"Of course," Isobel said, though they both knew it wasn't true.

The first half of Isobel's shift passed in a fog of heartsickness and worry for her future. She took no joy in the shipment of new dresses, barely noticing the quality and intricate details of each gown. When a young bride arrived for her fitting, Isobel only just managed to muster a whisper of fake enthusiasm for the woman's once-in-a-lifetime moment.

By lunch, misery weighed her down.

Hoping some fresh air might clear away her dark mood, she ventured outdoors for a walk, but the menacing gray clouds hovering overhead drove her back inside after a short trip around the block. In the break room, she plopped down in a metal folding chair to wait out the remaining minutes of her break.

Whenever she'd experienced times of intense turmoil, thoughts of her mom often visited her, and they did so then as well. Isobel didn't wish for answers to her questions or her mother's advice. She simply wanted her mom close. She wanted time for them to be together, talking about silly things, or shopping, or working side by side in the kitchen. It was ridiculous, but after all these years, she craved a parent's love.

Seeking distraction, she filched her cell phone from

her back pocket. When she swiped a finger across the screen, a notification reminded her that she had an unopened voice message several days old. She tapped the screen to dial her mailbox, then followed the prompts to replay the recording.

A man's voice crackled through the phone's low-quality speaker. "Isobel, it's Dad."

Shock flew through her and her hand shot to her mouth.

"I want to see you. I... I'd like to see you, if you can bring yourself to see me." In the long silence that followed, she could hear faintly the sound of his uneven breathing. "There are some things I need to say to you. Call me. Please. Okay, bye now."

Isobel lurched to her feet, dropping the phone on the table with a clatter of noise. In the tiny break room, she paced.

What did her dad want? Did he want to talk about what happened eighteen years ago? Was he going to apologize? Or did he still blame her for bringing shame on the family?

Her hands shook so badly she rammed the phone into the back pocket of her black jeans.

What if he didn't want to talk about the past? Should she bring it up?

Twisting around, she paced the other way.

But if he didn't want to discuss what happened, why was he calling? Was something wrong? Was he sick?

She lunged for her phone. Fingers poised over the screen, she hesitated, wanting so badly to call her dad and at the same time not wanting to want to call him.

Not unlike the tangle of conflicting desires she experienced for her husband.

Why? Why was she so frozen with indecision? What was she so afraid of?

The adrenaline drained from her body and she collapsed in the metal chair.

What was she afraid of? Heartbreak. She wanted love, all of the love, but none of the pain that came with it, those inevitable hurts and wounds inherent in the act of opening up to others. She wanted all the reward but abhorred the risks.

Her fingers started tapping out a text message on her phone's small screen. *How's it going? Everything okay?*

She hit Send to forward the text to her sister, then resumed pacing. Ava would know whether something was wrong with their dad.

When the phone chimed a few minutes later, she opened the reply from Ava. *Yeah. Why?*

At the brief blow off, relief flooded Isobel. Nothing was wrong. Their dad wasn't sick.

She typed hastily, then sent off her message. *No reason. Just checking. Have a good day. xoxo.*

The phone jingled right away. *You're weird.*

Entangled in inner turmoil, Isobel had no memory of the rest of her work day or the drive home. When she entered the house through the back door near dinnertime, silence greeted her. She hitched her purse on a hook by the door and moved through the kitchen. Soft voices pulled down the hallway to Maisie's bedroom door.

"I don't want you to go." Maisie's plaintive plea pinched Isobel's heart. "I want you to live here again. Will you?"

"No, kiddo, I don't think I will." Emotion thickened Shea's gravelly voice.

"Because Mama doesn't love you anymore?"

In the beat of silence that followed, Isobel's heart shattered and crumbled to dust.

"It's a little more complicated than that," Shea hedged.

"I can come live with you," Maisie said, her little girl voice taking on a determined edge.

"You don't have to do that, *a stór.*"

Isobel peeked around the doorjamb.

On the bedroom floor, Maisie sat in Shea's lap and frowned down at the doll in her hands, the long sweep of her eyelashes dropping shadows on her chubby cheeks.

She laid her head back against his chest. "Well, if she stops loving me, too, then I will."

The wall holding back Isobel's tears dissolved.

"Ah, kiddo, your mom will never stop loving you." Shea's hand smoothed over her dark hair. "That's not how love works. Your mom and I will always love each other, even if we're not living in the same house. I don't live with your uncles and I love each and every one of them."

"Me, too."

"They're pretty lovable guys, aren't they?"

"Yep." Maisie's small fingers worked a dress over the doll's head.

"And there's nothing in this world that could ever happen or that you could ever do to make any of us stop loving you. Not your uncles. Not your mom or your brothers." Reaching around her, Shea tugged the fabric down to cover the plastic toy's nakedness. "And definitely not me. I'm your dad. It's a fact that I will always love you more than anyone else in the whole wide world could ever love you. That's what it means to be a dad."

"Oh." Maisie craned her neck back to look up at her dad. "I'm hungry."

Shea chuckled. "Well if you're hungry, we should eat."

As Maisie bounded from Shea's lap, Isobel ducked into her bedroom and closed the door silently behind her. She pressed her back against the solid wood just as a sob escaped. She clamped her hand over her mouth.

Her fractured heart wept with the love pouring

through her. Love for her children, and love Shea. So much love. She loved him for his stubborn pride and maddening overprotectiveness. She loved him for erasing any and all doubt in their daughter's mind about his love for her.

Shea loved him, and yet...

Dammit, Noah was right after all. She'd done to Shea exactly what her dad had done to her. Her dad, who hadn't spoken to her in eighteen years, hadn't rejected *her.* Not exactly. Rather, he'd tried to block the pain, even if that meant blocking out the love as well. Which is exactly what Isobel had been doing these last two years and more.

With every fresh heartbreak she'd experienced, she had closed off her heart a little more, thwarting the flow of love in and out in a desperate attempt to protect herself against all of it, the joys and the heartaches. Somewhere along the way, she'd decided the love wasn't worth the risk of loss and despair. Of disappointment and rejection.

So she'd locked herself inside a box, one with sharp corners and neatly delineated lines. Then she'd waited for Shea to show up with the key and rescue her. But Shea didn't have the key. Hell, he couldn't even see her stupid invisible box.

Trapped and alone, she'd forgotten that even the darkest moments had allowed her to love more. Through abandonment and divorce, she'd gained more than she'd lost. Even now, when all seemed lost, she had family that loved her. A husband that fought for her even until the very end.

She'd been a coward for so long, could she muster the courage to change? She could she open her heart to husband? Where did she even begin to make right all the wrongs she'd committed?

We'll do it together. With our love.

Love is always the answer.

She'd do it little by little, every single day, until they'd forgotten when it was ever otherwise between them.

She pulled her cell phone from her back pocket and sank to the bedroom floor. Hands shaking, she punched the digits on the keypad. Each tap on the phone's screen hurtled a shrill beeping sound into the quiet room.

She pressed the phone to ear and listened to it ring once, twice, before his gruff voice crackled over the connection.

"Hey, Dad. It's me."

Chapter Twenty-Six

Dark clouds blotted out the sun, their menacing shadows hovering overhead with the storm that kicked up suddenly off the lake. The waves churned with agitation, loosening his boat's ties to the moorings, and cascading sheets of rain pummeled him as he worked to secure the rolling vessel to the dock.

The storm's ferociousness echoed the violent despair inside him.

He was out of time. With the rainstorm, a cool north wind swept over the island, foretelling of the colder months that lie ahead. Once the storm had passed, he'd need to pull the boat out of the water and place it in storage for the winter. Then he'd have to move inland to the loft. He'd waited as long as he could.

A wind gust snatched the rope from his hand, and a sharp curse shot from him. While he struggled to recapture the cord and knot it tight, the ridiculous belief that he and Isobel might one day find their way back to each other submerged beneath a vast sea of hopelessness. He could no longer avoid the truth—she either didn't love him or didn't love him enough to stop the fear from keeping them apart.

A crushing weight sat on his chest when he clambered aboard the boat and darted toward the stern. He leaned over the railing to catch the dangling end of an unfastened rope that danced in the wind. In his rush to attend to the boat's ties, he'd shoved the legal papers into his back pocket. Now, sodden with water and dislodged by his movements, they dropped heavily to the boat deck.

He crouched to retrieve them.

Just then, a prickle of awareness skittered across his skin, raising the hairs on his arms. He froze, unable to move as the driving rain pounded him. In the distance, a rumble of thunder growled, and a shudder chased through him.

Slowly, he stood. His head bent, he concentrated fiercely on the decking beneath his feet while chaos lashed at him.

"Shea." In the din of the storm, her voice sounded faint.

He lifted his gaze. Drenched with rain, her dark hair hung in heavy clumps and her breezy blouse and skirt clung to her body. They stood apart, she on the dock and he on the stern of his boat, like a pair of cold cement statues, while the storm whipped and whirled around them

"I'm not perfect." She called over the howling wind.

"I know."

"You know?" Accusation wrapped around each of her words.

"I lived with you for seventeen years." He squinted

against the raindrops pelting his face. "Of course I know."

She might've cursed. "Were you going to tell me?"

His shoulders moved. "I thought you knew."

"Yeah, well… I didn't."

"So you have flaws. So what? So do I. So does everyone we know."

She ducked her chin.

"So every minute of every day isn't perfect." His voice rose above the noisy storm. "You think that means I don't want to be with you? That I don't love you?"

"Kind of, yeah." Her head bobbed. "Yes. That's what I think. What I thought."

Beneath his feet, the boat rocked. She remained firmly on the dock.

"When my mom died–" He stopped, swallowing the sudden swell of emotion. "Right before she died, she made me promise to take care of my brothers. I cried," he admitted. "I told her I didn't know how. Shit, I was afraid."

Isobel took a wide step toward him but drew up suddenly when she reached the edge of his boat.

"She told me to do the best I could and that's all she'd ever ask of me. She said as long as I tried my best to take care of them, she'd take care of me." He pushed a hank of rain-soaked hair off his forehead. "Then she died, and we were sent here, to this weird place on the other side of the world, and I was so fucking mad at her because she'd lied to me. I was trying. I was doing anything and everything I could to help my brothers, and she'd abandoned me."

Stormy gray eyes seized on his face.

"Then I saw you."

"What?" she called out.

"That day on the pier," he shouted back. "When I saw you, I knew it was my mom. She sent you to me."

Eyes shining, her throat worked when she swallowed.

"That was her way of taking care of me, so that I could take care of my brothers." When a faint smile touched her mouth, the air squeezed from his lungs. "After that, I wasn't afraid anymore. Because of you."

Her smile broke loose, but the flash of beauty was brief before her gaze snapped to the soggy papers clutched in his hand. The clouds that tarnished her pretty features rivaled those darkening the sky.

Instinctively, he looked down.

"Are those our divorce papers?" Then, without an obvious thought given to the turbulent seas or the unstable watercraft, she lurched forward, stumbling onboard his boat to snatch the papers from him.

"Wait—" He reached for the document, but it was too late.

With a vicious wrench, she ripped the wet sheets in two. "Don't sign them."

"Isobel—"

She threw herself at him, slamming into his chest in a way that was neither gentle nor elegant but desperate and needy. "Shea, please."

"I can't lose you." She clutched at his T-shirt. "Shea, I... I'm not afraid anymore."

His heart thrashed, but he ruthlessly crushed the bloom of hope that tried to unfurl inside him.

"I'm so proud of you." Cupping her face with his hands, he wiped raindrops from her cheeks with the pads of his thumbs. "The storm, it's a bad one."

"The storm?" The pucker of confusion between her brows suddenly cleared. "No, not that. I'm terrified of that."

A trickle of surprise laughter leaked out of him. "Then what aren't you afraid of anymore?"

Soft eyes gripped him by the balls.

"Love. You. Us." She shook her head. "I don't know

exactly, except I know I'm not afraid to love you. Not anymore. I've been so blind, Shea."

She raised up on her tip toes to brush her mouth over his, and the taste of rain and Isobel and—God help him—hope, burst on his tongue.

The kiss ended too soon when she dropped back down on her heels and glared up a t him, her gray eyes electric with thunderous fury.

"Did you sign those papers?" She was shoving him backward. "Are we divorced?"

Beneath the cabin's overhang, he tripped on a bundle of rope and landed hard on the storage bench. She climbed onto his lap, hiking her skirt as she straddled his hips.

The blood left his head and rushed to his groin. He grunted, but then her small hands moved to the fastening of his shorts. When she freed him, her warm hollow sucked him deep and a desperate groan ripped from him.

While he stretched her wide, droplets of rain fell from her hair onto his wet skin.

She pressed her forehead against his and when she'd impaled herself on him completely, she whispered desperately, "Did you sign them?"

He managed only a tight jerk of his head before her knees pushed into the bench cushions and she slid up, then back down, his hefty length. Glorious sensation crashed over him,

"You bastard." Her choked sob punctured his heart and she tossed the tattered papers over her shoulder. "You're going to marry me again."

He gripped her waist to halt the erotic revolutions of her hips. He needed a moment to think, except she was reaching for the top button on her blouse. Working quickly, she exposed herself to his hungry gaze. When she reached back to unhook her bra, she arched, jutting her breasts high. He slipped a hand around her waist and hauled her to him. With his tongue, he took a tiny taste of one perfect, pebbled nipple.

Her warm hollow clasped him tight and he dragged his mouth to the side of her neck. His eager fingers danced over her warm skin and located the throbbing pulse point above her collarbone, then trailed lower to the swells of her lush breasts. In the valley between her ample mounds, he stroked the delicate silver chain.

He leaned back far enough to capture her gaze, then slipped his fingers under the cool necklace and clinched her wedding ring in his palm. He looped the metal rope once around his hand and tugged.

When the fragile chain snapped, a soft gasp escaped between her lips. Gently, he removed her left hand from the spot where it rested on his shoulder and slipped the ring he'd bought her eighteen years ago into place.

A ripple of light disturbed the sea of hurt and fear in her eyes.

"It's true I signed that document," he said. "But those weren't our divorce papers."

"They weren't?"

She shifted and he sucked in a sharp hiss of air when another painfully exquisite surge of sensation rolled over him. Teeth clenched, he shook his head.

"We're still married?" She swiveled her hips.

He gripped her waist with both of his hands, then started to move under her. "You are my wife, Isobel. Now and forever. Do you understand me?"

Pink rushed into her cheeks and she nodded, then her head lolled back. He plunged up into her and she moaned when his shaft rubbed her clit.

Together, they moved, riding the carnal waves of fire and love. She rode him faster, higher, and every moan of pleasure that fell from her lips wedged inside his heart.

Around them, the storm raged. For each thrust he pushed into her, he could feel another one of her doubts fall away. The wind snatched her fears and flung them out to sea. The rain dissolved their haunted memories like sugar on the tongue.

Their breathing became ragged, rapid, they hurtled toward the cliff.

Reaching up, he grasped her nape and pulled her face down to his. "I love you, *a chuisle mo chroí.*" He repeated the words, over and over. In between, he took little licks of her soft mouth. All the while, his hips moved, thrusting up into her in steady but languid glides. "I'm never letting you go, my Bell."

The heart of her clenched around him and she cried out his name. Soft whimpers sounded in her throat while the sensual spasms of her climax clasped him tight. With one final, shuddering plunge, he drove home.

Pleasure and pain burned through him and his mouth latched onto the column of her throat to quiet his roar of need.

His world had narrowed to only her, and slowly he became aware of the boat dipping and swaying under them. A gusty breeze sent a few tattered paper shreds swirling on the wind and one jagged square struck his cheek.

She lifted her head from his shoulder and peeled the saturated scrap away his skin.

White teeth scraped across her bottom lip. "So, uh, if that wasn't our divorce papers, what did I just tear up?"

"I made an offer to buy the store. I think you just destroyed Celeste's counteroffer."

Emotions chased across her features and he tracked every one of them. Shock, worry, excitement. Love.

So much love.

"You bought the store?" At the hitch of softness in her

voice, his body hardened.

"I don't know." His palms smoothed up her narrow rib cage. "You tore it up before I got a chance to read it."

"Celeste already told me she accepted the offer." Huge round eyes searched his face. "But... how? When?"

"I overheard Celeste talking to her realtor yesterday at the pub and I thought we better move fast."

"We?"

"I'm sorry there wasn't time to talk to you first, but I added a clause to make our offer contingent upon your agreement to buy the building."

She bit down hard on her bottom lip, as if to stop her smile from breaking loose. "You bought the store for me?"

"Well I certainly don't need it."

Her smile nudged a little wider. "But you didn't sign those papers?"

"I did not. Last night, I burned them and dumped their ashes in the lake." He winced with his confession. "I knew it wouldn't change anything, but dammit, Isobel, I couldn't do it. I couldn't bring myself to give you up. I'm a jerk, and I'm sorry for it, but no matter how hard I tried, I just couldn't let you go."

She rained kisses on his face, showering him with her love until he caught her mouth with his. With soft nips and licks, they nibbled and tasted, exploring and savoring each other as though they kissed for the first time rather than the first of their next one thousand kisses.

His shaft thickened inside her. In response, a lusty moan vibrated in her throat.

"I'm going to need a little more time," he murmured against her mouth.

She rolled her hips. "I'll wait."

"Is that all you want me for? My twelve-inch cock?" Despite his teasing, a pinch of vulnerability squeezed his chest.

With her fingertips, she traced the outline of his cheek. "I want you for so many reasons, it'd take me all day to list them."

He reclined deeper into the bench. "I'll wait."

Her expression grew serious, and in her eyes, a light radiated through the clouds. "Because I love you, and because after everything, you still love me. I don't know why you haven't given up on me, but after all these years, you've made me believe that I'm worth loving."

Words clogged in his throat when the wind pushed a strand of her hair across her forehead and be brushed it back.

"After losing my mom and my dad, somehow you made my heart whole again, Shea."

His hand squeezed her nape. "That's only one reason," he croaked.

Her smile filled his heart. "Yes, but it's the only one that matters."

Epilogue

Isobel poked her head around the doorframe to Connor's bedroom. On the bed, Shea's long, lean frame stretched out and the small forms of Connor and Maisie tucked into each of his sides. A book balanced on his flat midsection, he read the words with exaggerated enthusiasm.

Maisie glanced up. "Hi, Mom."

"What are you guys doing?"

"Reading." Connor tipped the book in Shea's hands.

"Is it a good book?"

"It has a princess," Maisie offered.

"And a dragon." Connor looked up at Shea, who looked down at his youngest son. Lips snarled, and two beastly growls erupted from father and son.

"Oh geez." Maisie's head dropped back onto the pillow.

Vivid blue eyes captured Isobel's, and as she gazed at her husband, her heart ached. But she knew it wouldn't break. Forged in the fire of passion and pain, her heart, like their love, was unbreakable.

"Your brother is here," she said softly.

With shrieks of excitement, Connor and Maisie clambered from the bed. Tiny footsteps thundered through the house as they charged down the hallway to greet whichever uncle had arrived to visit them.

But in the living room, their footfalls fell abruptly silent, and they craned their necks to stare up at a man they'd never seen before.

"Who are you?" Connor wanted to know.

Shea emerged from the hallway behind Isobel. "He's your uncle Aiden."

Maisie's cherubic face pulled into a severe scowl. "How many uncles do I have?"

"Four," Connor stated, holding up five fingers.

Isobel brushed a hand across his dark head. "Actually, you have five uncles."

"That's a lot."

"Yes, it is, *mijo*. We're very lucky to have such a large family." Her soft laughter trailed off when Connor tagged along after his sister to the toy chest where they rummaged around for their favorite playthings to show off to their new uncle.

When she turned back to the two men, she caught the last traces of their shared look.

Curious, she searched their faces. "What is it? What did I miss?"

"There's something more Aiden has to tell us." Shea spoke in a low voice. "Isn't there?"

Aiden's mouth pulled into a tight line. "As a matter of fact, there is."

In the beat of heavy silence that followed, all the air seemed to be sucked out of the room.

Aiden offered Isobel a weak smile. "The number's a bit bigger than five, as it happens."

"A bit bigger...?" Isobel frowned with her confusion. Then understanding slammed into her.

LAST HEARTBREAK

A hint of mild regret touched Aiden's handsome features. "I'm not Daniel Nolan's only bastard."

THE END

ABOUT THE AUTHOR

Amy Olle is a USA Today bestselling author of sexy contemporary romances filled with charmingly flawed characters and cozy settings. Her debut novel, *Beautiful Ruin*, is the first book in the series about the five Irish-born Nolan brothers. She is delighted to put her Psychology degrees to good use writing romance.

Amy lives in Michigan with her longsuffering husband, brilliant son, and (female) turtle named George.

Amy loves connecting with readers! Find her on the web at www.amyolle.com.

www.ingramcontent.com/pod-product-compliance
Lightning Source LLC
Chambersburg PA
CBHW051654180726
48284CB00006B/1991